A MOTH TO FLAME

A NOVEL

JOE CLIFFORD

*This book is dedicated to Lynne Barrett, without whom
I don't have a writing career. (It's okay. I don't blame you.)*

nyc·to·pho·bi·a

/ˌniktəˈfōbēə/

noun — *Extreme or irrational fear of the night or of darkness.*

THE NIGHT OF THE PROTEST

The Rider on the Plain, Broadcast Excerpt, Thursday, March 14, 1991, 11:49 p.m.

Lies. Bullshit. Spin. You know it. I know it. And trust me, the school board knows it. Brad Pearce was the best teacher we ever had. And they fired him. For what? For telling the truth—for challenging authority's self-serving deceptions, exposing the gross inequities of a system built to exploit us. But this is what they do, isn't it? Divide and conquer. Control. It's always about control. Get brother to hate brother, sister to hate sister. Misinformation. Don't trust your own eyes and ears. Believe what they tell you is the truth. They want you to travel down the road they've paved, the one that leads to profits for them, and ends in subjugation for us. They want to keep us caged like rats spinning wheels, fueling their power trip. The machination of oppression. The ones in control have been pulling this crap since the dawn of civilization. They isolate, subjugate, legislate, facilitate an economic divide favoring the ruling class, rendering a few royalty, the rest of us servants. And they keep us down by force-feeding propaganda, fattening us up like ducks so they can spread our engorged livers on their gold-dusted bread. Work us to the bone, break our backs, bleed us dry, toss the carcass. There's plenty more waiting to take their turn. Mr. Pearce confronted our perceptions, pulled back the curtain to uncover the master's puppet strings. We are meant for more than punching clocks, wasting our best years in boxes or factories. We are meant to live.

Right now, if they have their way, we're gonna die. Look at what's going on half a globe away. Iraq, man. Dropping bombs to keep the price of oil down and their stock options up. I'm telling you, this war, this war isn't over. It's going to rage on and on—it's our generation's Vietnam. How long before we get sent overseas, left in the desert to risk our lives to protect their interests?

This school doesn't foster independent thinking. They choose the curriculum, pick the books, redacted and chockful of revisionist history. Like Mr. Pearce said: you can't sell out if you never buy in. And what did he get for dropping that knowledge? Fired, that's what.

But I'm telling you, man, we've got them scared. We've started a movement! The Pasa Ardo Police Department—the FCC and FBI—are listening in on this right now—hello, you bastards!—they're closing in, trying to identify me. And they will catch me.

Because I'm gonna let them.

Sometimes winning means surrender. We only have a few minutes. Tonight, I'm sorry to say, our time together comes to an end. Right now, the pigs are triangulating this roving signal, ready to slap on the cuffs. Then what? No clue. What's the prison sentence in this country for telling the truth? Ask Leonard Peltier. Ask Mumia Abu Jamal. Ask Brad Pearce.

Brad Pearce was more than a twelfth-grade English teacher. He was an inspiration, the one person who had the balls to rage against the machine, to tell it like it is and not regurgitate homogenized agendas. Thanksgiving and the Fourth of July are myths. We didn't eat turkey with the Indians. We slaughtered them. This land isn't our land. It's their land. No one told me about Wounded Knee until Mr. Pearce. Fourth of July? More blood and bullshit. When fascism comes, Brad said, it will be wrapped in the flag and carrying a cross. God? The only god they worship is the almighty dollar. Brad was the one adult who gave it to us straight. He talked to us like regular people and not little kids. But he's gone now. This is our fight. We will not sit down. We will not shut up. We will rise up and tell Principal Sheinbaum and the rest of the school board that no, we will not respect their decision to fall in line and salute their flag. They had their time. Now it's ours.

It's almost midnight. The Feds are en route. This radio broadcast was never about me. It was never about Mr. Pearce. It was about all of us, a unified scene, fighting together.

You hear that, man? The sirens? Right on cue. They got me surrounded. They want me to come out with my hands up. Like a goddamn movie.

I'm pulling over.

It's been an honor to be your captain and I am proud to go down with this ship. Let this be our reminder that we can all be something bigger.

Rider out!

THE MORNING OF THE DISAPPEARANCE

Friday, March 15, 1991, 1:12 a.m.

It had been over an hour since the Pasa Ardo PD and Feds arrived in Soledad Gorge, squad cars screeching, followed by several unmarked sedans, men in dark suits and darker sunglasses at night, all to take down … the Rider. Jess Barrett never got to see who the Rider was, the mystery man behind the garbled, disguised voice, the one who helped start a revolution. The scene pure chaos, everyone running in different directions, screaming, bullhorn blasting, shouting for the riot crowd to disperse. *Stop where you are! Every one of you punks is in trouble! You are going to jail!* Yeah, right. Like they were piling a hundred students from the privileged valley into the back of the prison bus. The Class of '91 should've stood their ground, fought back like Rider had rallied them to do, but seeing those flashing blue and red lights was scary. Talking tough is harder to do when you're staring down a gun.

Jess had drunk more than she'd intended. She wasn't much of a drinker. Add a few pills… This night was a big deal, a celebration. A declaration. A creed.

Hearts were also broken.

Jess had been more optimistic before the fight with Cam. She and Cam never really dated. They'd hooked up a few times. Okay, it was more than that. They had feelings for each other. Strong feelings. She was downplaying their relationship because she didn't want to be the bad guy. It's not you, it's me. Empty excuses.

She hadn't been totally wasted, but after their fight, she wanted to be numb, obliterated. Mixing meds and hard liquor was never a good idea. Turned out worse than that.

Can you love more than one person? Jess was pretty sure she did. Cam was special. He was also a boy—a cute, interesting boy. That didn't compare to a man. Cam was more mature than any other person her age. Being the chief of police's son—as well as the only black student at Pasa Ardo High—Cam had to deal with shit Jess couldn't imagine. Nothing seemed to rattle Cam. He was smart, strong, self-secure, and now Jess was thinking maybe she'd made the wrong choice. Or maybe she didn't love anyone, and recent decisions had been a chain reaction of chemical interaction, sexual attraction. Longing. Desire. Pure wanton, animalistic lust.

What did it matter now? Neither one was here. She missed him so much. How he smelled. How intelligent and sophisticated he could be. Society said it was wrong. She'd heard the whispers. In the hall. Tonight on the hillside. Saw the greasy smirk on Geremia's face when he palmed her the pills. In a way, she was relieved. She wanted people to know the truth. The weight of secrets drags you down and broken hearts are as heavy as stone.

What had she hoped to accomplish tonight? What had any of them hoped to accomplish? She had time to mull this over now as the sounds of law and chaos faded behind her.

Jess stumbled in the darkness, unsteady on shaky legs, the crunch of dry brush and dead twigs beneath her feet, echoing throughout the valley. With each step, she distanced herself further from the bedlam, walk turning to jog, jog to sprint. The night dipped colder, her skin clammy. She didn't stop running until she was far away and alone.

Why had she run in the opposite direction from everyone else? Because Jess Barrett wasn't a sheep. She listened to her own beat, made her own rules. And she always would.

Jess swigged the rest of the bourbon, washing down the remaining pills. She'd planned on taking one. She ended up taking all four. Bourbon mixed with the meds, and the rush hit her at once. And it was beautiful. She could smell the far-off citrus orchards, the air piquant with spritzed orange and lemons. A kiss of sunshine in the dark valley in the dead of night. The hillsides blazed with yellow mustards and red brome juxtaposed against blacks so black they appeared blue. The shrubs on the prairie. The wild grasses of the valley.

Jess's run slowed to a walk. She walked a long way.

When Jess heard crunching leaves and cracking twigs, she thought the disturbance came from her steps. Time was playing with her, like a recording on a half-second delay, the opening to a Pink Floyd song. Until she looked down and realized she hadn't moved. Must be a rabbit or other woodland creature. A squirrel skittering around a tree. No, whatever was out there was bigger, heavier, deadlier; a disruption of ground cover unearthed a slinking beast stalking its prey, the movement too methodical. A coyote, bobcat, mountain lion. The valley was filled with terrifying creatures that hunted at night. She waited for yellow eyes piercing the dark, the sharp claws that would tear her limb to limb.

Could she outrun it? Fight it off? Jess was tall but slim. She didn't like her chances against jagged incisors. Through wobbly eyes, Jess scanned the forest floor, trying to focus enough to find a sharp stick. She reached in her pocket, extracted her house keys, slipping metal spikes between her knuckled fist.

Then the sounds stopped. The beast had changed its mind, didn't want the hassle, had retreated.

Or whatever was clocking her had its timing down and prepared to pounce…

Jess spun and locked eyes.

It wasn't a wild animal.

The thing that stared back was far deadlier.

CHAPTER ONE

NOW, Tuesday, July 19, 2016, 4:59 p.m.

The bright, white lamp blazed overhead, illuminating the cold, blue corpse. You can feel the presence of death, addition by subtraction. It's more than the fish belly flesh or ungodly odor. Life possesses an essence. You can feel when it's there. And you know when it's gone, a soul extracted.

Chest cavity sawed open, hard bone split, cartilage cut, parted, peeled like thick plastic casing. Lydia Barrett slipped her hands into the slick slime, extracting the heart meat. She held it in her hands. The organ was more than a knotted lump of muscle, a vessel to pump and filter blood; it was a lifeforce, a battery that had once powered a full-fledged human being. When it stopped functioning, so did we. Maybe one day modern medicine would crack the code, figure out how to get it beating again. Immortality. Until then, the dead stayed gone.

When the cell buzzed in her pocket, Lydia mentally chastised herself for leaving it there in the first place. A rookie mistake. Maureen Gearon, friend, mentor, confidante, loomed nearby, studying Lydia's technique and methodology, pretending she didn't hear the iPhone's vibration. Maybe she didn't, Maureen so engrossed in Lydia's process and procedure, unable to hide her satisfaction. Just because you stop being someone's student doesn't mean you stop learning from them. Maureen Gearon had been Lydia's life coach, in one form or another, for more than half her life.

Lydia was thankful when the cell stopped droning, a temporary reprieve, only to have it immediately start up. Which told her who was calling. The last person she wanted to talk to: her mother, Gloria.

Lydia ignored the distraction and placed the cold meat on the scale, jotting the data, reporting numbers into the recorder. Swapping out sharp metal objects, she selected needle and thread, piercing together leathery dead flesh, sewing whole what had been torn apart.

Autopsy over, the two women retreated to the adjacent room to clean up and confer behind closed doors. Beyond the big glass window, the naked dead man lay on display.

Lydia peeled her gloves, snapping them in the trash with pinpoint precision, nothing but net. Reaching in her pocket, she stealthily attempted to slide off her phone before Gloria had a chance to hit redial.

"What do you think?" Maureen asked, hands soaping under hot water, steam rising, eyes cast askance, a casual question to mask serious inquiry.

Lydia knew what Mo was doing. Her old instructor often called her in to assist with autopsies like these. There was always a rub, no different than when Lydia first began her apprenticeship. Appearance versus reality, identify the abnormality. A test to evaluate if her former star pupil was still as sharp. This one was a big ol' softball.

"What?" Maureen teased. "You don't agree with the diagnosis of a heart attack?"

"We both know it wasn't a heart attack."

"All the symptoms—"

"Pulmonary embolism," Lydia said. "Come on, Mo. You used to try harder."

"I used to think I was prepping you to take over for me." Maureen feigned disappointment, affecting the posture of a tired old woman.

Nice try. Lydia could only hope to look that good when she was fifty-nine. Maureen Gearon was grace and dignity personified, projecting the classic beauty of a latter-day Michelle Pfeiffer. At thirty-eight, Lydia felt exhausted, beat-up, aged. *This job gets the best of us all. Except Maureen, apparently.*

Maureen's expression washed earnest. "Please reconsider."

"I like where I'm at."

"You're overqualified where you're at."

Lydia offered a wry grin. "Oh, but you meet the most interesting people."

Despite being a shoo-in for the county medical examiner's office, Lydia had opted for the less glamorous—and lower paying—position of coroner's investigator on the graveyard shift. The reasons for this were complicated. Or maybe that was how Lydia justified her decision to most. Of course, Maureen knew better.

"You're wasting your talents. That job is a stepping stone for recent grads. Or where washouts go. I'm not saying that to be mean. I know Ward and a lot of others who've worked the job. They're good people."

Ward Haynes was Lydia's latest partner on the overnight. He was nice, borderline competent, and mailing it in until the Social Security and pension kicked in next year.

"It's an important job," Maureen continued. "A necessary one. You were meant for more. I'm offering what you trained to be. You didn't earn a medical degree to be creeping around Los Angeles at all hours of the night—"

Lydia stifled a yawn.

Maureen's face fell sour.

"Sorry," Lydia said. "That wasn't intentional."

Maureen grimaced. "How's the insomnia?"

"I'm here, aren't I?"

Lydia got enough rest before and after her shift, even if she had to cobble it together. She didn't require much sleep—four or five hours did the trick—if not always in a row. We learn to live with what we cannot rise above. Lydia made the schedule work for her. Every day, she got in her jogging or yoga, was able to run errands, respond to emails, which still left time to shower, grab coffee, and make it to work on time. But rest isn't the same as sleep. It had been a while since Lydia slept well. That was if she ever did. Maureen knew the backstory few did.

"How are the night terrors?"

"I wouldn't call them 'night terrors.'" Lydia waited. "Sometimes, when I'm stressed, my dreams disturb … more easily."

"And keep you from falling back asleep."

"I'm a light sleeper."

"Underlying issues only burrow deeper—"

"You sound like a therapist." Lydia made sure to catch Maureen's eye. "I'm okay, promise."

"When you follow me," Maureen said, "and I hope you will—medical examiners work during the day."

"I am well aware."

"The assistant position is yours. Say the word."

Lydia's cell buzzed, making it clear her first attempt to silence Mom had failed. She had no choice but to abandon the subterfuge, pulling the phone from her pocket. Five missed calls, all but one from Gloria. Adjusting her thin-rimmed glasses, Lydia made sure to get it right this time, powering the damned thing off.

"And how is Mom?" Maureen asked.

"She hasn't grown nicer in her old age, if that's what you mean."

"Y'know," Maureen said, respectfully, "you can Google 'how to deal with toxic family members,' and you'll get a thousand results." Maureen reached out, rubbed Lydia's arm, a show of maternal affection, a gesture Lydia had lacked her entire life. Gloria might've been her mother. But she sure wasn't a mom. Since meeting Maureen, Lydia had been blessed. With a seat on the board, Maureen did more than offer a scholarship. Maureen Gearon had taken up the mantle of caregiver, a job she was under no obligation to shoulder. Without Mo's influence, who knows where Lydia could have ended up?

Blood is blood.

"She's my mother," Lydia said. "She doesn't have anyone."

"What about the old guy? Still hanging around, holding out hope?"

Lydia laughed. Poor old Richard Fontaine. He was so in love with Gloria. Her mother had been stringing along the handyman to do free work since Lydia was a kid, back when her older sister Jessica was still alive. Richard always seemed to be lurking. He'd disappear for chunks of time, and then there he was, like he'd never left.

"He's still in the picture," Lydia said. "I'm her daughter. You know how she milks that."

Lydia checked the big clock on the wall. "I owe her a visit." She grabbed her windbreaker off the rack, scrunching it up. "Promised I'd head over before my shift."

"Want some company?"

"You don't have to do that."

"I know." Maureen smiled. "Purely selfish reasons. I could use more time with my favorite protégé. Besides," she added, "we both know your mother doesn't cook. And you need to eat."

"Please don't say I'm getting too skinny."

Maureen laughed. "There's a great Vietnamese place on the way. Terrific phở. My treat."

"I won't say no." Lydia relished the buffer when it came to dealing with her mother. "If you'll promise to ease up on the hard sell."

Maureen blessed herself in the name of the Father, Son, and Holy Spirit.

Which earned a courtesy chuckle. Neither was a believer. Students of science, each favored the quantifiable over the supernatural.

The drive back home to Pasa Ardo offered pleasant views of the SoCal landscape. Evening settling, horizon a fiery auburn as the sun bobbed behind the hills. Maureen and Lydia had known each other long enough that they didn't need to fill empty spaces with meaningless chatter. The shared company of mutual silence.

Lydia appreciated Mo's tutelage. What she'd told Maureen outside the autopsy room was true. She *did* plan on working for the medical examiner's office. Someday. Lydia was more than qualified, having graduated top of her class, the recipient of countless awards and commendations. Bouts of insomnia aside, Lydia could adapt to sleeping during the night same as anyone. Yes, she suffered from nyctophobia. A fear of the night. A mild form. Situational, therapists suggested, stemming from the loss of her sister. Lydia didn't feel sorry for herself. Others suffered far worse. Lydia had learned to adjust. Truth was, she *did* prefer being awake when everyone else was asleep. There was solace in the still, quiet hours. A form of meditation. Which was an odd comparison, given what she was doing during that time.

Each night, Lydia hit the mean streets to stare in the face of death. She was a detective, even if her clientele landed a long way from the deep pockets of desirable. The people she investigated were often the ones society shunned, discarded. In the shadows, there was less judgment. Night lacked the urgency of day. This soothed Lydia. What did it matter where you slept if you didn't have a home? Flattened, oil-stained, cardboard mattresses made for the same uncomfortable bed regardless.

Do we choose our professions, or do they choose us? Lydia thought about this often. She was thinking about it now, tooling along the freeway, Maureen resting her head against the cool glass, enjoying a power nap after a hearty bowl of phở áp chảo gìon.

Would Lydia have entered the medical profession if Jess hadn't died? Lydia excelled in science classes. Biology, anatomy. It was taking home the National Science Prize that caught Maureen and the board's attention. But the *field* of medicine? Majoring in such a macabre facet?

She should've gotten more sleep last night. Thinking wasn't helping, these questions better exhumed in therapy.

Entering Old Town, the historic section of Pasa Ardo that survived gentrification, Lydia took in the whitewashed windows and boarded-up buildings, feeling the anxiety and dread of darkness creeping in. It was a symptom of her phobia, which is why she chose to be active and outdoors whenever possible. It beat being locked inside a cage.

The sun had just set, enough light left for Lydia not to experience the more debilitating effects of the condition. Plus, she wasn't alone.

"You look like you got the weight of the world on your shoulders," Maureen said, coming to, glancing over.

Lydia grimaced a smile. Her friend wasn't wrong.

Sometimes Lydia felt the weight of it all, unable to withstand the burden, fearful one day she'd be dragged down by the stone.

CHAPTER TWO

THEN, Night of the Protest
Thursday, March 14, 1991, 9:18 p.m.

Jess waited for Sarah and Renee in the dark woods before the cul-de-sac, feeling silly. Needlessly clandestine, peeping out between branches, an operative with a price on her head. Better safe than sorry. No reason to risk bright car headlights spreading up walls, alerting Gloria. Not that a seven-point-eight quake could rouse Mother from her nightly sleeping pills and bottle of chardonnay.

The street was dark, save for the soft, white halo of their porch light, always a welcoming sight, regardless of the dysfunction swirling inside. There were no streetlights on their road, house so remote. That was the point, why folks paid big money to live in Pasa Ardo. Few neighbors. Fewer hassles. Most everyone looking, thinking like you.

Gazing back at their house, Jess didn't see lights on in any of the guest rooms. It was doubtful her little sister would've returned to their shared bedroom so soon after an argument. Lydia must be asleep.

They were sisters. Of course they fought. Sometimes it got bad. This fight was worse, escalating quicker than usual. Jess was turning eighteen in a few days. No one that age wants to share a room with their thirteen-year-old baby sister. Their house was huge, with multiple spare rooms. But Lydia was scared of the dark and didn't like to sleep alone. Jess had long acted as caretaker. Mom sure wasn't up to the task. Dad was out in Santa Barbara, banging actresses. Jess would be leaving soon. That's what caused the fight.

Jess wasn't hiding the acceptance letter from UCLA. She wasn't ready to broadcast the news either. Lydia got the mail first. Jess' decision to attend the University of California, Los Angeles was more nuanced. Lydia couldn't understand. What does a thirteen-year-old know about true love and soulmates?

Panning from dark house to darker street, Jess wished Sarah and Renee would hurry the hell up. She didn't need Lydia waking to pee and noticing she was gone. Her baby sister was nothing if not inquisitive. Crazy smart, too. Probably grow up to be a mathematician or scientist. Jess didn't have time to explain where she was going.

Tonight's meeting at the water tower was the start of a revolution.

When Lydia stormed from the room, Jess didn't stop her. Her little sister was never short on theatrics. Blame it on hormones or Hollywood, whose reputation loomed large, throwing shade across the valley. They filmed quite a few movies around their little town—exterior shots of markets or coffee shops—Pasa Ardo granting instant, easy access for authentic color and local flavor that couldn't be manufactured on a soundstage. Only the bigger, more commercial movies could afford the assorted fees California tacked on for the luxury of filming on location. Jess knew all about how the movies worked from their father Alan, who made his name behind the scenes, financing some of the biggest and most profitable. The movies he helped produce were so big-time that Jess seldom brought it up to friends, even if they were in the theater watching one of them. Felt too much like bragging. Plus, Jess preferred the indies, cinema driven by passion and soul instead of bottom-line profit.

Jess acknowledged she was biting the hand. Jess and Lydia lived the way they did because of Dad's money. It was hard for Jess to take sides in the divorce—both her parents were awful. Their mother Gloria was one of a kind. You never met a more passive-aggressive, gaslighting bitch in your life. A real piece of work. That's what her dad used to say. He wasn't wrong. Jess appreciated the money her father supplied, even if it was court-ordered. Without it, the girls don't get to keep the big house and privileged Pasa Ardo zip code. Then again, if Dad wasn't off screwing prospective talent on casting couches, maybe her parents don't get divorced. Not that they'd been one big happy family when they were together. For two people who had no business being married in the first place, Alan and Gloria Barrett deserved each other.

If they hated one another while they were married, Gloria saved the real vitriol for when Dad's career took off, after the split. Meaning Mom wasn't entitled to as much money, which drove Gloria endlessly irate. That part was amusing at least. In a way, it screwed Jess and Lydia as well. Except their father was plenty generous with them. Gloria didn't make it easy, wielding her daughters like weapons. Since she had custody, Gloria attached so many strings and stipulations to visitations, Dad often grew weary and gave up. Jess was happy to accept his offer to pay for college.

College. The fight. The acceptance letter from UCLA. No matter how many times Jess assured her little sister she'd be back to visit frequently—the university was just over the mountains—Lydia couldn't hide the hurt. Jess understood. She wouldn't want to be left behind with Gloria either. Lydia had already been abandoned by their father. Now the only stable figure in her life—Jess—was bailing too. We all must follow our own path. Sitting around, waiting for her life to begin, would only foster animosity.

Jess understood that now. *Carpe diem.* Seize the day.

She'd first heard that phrase from Brad, back when he was Mr. Pearce, the hot, young, new English teacher, and not the man who changed her world. All the girls were in love with him. But that was because of the way he looked. Jess' attraction sprouted from deeper, more intellectual seeds. Brad was the first teacher to reach Jess, the first to get her to take her studies seriously. After Brad, Jess stopped viewing her father's money as a luxury and more like a useful resource to harvest the best version of herself. Without Brad, no way Jess turns around a lackluster scholastic career. That's what made Brad so special: he made every student feel like he'd taken a special interest in them.

Now it was their turn to return the favor.

The wide-open night skies, so clear above Santa Clarita Valley, exploded with stars, a living planetarium, which only added to how massive this moment felt. Up above, you could see a million distant suns blazing bright, alien worlds lush with the unknown, horizons expanding beyond comprehension. They were going to make big changes in this town.

Before the high school hired Brad, Jess hadn't cared about books or learning, period—she had no plans for after high school, no clue what she wanted to do with her life and was happy to mock anyone trying too hard. Dad's money would allow her to drift from party to party, hanging out with friends, having a good time, letting time pass her by. That was surviving, Brad told her; it wasn't living. Brad introduced her to literature, real literature, not board-approved, boring, canonical crap. He got her to read Dostoyevsky, Proust, *To Kill a Mockingbird*, which she'd been assigned to read several times, never once cracking open the spine.

Jess' senior year had coalesced in a series of life-altering events: Cam Rawls and Brad Pearce; embracing learning, falling in love; and a renegade radio show that served as a voice for the voiceless.

Tonight was made possible because of the Rider.

It had started as a joke, the pirate radio program, because that movie *Pump Up the Volume* had come out last year. Typical Hollywood misrepresentation of what it was really like to be in high school, all the actors in their twenties and super slick and sexy. Then there was this Rider on the Plain joker pulling the same stunt. But, like, in a totally ironic way, making fun of that film's earnest message of teen angst. Being judgmental came easy in SoCal. Putting yourself out there left you exposed to ridicule. That was another debt she owed Brad, who was the one who told her, "It's easy to make fun of everything when you don't stand for anything."

Whoever this Rider was, he'd taken a risk, put himself out there, and had come to represent possibility, hope, and change.

The car rounded the corner, headlights off, drifting in neutral, tires rolling over soft sand.

Sarah and Renee pulled alongside Jess, sliding up the seat so she could climb in back.

"You ready to do this?" Renee said.

Sarah passed the bottle, Renee checking the rearview as if to make sure they weren't being followed. And even if Jess felt self-conscious at the spy-game gesture, she allowed herself to be swept up in the moment and celebrate the cause.

Nothing would ever be the same after tonight.

CHAPTER THREE

NOW, Tuesday, July 19, 2016, 8:29 p.m.

Pulling into the driveway of her childhood home, Lydia spied Richard Fontaine's battered green Ford Ranger pickup truck. Poor guy was a lovesick puppy dog, forever lapping at the heels, desperate to suck at the teat. Floodlights splashed over the courtyard around back, meaning the old guy was still hard at work. Before she even opened the door, Lydia knew where she'd find her mother. Lounging, sipping white wine.

When she entered the house, Lydia was aware how fast she stepped in front of Maureen, as if to shield her from Gloria's wrath.

Gloria, fluffy, pink-slippered feet propped on the recliner stool, bottle of white on the glass table beside her, peered over her shoulder, scowling.

"You remember my friend, Maureen?" Lydia said.

"You work together at the morgue." Gloria wrinkled her mouth. "Did you dye your hair darker?"

"It's the same color it's always been."

Regarding the job, Lydia didn't bother correcting her mother's oversimplification. These were the subtle daggers Gloria excelled at wielding. Her mother's world yielded no nuance. There was no coroner's investigator or medical examiner, only the mindless task of herding the dead.

"How are you, Gloria?" Maureen asked, rising above the slight to extend manners that would not be reciprocated. "It's nice to see you again."

"I'd be better if my daughter answered my phone calls." Gloria's focused on the giant flat screen. Crime. Blood. Gore. Some program Lydia had never seen. No surprise. Lydia didn't have much downtime for television.

"Mom, we were conducting an autopsy."

"I still don't understand why people care so much about how someone dies. Dead is dead. Seems like a waste of taxpayer dollars."

Gloria Barrett was not a stupid woman. She recognized the need to determine a cause of death. Legality. Bureaucracy. Closure for a family. When Jess died, Gloria had been the loudest, most vocal proponent, demanding answers from then-chief of police Delmar Rawls.

When neither Lydia nor Maureen took the bait, Gloria peeked over her shoulder, nose wrinkled, unsteady eyes angled at her daughter. "Why didn't you call me back?" The chastisement was delivered via slight slur.

"I told you. I was working this afternoon."

"I thought you work nights?"

"Yes, Mom, I work nights. Sometimes I help out Maureen with autopsies during the day."

"Help?" Her mother spat the word like an epithet. Her stare remained fixed on Lydia, unwilling to acknowledge anyone else in the room. "You're not getting enough sleep. You look tired. Too dark." Then to Maureen: "I hope the county is paying my daughter for all this overtime."

"I personally make sure of it." Maureen smiled.

This was the difference between Gloria and Maureen. If the situation were reversed, Gloria would use the platform to push her own agenda. She'd play the martyr, parlaying abuse to press Lydia to take the assistant M.E. job. Gloria loved leveraging people against each other. Mo would never manipulate her like that.

Gloria's attention returned to the television as she spoke behind her back. "I wish you returned my calls. I left several messages. I'm out of groceries."

Lydia walked into the kitchen, opening the fridge, every square inch stocked with leafy greens, overpriced soft cheeses, and rare roasted meats. Untouched cartons of oat and almond milk, fresh-from-the-farm eggs at ten bucks a dozen. Four variations of tapenade whose seal her mother would never break. Mom survived on a liquid diet of rotating herbal smoothies to keep her figure. Lydia gazed through the window, where hunched-over Richard Fontaine drove a shovel into the hard earth along the pathway, tearing up chunks of tough terrain in a violent motion. Sacks of mulch and slabs of marble piled behind him.

Lydia came around to her mother's side. "Why didn't you have Richard get … groceries … for you?" Lydia tried to soften the sarcasm. She hated when she sounded like Gloria. There was plenty of food. "Groceries" was code for wine.

"Dickie's working," Gloria said, oblivious to the setting sun.

"You know how late it is? It's dark. There are mountain lions and bobcats out there. The guy is what? Seventy-five, eighty?"

Gloria waved a hand. "Dickie likes to keep busy. You know what they say about the devil and idle hands." Her mother cleared her throat. "I'm having him and his boys put in a new walkway to the pool."

"Didn't you do that last year?"

"Yes, I did. But I didn't like it. They used brick. It looked cheap. I want marble."

Lydia and Maureen exchanged a look. There was no one outside except Richard.

"He sent his crew home at five." Mom lifted the wine bottle, double checking it was dry. "Like they're actual employees. They're trouble, those charity projects of his. I wish he wouldn't bring them here. You know one of them tried to use the bathroom—inside?"

"People need to go to the bathroom, Mom."

"They can do … that … elsewhere. I'm not letting those people in my house. They're all crooks."

Maureen touched Lydia's arm, with a soft head shake to prevent Lydia's engaging. There was no point checking her mother's racism. That's what it was, plain and simple. Bigotry. For larger projects, Richard used day laborers, who were often Mexican, undocumented immigrants who huddled by designated intersections or outside the Home Depot, hoping to be picked up for ten dollars an hour. Hardest working people Lydia ever saw, doing the jobs no American wanted, and for a fraction of the cost. Schrödinger's Immigrant: both lazy and stealing our jobs. Lydia remembered when Richard first dug the pool in 1990. Back then, the old guy carried a steady crew. She and Jess would sit upstairs by their bedroom window, giggling over shirtless, young men, slathered in sweat, roughhewn, chiseled bicep and pectoral muscles glistening in the noonday sun. God, her sister was boy crazy.

"I liked it better when Richard hired … our people."

Our people. Lydia was mortified for Maureen's sake. At least her mother didn't say "whites."

Gloria pawed for her wineglass, palsied fingers dancing around the stem. "It's nice to see you, dear," her mom said without turning around.

Revisiting a childhood home is a bizarre experience. You get older, but the house never changes. Maybe a metal sculpture is erected on the porch, a burnished sign gets hung over the doorway, a new portrait goes up in the hall. But at its core, the house remains the same, retaining what it has always been—it's you who has changed, altering perception. Since Lydia last visited two months ago, the family room had been painted a more soothing shade of taupe.

With each visit, the home felt smaller, regardless of its thousands of square feet or sizeable acreage it sat on. The space could no longer contain Lydia. Like Alice popping pills, forever shrinking. By many standards, the home was a mansion. In Pasa Ardo, it was par for the course. An apt comparison with the country club up the road, cresting the hill, sucking up precious water high in demand, short in supply. Ninety million gallons a year. Lydia had read that somewhere.

"If you'd called ahead," Gloria said, "I would've made extra for dinner."

Lydia didn't need to mention she and Mo had already eaten. The statement was absurd. Gloria didn't cook. Anytime she *did* eat solid food, it was delivered, unless she had Richard grill salmon.

Lydia stepped into the living room, Maureen lingering in the kitchen.

Nearing Gloria, Lydia studied the TV screen. A dramatic recreation depicted a gruesome murder, index cards encircling blood splatter. "What are you watching?"

"Netflix. Documentary. Serial killer. They always recommend these shows. I let them play. Surprise me. All these programs are the same. So … sensational." The remote rested by Gloria's hand. She could change the channel anytime she wanted.

Her mother pushed herself to her feet, making the effort appear greater than it was. As her mother came nearer, Gloria's face seemed unnaturally taut, stretched with recent injections. The doctors used a heavy pour this time. Her skin looked like it had been sealed in plastic wrap.

Gloria leaned in, brushing Lydia's skin, kissing air.

"It's good to see you, dear," she repeated, patting her daughter on the shoulder, making for the kitchen. At the pantry, Mom brought back a warm bottle of chardonnay, reaching for the freezer and ice. "Seen your father lately?"

"We had dinner last month."

"Dinner," her mother spat. "How's Heather? Still prancing around half dressed?" Gloria never hid her disdain for Alan's wife. Heather was an actress, if not a terribly successful one. She was one of her father's many affairs. Lydia didn't know why this one stuck. The age difference was off-putting at first. Still, when Jess went missing, Heather, only twenty-five at the time, had been far more supportive than Gloria had ever been.

Richard came in through the back door, eyes lighting up, crow's feet crinkling with kindness. "Lydia!" He came in for a hug, stopping short, staring down at his dirty hands and stained shirt, settling on a pleasant smile to avoid soiling her clean clothes.

"What have you been up to?" he asked.

"Work." Lydia broke into a grin. "You remember Maureen?"

"How could I forget!" Richard beamed like a proud dad. "She's been grooming you for the big time half your life."

"What's Mom got you doing these days?" Lydia asked, dodging the subject of becoming full-time medical examiner.

"Oh, y'know, this and that." Richard smiled, thumbing over his shoulder. "We're sprucing up the pool." He pointed at the sky. "I was installing motion sensor lights."

"Right. The crime rate in Pasa Ardo." Lydia smiled. "Good to see you're keeping busy."

He laughed. "Back barks nonstop." Richard reached for his lower lumbar. "I'm like a shark. Gotta keep moving to stay alive."

"Will you be spending the night?" Gloria asked her daughter. "Your old room is as you left it."

"Mom, I told you. I have to work." There was no need to point out she'd come with Maureen. The offer was perfunctory. Gloria liked knowing she could demand Lydia's presence. Didn't mean she wanted her staying long.

"I thought you worked earlier."

"Yes, I assisted Maureen with an autopsy. I still have my night shift."

Gloria cast her eyes wearily over both women. "I don't get it. All those years of medical school. For what? Examining dead bodies? How is that a real doctor? Real doctors save lives. They don't dissect them like frogs in biology class."

Maureen had too much class to respond, and Lydia, as she did with most of the offensive things that came out of her mother's mouth, let it be.

"I guess I'll go to bed," Gloria said. "Nice to see you again, Maureen." Gloria couldn't have said it with any less sincerity. "Too bad you have to leave, Lydia," she added, glancing toward Richard, laying the bricks of the guilt trip to come. "Dickie will be going soon. I get so lonely in this big house. And I only have the one daughter."

CHAPTER FOUR

THEN, Random Weekend After the Divorce Became Final, 1989, Late Morning

A fifteen-year-old experiences a parents' divorce differently than an eleven-year-old does. Whereas an older sister might embrace peace after years of endless warfare, the younger one only sees her world falling apart.

Late Saturday morning, Jess was supposed to be hanging out at the mall, but called her friends to bail. Jess decided to stay home with Lydia, after her baby sister spent the night crying in the closet. Their father Alan was coming by today to pick up the rest of his stuff, which had been boxed and gathered for easy pick up, meaning he could've sent a messenger service or any of his lackeys to fetch these items, which were frivolous anyway, at least compared to the grief of his own children—a charity-raffled guitar signed by Bruce Springsteen, an artist he didn't like; a set of old golf clubs for a sport he seldom played; records for the player he didn't own. Jess would've loved to believe their dad wanted the opportunity to see his daughters. That wasn't it. Alan wasn't a bad father. He loved his girls. He was kind and gentle, but never present. If he could be elsewhere, Jess got the impression he would be.

Alan, who produced movies, cheated on Gloria. Normally that

would make a girl like Jess side with Mom. But you didn't know Gloria. Watching the way Gloria treated their dad, her sense of entitlement—the way their mom treated her new boyfriend Richard (Jess thought he was a boyfriend)—how she treated everyone, but men in particular, like they were born to serve her—was sickening. This didn't excuse her father's affairs. Even at fifteen, Jess could see how those affairs happened. Yes, there was opportunity. Alan didn't work on straight-to-video production—he helped finance major motion pictures. Box office record breakers. Academy Award nominees, winners. Actresses had to be throwing themselves at him. Maybe their dad was a sleazeball. What did Jess know about adult relationships? She'd look around at her friends' parents, half of whom were divorced. Few spoke kindly to each other. In the middle was a math equation that didn't add up, two oddball parents who actually enjoyed one another's company.

Waiting for Dad to show up, Jess watched Richard with his makeshift construction crew break ground on the new deluxe in-ground pool. Gloria had her lawyer tack it on in the divorce settlement because she could. Mother delighted in extracting every bloody red cent she could. Gloria didn't like to swim. It would be wonderful to say she got the pool for her daughters. Lydia might believe that. Jess knew better.

The pool was going to be nice, though. Jess had seen the plans. Of course her mother picked the most expensive options, only to turn around and have her boyfriend Richard do the labor on the cheap. Jess had to stop calling him that. Gloria didn't treat Richard like a boyfriend. But, boy, did that guy love her. You should've seen it. Old man Richard lifting heavy sacks of concrete, buckling his knees, hunching his back; you couldn't help but root for the guy. Jess didn't remember when Richard entered their lives. The handyman always seemed to be around. Didn't matter if today was a weekend. Jess knew Gloria instructed Richard to be there because she wanted Alan to see she too had moved on.

Gloria sashayed around the kitchen in a silk robe, clutching her morning bloody mary. Every time she passed the sliding glass patio doors, she let a shoulder slip, taunting the men outside. Gloria was pretty. Jess knew having Richard there was part of a plan. But if that plan was to make their father jealous, Gloria ought to have picked a better boy toy than battered, bent, and broken Richard Fontaine. Perhaps since Richard had worked for the family while they were married, Gloria wanted Alan to believe he wasn't the only one getting some on the side.

Lydia, glasses crooked, bedheaded hair, rounded the corner, wiping her nose with a pajama sleeve, before reaching for cereal in the cupboard. Jess heard the car pulling in the driveway. You could feel the air sucked from the room. A few moments later, Alan entered through the garage door into the foyer, falling for Gloria's trap.

"You can't just walk in," Gloria snapped. "This isn't your house anymore."

Alan winced a smile, retreated the way he'd come, shutting the garage door, walking around to the front and ringing the bell.

"Stop being so dramatic!" Gloria shouted.

Still, Alan wouldn't come inside, like a vampire waiting to be invited.

"Oh, for Christ's sake." Gloria turned to Lydia. "Get the door."

Jess, who was on the other side of the living room, said she'd do it.

When Jess opened the door, her dad affected enhanced manners, further irritating Gloria. This was shaping up to be a helluva morning. Petty antics by petty people, playing stupid games to win stupid prizes.

"Hello, Jessica," her father said, pretending he didn't see Gloria looming in the kitchen. "Would you mind asking your mother if I may be allowed to enter the one-point-nine-million-dollar home I purchased and gave her?"

"Stop it," Gloria said. "Just stop it."

Alan Barrett wasn't a big man. He wasn't a small one. He was average in almost every regard. But he had a temper. It didn't often show—her dad did a great job suppressing it. Through his restraint, his rage radiated off him. How could two people love each other enough to buy a home, start a family, sign up for a lifelong commitment, only to have it turn into this? Her dad was never violent. But if looks could kill…

After Alan hugged his girls, he headed upstairs to pick up his remains, leaving Gloria to mutter assorted curses under her breath. Lydia retreated from the kitchen, slinking up a different set of stairs to seek shelter.

The slider door opened, and Richard walked through with another man. Most of these employees Richard hired looked the same—hard up having survived a hardscrabble life, subservient to the point of spineless. Which Jess knew her mother loved seeing: men with their spirits trampled.

"This is Mark," Richard said. "Wanted to get him a drink of water."

"Of course, dear," Gloria said, loudly, with rare fondness and generosity.

At that moment, Alan pattered down the stairs, clubs slung over shoulder, box in hand, pausing. "Do I need to go around and knock again. Or am I allowed to speak?"

With the two other men standing there, Gloria didn't condescend to answer, painting the impression of one above such childish behavior.

Alan set down his things and walked over. "I'm officially moved out."

"Wonderful." Gloria rubbed Richard's arm. "Please make sure the child support arrives on time. As stipulated by our arrangement."

This time, Alan took the high road, extending a hand. "Good to see you, Richard. Looks like you're getting to work on that pool."

Alan grinned. "Don't let this one"—he thumbed at Gloria—"work you too hard. She's a real slave driver."

The comment earned a courtesy chuckle from everyone, save Gloria.

The other man, Mark, raised the glass of tap. "Thanks for the water, ma'am."

Gloria howled with raucous laughter.

"Please, it's Gloria," she said. "I think I'm a few years away from 'ma'am.'"

The man's faced flushed. Jess felt sorry for him. He was trying to be polite. Why did Gloria have to humiliate people like that?

"Alan," Richard said, maintaining the decorum Gloria lacked. "This is my friend, Mark Burns. He's one of my best men."

Mark Burns did not look like anyone's "best man." He wasn't as old as Richard, but his face was gaunt, scavenged, body leaning in ways Jess knew weren't normal. Giving him a name afforded the man dignity.

Alan reached over, shook the man's hand, and said it was a pleasure to meet him.

Then Richard and Mark returned to work. Alan and Gloria narrowed stares. They spat a pair of parting quips, before he left and she refilled her cocktail.

Jess stood in the middle of the big kitchen with its large island and hanging pots, staring at all that gleaming metal and ample counter space, left to wonder how people ended up so callous and inhumane when they got older. It was like age was a disease. Eventually everyone caught it. The symptoms might be different for each. For some, the condition stripped your pride. For others, it turned you into an arrogant asshole, another a bitch. But no one escaped uninfected.

CHAPTER FIVE

NOW, Wednesday, July 20, 2016, 5:31 a.m.

Bright artificial light blistered around the office. Lydia Barrett and Ward Haynes had endured a long, mind-numbing shift at their desks, the pair tasked with the tedious administrative duties of the position, compiling causes of death, which ran a comprehensive gauntlet, from bullet holes to stab wounds, the one constant more prevalent than not: violence. There was no shortage of how horrible we humans could be. Even suicides, harm inflicted upon oneself, stemmed from the darkest recesses. Most of Lydia's job comprised this minutia, cataloging gruesome physical evidence of death. Ligature scraps, gunshot residue, skin flakes under fingernails, flesh rubbed raw by rope, samples collected, marked, stuck in assorted tubes and labeled, sealed in plastic baggies and logged into evidence. Some clues were smoking guns; some as innocuous as miscellaneous art supplies. All were potentially vital in solving a crime, especially one as heinous as murder. After death, the real work began.

Then it was all hurry up and wait. Compile, sort, send off for analysis, moving body to body, biding time for algorithms to interpret, compare and contrast, spit back data, point investigators in the right direction. Death was subjected to the same procedural bureaucracy as any other life event. Sometimes it felt like there was never closure, just one long open case.

Out the window, Lydia observed L.A.'s jagged skyline, sharp points and razored edges slicing the darkness, carving the night bleak, the horizon another cavity to penetrate and crack open, exposing what lay beneath.

Though the sun would be up soon, there was a whole world out there that never slept, partiers and ravers, late-night pub crawlers and frat boys grubbing at twenty-four-hour diners, sloshed beer bellies sopping up greasy fried foods, raucous laughter and bloodshot eyes. A mournful feeling overtook Lydia. Remorse? Regret? Sometimes, Lydia felt like she had missed out on that part of growing up. The careless, reckless part. After her sister died, Lydia had been sent away to boarding school. Sometimes it felt like she'd gone from thirteen to thirty-eight overnight.

Night surrendered. Morning started to bleed daylight. Bruised purple toiled, rumbling through rich reds to rosier pinks, more honeyed rust, the restoration of the illusion that there could be peace. Burnt orange slathered pavement, highlighting the cracked rubble and ruptured fissures of a broken city, Southern California plate tectonics forever shifting, buildings in a permanent state of settling, rendering the entire panoramic disturbed. It was subtle. You had to know what you were looking for. A bend here, a fracture there. When you experience a city so often in the dark of night, your perceptions are altered by the light of day, disruptions more pronounced. You can see the world for what it is: off-kilter, off-center.

That's when the call came in. Female. Mission Junction. River's edge. Dead. Police on the scene were unsure whether it was an accident. No visible signs of struggle. That's all they were instructed to say. Detectives were en route.

When she and Ward arrived, the first detail Lydia noticed was the way the woman's neck lay over the edge of the concrete riverbed, her crooked body unnatural, suspended improbable, violating laws of gravity. The Jane Doe hovered inches above the trickling urban cast-off, tendrils of hair dipping in sludge littered with broken glass, used syringes, cigarette butts, and the odd candy wrapper. The woman seemed emptied. An inflatable doll with the air let out, her entire person deflated.

The Jane Doe appeared to be in her early fifties. Attractive, fit. It was tough to tell, especially in Southern California where nipping and tucking could obfuscate nature's timetable.

The next observation should've buoyed hope. The woman was fully clothed. Well-dressed, in fact. While no one was happy to encounter a sexual assault, it made the job easier. Such a death adhered to logic, however depraved. Unchecked animalistic impulses, the need to exercise power, the rage and domination. People—men—and the violence they perpetrated disgusted and terrified Lydia. But it offered an explanation. Of course, it was possible for a rape victim to be assaulted and redressed. Lydia had encountered odder postmortem rituals, rapists who'd cut and clean nails, even bathe their victims after they'd killed them. That didn't appear to be the case here.

Silent squad car lights splashed off hard surfaces, rendering the picture unclear. Though the riverbank was caked in mud, the dead woman's clothes remained unsoiled. As if someone had gently laid her by the water's edge. There wasn't enough liquid in the parched riverbed to get in the lungs, nor did the body appear bloated. The death smelled fresh.

After speaking with police, Lydia had a name: Rhona Clarion.

Rhona's purse had been left behind, credit cards and cash intact.

A wedding ring remained on her finger. Her iPhone lay in a shallow puddle of water nearby. Valuable items that would've been taken if this were a robbery gone wrong. Rhona's address read Ridgemont Avenue, Fairfax. Nice neighborhood. Good street numbers.

The possibility of a thwarted drug deal flashed through Lydia's mind, a thought she dismissed as quickly. Never mind Clarion's attire—addiction didn't discriminate—Mission Junction wasn't a great section of town, but it wasn't associated with street-level dealing either.

The one photo in Rhona's purse showed her with her arms around a slight, balding man. Sixty-something? Young enough to not come across as Rhona's father. The pair was bookended by two teenage girls. Fifteen, sixteen. The man displayed dead eyes and the wan pallor of an anemic vegan who didn't get enough sun.

Snapping on her latex gloves, Lydia admitted, if only to herself, that it would be odd—though not out of the realm of possibility—for an aneurism or blood vessel to burst at an inopportune time. Improbable but not impossible. An investigator must remain open to the unlikely. Although that wouldn't explain why a woman dressed like this would be walking in this part of town. No car was found in the immediate vicinity. Not one registered to anyone named "Clarion." Divorced women change names. This woman lived comfortably. Or had until this morning's tragic outcome. According to her driver's license, Rhona Clarion was fifty-one.

End of shift came and went. The new crew arrived with fresh coffees. The early morning sun shone brighter. After five minutes of unpaid overtime, Ward slinked off. Lydia remained.

The iPhone, damaged and unable to turn on, might yield answers. The police would require time, perhaps days to pull records. This was an odd spot for a suicide…

Lydia talked to the officers who answered the call, and then the detectives who arrived later. Nobody had reported Rhona missing during the night, which was strange. She could've been working late, meeting friends—meaning Lydia wasn't ready to blame the husband. Yet. By now, he must have noticed his wife and the mother of their children hadn't come home. Morning had broken. Still, no one had reported Rhona missing. Lydia was making assumptions, which she didn't like to do. There was no evidence to say the man in the photograph was a husband. Could've been a friend, perhaps an older brother, the girls, nieces. This didn't sit right. Instincts said husband, daughters. Lydia trusted her instincts.

While the forensic team bagged the body for transport, Lydia jotted down the address.

Despite repeated urges to head home and get some sleep, Lydia insisted on being the one to deliver the news. This was part of the job, the worst part of it: notifying next of kin. And it was ten times worse when you didn't have all the answers. There was a good chance the husband was responsible because math. That was the sad truth of domestic murders—though Lydia had no way of knowing if they were dealing with a murder. Let science do its job. Meanwhile, Lydia reminded herself to remain impartial, compassionate. A father would have to tell children their mother was never coming home again.

Lydia slogged through morning gridlock. The drive along the freeway was a solemn one, passageways, detours, and reroutes clogged because this was Southern California. The radio filled the silent spaces with pointless chatter, morning DJs trying too hard to be funny, the occasional overplayed pop song, talk radio with too much talking.

Caught in the morning commute, Lydia felt her mind drifting, called back to an earlier time, the precipitating event that had delivered her to this exact moment. This wasn't a place she visited often, mainly because it failed to provide any relief.

Lydia felt conflicted recalling her schooling, a bittersweet experience. She'd excelled at school, education her salvation. It was the one area of her life she could control, a means to ignore the loss of Jess, her sister and best friend. It was easy to keep her nose in a book, a form of disassociation to push herself to be the best by staying in the well-lit dorms to study instead of going out to party. The truth was Lydia didn't want to be getting soused at campus bars. Lydia had plenty of friends, enjoyed the occasional beer, but she never got caught up in that rowdy rite of passage like other classmates or friends. Whereas most people partied to numb themselves from the pain, Lydia had, in a way, done the opposite to achieve the same effect.

After Jess died, Gloria couldn't hide her disdain for her remaining daughter. The more her mother drank, the looser her tongue became and the sharper the barbs lashed. Being told by your own mother that you, and you alone, were responsible for the death of a sibling can crack the sturdiest self-esteem. The years away from Pasa Ardo saved Lydia. Without parents, she flourished. Teachers, therapists, and instructors helped carry the load. People like Maureen. But that's what we do, isn't it? We instinctually fill voids. We find mothers and fathers to replace the ones we never had.

Rhona Clarion's address delivered Lydia to a posh neighborhood, streets lined with tall palms and intricate pathways paved with small, smooth stones.

The Clarions lived higher on the hill, where the bigger houses began to spread out, offering more privacy. Lydia parked in the driveway before making her way up the steps.

She had made many similar house calls over the years, enough to know people reacted to bad news in all sorts of ways. Response to grief was personal. Some went silent. Some wailed. Some took it out on the messenger. While Lydia didn't yet know if they were dealing with a homicide, initial examination at the scene and professional experience told her that, yes, unfortunately, that was the case.

The first person suspected in a domestic homicide was the spouse.

One look in the man's eyes gave Lydia her answer.

CHAPTER SIX

THEN, Same Random Weekend After the Divorce Became Final, 1989, Early Afternoon

As soon as Alan walked out the door, Richard went to hug Gloria, but she pushed him away.

"Not now, Dickie." Gloria stared at the closed door, the sound of her ex-husband's exquisite German craftsmanship purring in the distance. "Why should that sonofabitch get everything and I get nothing?"

Jess stood in a corner, trying not to giggle. *Nothing?*

Richard echoed her thoughts. "I don't know if I'd call this *nothing.*" He gestured around the spacious, well-decorated home, then pointed outside to the large yard and massive excavated hole for the new pool, the expansive emerald lawn, before returning his attention to four thousand square feet of mid-century modern design, a home many would kill for, where they all stood warm, cozy, and well-fed. If he was hoping to elicit gratitude, he was talking to the wrong person.

Gloria seethed. "You know goddamn well he waited to sign that last movie deal until the divorce was final. He's going to make a fortune!"

"Gloria," Richard said. "You're letting him live rent free inside your head—"

"Save your Alcoholics Anonymous bumper sticker slogans for someone else, Dickie." Gloria pointed at a sheepish Mark Burns who remained frozen, scared to move for fear of being noticed. She snagged her bloody mary. "Why don't you and your little AA pal get back to work? I'm not paying you to stand around."

At this Jess couldn't *not* laugh. She knew, for a fact, how chintzy her mother was. Whatever Richard paid his workers, guys like this Mark Burns, came from his own pocket.

"And what's so funny, Jessica?"

Jess watched Richard lead his sad-sack buddy outside, too beaten down to stand up for himself. Jess wasn't intimidated.

"You're ridiculous," Jess said. "That's what."

Gloria finished her cocktail. "Why am I not surprised? You've always taken his side. No matter how many whores he was sleeping with. You have no idea what I put up with for you girls to keep this house."

"The house that wasn't good enough two minutes ago?"

"It's so easy at your age."

"Yeah. I know. Best years of my life." Jess pretended to stifle a yawn.

"I used to be your age once."

"Once." Jess rolled her eyes and folded her arms.

"I know you think I'm an asshole. And maybe I haven't always been the best mother. But you reach this age and tell me you managed to hold onto all your lofty ideals, especially if you have children. Let me know the bad taste left in your mouth from all you had to swallow."

"I won't be a hypocrite, I can tell you that."

Jess had gotten into plenty of shouting matches with her mother, escalating over the past couple years, this last year particularly bad. In these fights, Gloria could be spurred to histrionics. It was hysterical watching Gloria lose it, playing the victim, dabbing crocodile tears. Her mom never had to work a day in her life. Her father was no saint. That didn't make her mom any less of a bitch.

Instead of shrieking dramatically, this time Gloria adopted a sad smile, as if she were remembering a different time, a better life, one with rosier futures. It was an odd expression.

"That's the funny part about hypocrisy, dear." Gloria set down her empty glass. "It's death by a thousand paper cuts. You won't survive long if you don't learn to live with it."

"Sure, Mom." Jess okayed her fingers. "Great talk."

"Your father was never faithful. I knew it on some level of course, but I looked the other way. He made it easier back then. He at least had the decency to be secretive. Then you girls were born and he didn't bother hiding it. Condom wrappers in his pants. I had my tubes tied. Credit card receipts for Tuesday afternoon hotels while I was still recovering from having my body ripped open. It's easy when you're a man. Back then, he was getting started in the industry. He could walk away from me whenever he wanted. I'd hitched my future to his. And when you girls were born, I lost any luxury of taking the high road. Yes, I am a hypocrite, Jessica. I lied to you every day I was married to that man. I'd never encourage you girls to tolerate being treated like a dog, groveling for scraps of affection, getting kicked around. But if I left"—Gloria spread wide her silk-wrapped arms—"we'd be living in a one-bedroom dump in Reseda while I waitressed at Denny's. So I stayed and suffered his infidelity. I raised you girls, washed the semen stains out of his underwear and cleaned the lipstick off his collars as he threw the freedom he enjoyed in my face, humiliating me with how little of it I had. Each morning, I woke, waiting for night and the sweet relief of sleep. Because dreaming was the highlight of my day."

"Mother of the year material." Jess faux clapped. "Magnificent."

Gloria had stopped listening to or conversing with Jess. She continued her monologue as if performing her own eulogy, staring out the windows toward the Hollywood Hills.

"I did all the cooking and cleaning and shopping and homework with you girls. I wasn't always this broken. I brought you to birthday parties, stood around, enduring banal talk from vapid, brainless mothers. Vacations on Catalina Island. Investment options. Who knows what the hell they were talking about? Stepford wives. Oh, and I know that doesn't sound so bad." Having slurped her bloody dry, Gloria refilled the glass with straight vodka. "And it wasn't. It was … fine." She waved a hand over her home, balance wavering enough for Jess to start toward her in case she fell. Gloria protested. "I'm fine. And you might not believe this, but I love you girls more than life itself. You can't understand a mother's love for a child until you have one. It's like having your heart walking around outside your body."

Jess wanted to whip back a snarky retort. This self-pitying martyr speech was making her ill. She didn't buy any of it. Jess also wanted to see how it ended, her mother's rewriting the tragic fall of Gloria Dunn Barrett inside her hallowed marble halls.

"I gave the best years of my life." Gloria glanced down at her body, which was still fit for its age, Jess supposed. "I gave my body. You don't know what it's like carrying two pregnancies to term, the toll it takes. What it looks like … down there. It wrecks you."

"I'm pretty sure Dad paid to get *it* fixed." Jess knew about her mother's assorted tummy tucks and plastic surgeries. Gloria milked the recovery, asking the housecleaner to sleep in a guest room for two weeks to tend to her every beck and call.

"It was the least he could do." Gloria turned to the window, watching Richard, Mark Burns, and the rest of the Twelve-Step gang of losers he'd assembled. "You think I'm settling for that?"

Jess assumed she meant Richard. Or maybe she was talking about the pool. Or maybe she meant all of it, the severance package for enduring fifteen years of a miserable marriage.

"You really are a bitch," Jess said.

"Maybe I am. But all that—" Gloria gestured over Jess' young body. "The tight jeans and budding breasts, your fine little ass and flawless skin? You'll peak. You don't think so. But one day will be your last best day. Then you'll slowly start trudging toward your expiration date. One morning you'll wake up like this. And you'll find there isn't a doctor in the world who can give you back the years you lost."

CHAPTER SEVEN

Lydia Reavis. That could've been her name. Sounded horrible. Like a sci-fi villain or venereal disease. She'd never considered whether she'd take Gil's last name, even when it felt like they were on the verge of getting engaged. The possible lifetime commitment was less about being in love and more the timing, having reached an age when one made that decision. Neither she nor Gil wanted it, and it was a relief when both agreed they were better off roommates and friends than another loveless married couple.

Walking up the stairs to their second-floor apartment, Lydia didn't know why she was thinking about this. Probably because she'd just seen Gloria, which reminded her of her parents' disastrous nuptials. No, she thought, she'd have kept her last name. Lydia couldn't see herself surrendering her identity like that.

When she walked through the door, Gil was making coffee. Each froze. Yes, they shared an apartment. Their alternating schedules seldom allowed face-to-face interaction. Gil kept staring even after Lydia had tucked away her keys. Seeing him there with his shirt off, Lydia didn't allow old feelings to stir. Her girlfriends never understood how she let Gil go. Looks aside, he was a fireman. That part didn't impress

Lydia. Or maybe it did. Caught in his piercing gaze, like she was now, sometimes she didn't have a good answer.

"What?" she asked, depositing her bag and belongings, including her department-issued firearm, in the chair. Lydia hated guns. Now that her workweek was over, she couldn't leave it locked in her glove compartment, its normal storage place. In ten plus years on the job, she never once had to use the damn thing. The dead seldom fought back.

Gil backed off, returning to his coffee. "Looks like you had a rough night."

He peered out the window, over the northern hills, into the new day's buttery sunshine, slathered in that special way you only find in Southern California, perfectly toasted grains glistening. He snagged his tee shirt off the counter. "Overtime?"

"Not exactly." Lydia ran her fingers through her long hair, tangled knots slow to unravel. "Rough night?" she repeated.

"Sorry. Didn't mean it like that."

"Like what? That I look like shit?"

Gil held up the pot of coffee. "Peace offering?"

Lydia preferred not to sleep when she got off shift, scattering strategic naps throughout the day. Graveyard ended at seven, even if this morning had run closer to ten, which offered fewer options. She could try to force it now, but she was wound too tight, which meant resting later in the day. She hated that switch over, going to sleep while it was light, waking in the dark. She found the sensation jarring, unpleasant. Those first few seconds of consciousness came on overwhelming, like tonight might be more than she could bear. It was a symptom of the nyctophobia, she knew, the confusion and agitation that came with the dark. She was able to combat it. If she could keep moving. It was a constant battle.

She nodded, accepting Gil's caffeinated apology, and turned to the flat screen, which he had on, sound playing low. A reporter stood along the edge of a forest, the soft glow of fire and plumes of smoke rising behind her in the distance.

Gil passed along the mug of coffee. Black. One sugar. There was comfort in familiarity.

Lydia nodded at the television, whose screen filled with increasing smoke as a hovering copter filmed live eyewitness coverage.

"That time of year." Gil shrugged. "Wouldn't worry about it. Nowhere near us."

Welcome to California, the promised land of wildfires and earthquakes. Both were such a daily presence, threatening apocalyptic destruction that they, strangely, stopped being a concern. Once fire season started—and it had—the flames would pick a spot to scorch and get to work, ravaging thousands of acres in a few days. You could pray to God or hope for rain. Neither worked. And the big one could hit any minute. When total annihilation is only a moment away, what's the use in worrying? You'd drive yourself mad thinking about it.

For a firefighter, Gil did little actual firefighting. Early in their relationship, he explained that the danger wasn't as prevalent as Hollywood would have you believe. Most of his job consisted of responding to other kinds of emergencies, medical and domestic, serious and benign, from motorcycle accidents to the proverbial cat stuck in a tree. When she was his girlfriend, Lydia thought he was trying not to worry her. But he wasn't lying. Despite the persistent wildfire threat, like so many of our fears, perception trumped reality. The truth was there were far fewer forest fires than there used to be. You wouldn't know it by listening to the news. A thousand years ago, fires burned unchallenged, consuming miles until they grew bored, humanity helpless to stop them, which left two choices: run or die.

In many ways, Gil and Lydia had the same job, both on call for tragedy. With one glaring difference: when Gil was summoned, the possibility of life was still on the table. Lydia was brought in after the fact, after it was already too late. He saved. She recovered.

"Want to tell me about it?" Gil asked, eyeing Lydia, who was engrossed by the talking head, motioning over parks and preserves she didn't recognize, camera lens at such a distance the devastation scorched in the abstract. Though it had been a while since they'd been a couple, Gil knew her well enough to read her emotions, which Lydia never did a great job hiding.

"My night?" Lydia said.

Gil took a sip of coffee, face remaining pleasant. He was a much better friend than he was a lover. Or maybe it was the other way around, Lydia the better friend. She had to admit she found intimacy easier when sex wasn't involved.

They plopped on the couch. She recapped her night, trying to put her finger on why she'd been so shaken over finding Rhona Clarion's body by the muddy banks of a concrete river. She knew Gil must be thinking the obvious: it triggered memories of her sister. Had he voiced this, Lydia's kneejerk response would be that every death didn't have to involve Jess. So she brought it up first, addressing that line of logic before Gil had a chance and she jumped down his throat. Lydia still hadn't wrapped her head around Rhona Clarion. Yes, it struck a chord, Jess the obvious transitional note, but there was more to it than that, an intangible component Lydia couldn't comprehend. She *felt* it. She couldn't find the right words though. Because it was more than Jess, greater than the cruelty of this life, how unfair it could be, how a loved one could leave the house alive one evening, only to wind up dead before dawn. It was the darkness that got to her most—the dark heart of man, the reach of evil. The scariest monsters are often right in front of us. We just can't see them.

Maybe she was overthinking it. Maybe Lydia was so disturbed because there was no cohesive answer, no comforting solution. When she'd told Dan Clarion the bad news, Lydia knew, statistics be damned, this was one instance where the husband could be ruled out. Never mind the credible alibi—in this case, Dan had returned from a conference in New Orleans this morning, plane ticket in hand. Never mind a vouch of character—Lydia spoke with the housekeeper, who lauded Dan's unassuming nature and limitless devotion to his wife; the daughters, who, while devastated, clung to their father's side, searching for security, displaying no signs of fear. So too set aside his slender, diminutive build—Lydia had seen murderers kill victims twice their size. Lydia saw it in his eyes. Perhaps it would turn out Dan Clarion was a helluva actor, one stone-cold SOB who'd hired a hitman to take out his wife. Until then, she'd trust her gut.

Gil gave her shoulder a squeeze. "You might want to get some sleep. Sooner than later." He held up a hand. "Not an insult. Sounds like you've earned a little self-care." He pointed out the window. "I'm teaching a session. After that, I have a couple days off. I was thinking of driving down to San Diego, see my folks and sister—"

Lydia couldn't hide the disappointment. For once, she didn't want to be alone.

"Unless … you need me to stick around?"

"I'll be fine. Say hi to your parents and Jen. I miss your sister."

"She misses you too."

After Gil left, Lydia tried taking his advice. *Get some sleep.* She did attempt to lie down. But she was too wired. Lydia couldn't blame caffeine. She hadn't touched the coffee. Like at the crime scene, anxiety gnawed, her mind a hamster wheel spinning relentlessly.

Lydia hopped out of bed, found the cold coffee on the counter, and reheated it in the microwave. The TV had been left on. The news report still showed a fire raging, advertisements slapped between the flames. That's all the news was: death and consumption. Report one, encourage the other. Ticker rolled at the bottom of the screen. Gil was right. The fire was nowhere near them. Didn't feel that way. Like any second she'd be consumed by it.

Hours drifted by while she surfed the internet, punctuated by futile attempts at napping. As soon as she'd begin to fall asleep, she'd wake with a start, panicked that she'd be late for work, only to remember she had the next few nights off.

Lydia pulled out her phone, scrolling through the few names and numbers of people she wouldn't mind meeting for dinner or drinks, but even that effort felt forced.

All of humanity's problems stem from an inability to sit quietly in a room alone.

When you're right, Pascal, you're right.

Before tucking away her phone, Lydia revisited yesterday's missed calls from Gloria. God, she wished she could take Maureen's advice and cut ties forever. Lydia erased all her mother's voicemails without listening to one.

There was another voicemail, though, from a number Lydia didn't recognize.

Probably an unsolicited spam call. She hit playback anyway. A woman's gentle voice came over the speaker.

"*Hi, you don't know me. I'm sorry to call like this but …*" (long pause) "*I'm not trying to touch a raw nerve. It's about your sister? Jessica?* (longer pause) *Uh, can you call me back? I don't feel comfortable leaving this over voicemail.*" The woman supplied a number.

Lydia was already shaken, tiny arm hairs standing on end, before the caller added one more chilling detail to the gooseflesh.

"*Oh, I almost forgot. My name is Rhona. Rhona Clarion.*"

CHAPTER EIGHT

THEN, Tropicana Motor Inn, North Hollywood, Room 23, Monday, October 8, 1990, 3:45 p.m.

Mark Burns set down the works, his needle, spoon, rig, spongy wad of wet black cotton. He undid the tourniquet, a dirty sock he'd wrapped around his skinny arm three times, pulling so hard he feared he'd tear his rotator cuff. Wasn't much meat left. Just a thin rail of bone. No blood either. He hadn't been able to find a vein, settling for muscling the dope. A quick jab in his skinny butt. Didn't produce the rush. But in a few minutes, he'd stop feeling sick. Mark wondered how he managed to keep alive without blood flowing in his body. He must have veins *somewhere*. Damned if he could find them. He'd lost so much weight.

A river of blue streaked along the bottom of drawn blinds. Mark stood at the window of his second-floor room, cracking the shutters, shielding his eyes from the glare. Street kids and crusted punks huddled in doorways. Skateboarders zoomed along the sidewalk.

Mark had rented the room for a week using his SSDI check. Social Security Disability. He used to work a regular nine-to-five, meaning he'd paid into the system. Back then he had a wife and two daughters. Factory job. Shipping and receiving. Didn't last long. Sometimes he thought about renting an actual apartment. No point trying. He'd never pass the background check. Criminal record. Mark wasn't working now. Any money left over went to heroin.

Last year, he'd had a good gig going as part of a construction crew for this guy Richard Fontaine. Mark was sober. He'd been attending meetings. Even got his ninety-day chip. There weren't many people who'd hire a guy like Mark, who came with trouble written all over him. He'd met Richard Fontaine at a Big Book Meeting. Richard owned a small general contracting company. It was hard work but honest pay, if under the table. Although most of the time, they seemed to work at this one house out in Pasa Ardo. This rich lady named Gloria. She wasn't nice. One of those snobby suburban alcoholics who thinks she's better than you because she has money and drinks forty-dollar wine. She had two daughters. The oldest one, Jessica, reminded him of his own girl, Beth. God, she must be ten by now… Mark hadn't spoken with Beth or Emily, his youngest, in a while. First there was the restraining order from his ex, Abby, and then… Mark knew they were better off without him. Addiction was a beast he'd never be able to tame.

That's how he felt, standing at that window, observing a world operating in sync without him, inconsequential and worthless. Cars with men returning from work. Women and children shopping for groceries. Boys and girls laughing. A regular life. Mark would've loved a regular life again. When he'd had that old job, he'd thought it was bad. Now that he'd lost it all, he was finding out how bad bad was.

Mark picked up last night's sandwich, which he'd fished from the dumpster behind Hanno's, where he'd been hanging out with Larry. Larry was a good guy, good friend. A screw-up like Mark, sure, but he had honor, a rare commodity these days. Larry reminded him a lot of Richard Fontaine. Except Richard was able to put down the bottle and keep his shit together. Mark never understood why Richard was so dedicated to that Gloria lady. You should've seen it. She'd bark and he'd come running. Like a whipped dog. Maybe Richard thought he could save her too.

Mark wasn't always like this. He used to have dreams. When he was nineteen, he had a band. Didn't talk about it much but they'd been signed to an actual label. They were called Feral Cat Fail and put out one record, *Cat Scratch Fever*, which was released one year before Ted Nugent recorded his own song with that title. Mark didn't think anyone stole their title. It was a coincidence. In the world of rock and roll, coincidences happened all the time. You only have twelve notes to work with. It's why so many songs sound alike. One, four, five. Plus, you can't copyright titles. Their record came out with a small indie label. It didn't sell. The label went under years ago, so it's not like Mark was missing residuals. They were all partying back then. Those were good times. Felt crazy to think about it now, but there was a moment where it looked like they really might make it. They played a show on the strip, and a record guy was there—a big-time record guy—and after the show, he talked to Mark and the band and said he wanted to make an offer. Then … it never happened.

Mark couldn't remember why. His whole life had been like that. Just when it looked like things might work out after all, the Universe would yank the rug. He never knew why the cosmos seemed to conspire against him. Bad things just happened to him. Or maybe it was because, like his sponsor once said, Mark lacked gratitude. Even after his rock-and-roll dream died, he still had Abby, and, God, he loved her. He loved being a dad. And he was happy. Sometimes. But he was never satisfied. Always wanted more. Thought he *deserved* more. That's called entitlement. The Universe does not like when we act entitled.

Sitting on the unmade motel bed hopping with bed bugs, which bit and shit inside him every night, choking down cold gray meat sogged inside stale bread, Mark wondered why he couldn't live like other people. He'd see them, every day. All the ordinary people with their ordinary concerns. Didn't know what they were doing with their lives. Maybe he was, like Abby maintained, a *bad* person. And she didn't mean a bad *person*, but a bad person. Like he wasn't any good at living.

The motel television was on. Mark didn't know the name of the movie. He wasn't watching. The sound played low because he couldn't withstand silence. It was an old-timey war picture with lots of *rat-ta-tat* gunfire and cries of pain. The low murmur drowned out the worst thoughts in his head. Soothing. He was thinking bad thoughts now. You should've heard the things he'd think in a quiet room. If anyone heard all the horrible things his own brain would tell him to do, they'd lock him up or put him down, like a rabid dog. They'd be doing him a favor.

Why couldn't he stay sober? Maybe he'd get a little clean time, find some honest work, even meet someone, someone he could see himself having a regular life with again. But then he'd screw it up. It wasn't even the drugs, though they were never far behind. Like this one time he had this great girl. Darlene. God, she was beautiful. And then he cheated on her with some girl from AA that he didn't like. Why?

Later, when he was back in rehab, one of the counselors, Dr. Miller, said it was because Mark "self-sabotaged." Which Mark thought meant he *wanted* to fail. Mark said that wasn't true. He believed in himself. He talked about his music, how they almost hit the big time, and how maybe one day he'd play again—Mark set high standards and big goals for himself. When he was with Darlene, he was making good money with a messenger company. Practically ran the place. Back then, Mark saw himself taking over, and then acquiring more messenger companies, maybe starting a franchise. He was clean and sober, putting in the work. He wanted to marry Darlene. They could almost afford a house. He was going to reach out to his daughters soon. They'd see he'd changed and maybe they could restart a relationship. Mark was at an age where he knew this might be his last chance. And then he goes out and blows it, sleeping with some ugly girl he didn't like. Darlene dumped him. Mark started using. Of course he got fired. So close he could almost touch it, taste it… That, he'd told Dr. Miller, is what hurt the most. Mark knew he had it in him, that he could be a good *person*. Maybe even a *great* one.

Dr. Miller said something Mark would never forget. The doctor said some people set such high standards for themselves, not because they believe in their abilities or have faith they'll succeed, but because, secretly, they know they're going to fail, and that'll provide the excuse to hate themselves, which is their real goal. That's how much self-loathing they have.

Blew Mark's mind when he heard that one.

It was true. Mark hated himself. Mark hated himself more than any-one he knew.

Mark's life really turned to shit when he lost the job working for Richard Fontaine. That ninety-day chip? Traded it in for a free wel-come-back bag. He didn't blame Richard for letting him go. He gave the guy no choice when he started showing up high, asking to borrow money, stealing things from Richard's truck to pawn, calling in sick.

Wiping the crumbs from his scratchy beard, Mark walked shirtless to the motel mirror, staring at that man he hated so much, counting the ribs sticking out. If he struck them with mallets, Mark bet they'd sound like a xylophone. *Welcome to the Feral Cat Fail one-man reunion tour! Featuring Mark Burns and his amazing xylophone ribs!*

Maybe he was directing his anger at the wrong person. Why should he hate himself so much when there were so many more deserving of his scorn? He didn't make himself this way. He was born with busted gears, rusted circuitry, crisscrossed wires. That was God's fault. He stood glowering at that man in the mirror, at those bony appendages poking out, growing angrier by the second. That was Mark's other problem. Rage. It could come on fast, sudden, without warning. Especially when he felt he'd been wronged. This world was one big miscarriage of justice. God, Higher Power, the Universe. Hand out a pile of gold to some, a fistful of shit to others.

Like that rich bitch Gloria in Pasa Ardo, with her wine cellar and fancy sculptures. But, no, he was the addict, the bum, the piece of shit.

Why should some people have everything while others had nothing?

It wasn't right.

Next thing he knew he'd put his fist through the mirror, glass shards everywhere, sharp, jagged points jutting from his knuckles. He stared at the blood dripping down his shredded fist.

No one was coming to his rescue.

It was up to Mark to be the change he wanted to see.

And that started with money.

Maybe it was time to reach out to Richard, see if he could convince his old boss to take another chance on him. Richard Fontaine had always been kind. He didn't seem the type to hold grudges. Mark would come to him with a new attitude, a positive one. He'd show initiative. Bring ideas. Richard had the connections and means to make dreams come true.

Then Mark could get out of the Tropicana Inn, return to the world, put down the needle and spoon, stay sober. Maybe even see his girls again. Would just take a little planning.

With that, Mark drew up another hit.

When you're an addict, you can't even think about getting straight until you're high.

CHAPTER NINE

NOW, Wednesday, July 20, 2016, 3:54 p.m.

Rhona Clarion. The dead woman in Fairfax. Lydia didn't know Rhona. Had never heard of her, never seen her face. Could honestly say she'd never met anyone with that name her entire life. When she'd delivered the news to Rhona's husband, Lydia hadn't recognized the neighborhood. Which itself was weird. Lydia had driven all over L.A. for her job, including large swaths of Fairfax. This might've been the *one* section she'd never traversed. She felt no tug of remembrance for the house or its décor. Witnessed no familiar qualities in Dan Clarion's face. Lydia had no ties to this woman. Yet, she'd called her. The day before she died. A message from beyond the grave.

Lydia replayed the voicemail, making sure she heard what she knew she'd heard correctly the first time, hoping an overworked mind had filled in blank spaces because the subconscious wanted to. Like those internet videos where they present two different words and you hear whichever one you are thinking of. A parlor trick. A flat-out hallucination. Anything would be preferable to the alternative. But, no, that was the name. Rhona Clarion. Clear as a bell.

A ridiculous thought entered Lydia's brain. Maybe it was a different Rhona Clarion. Not that such a coincidence would be any less baffling.

Besides, as Lydia learned early on, in the world of investigation, there is no such thing as coincidence.

Crime is no different than any other human behavior; it adheres to logic, order. Even a random psycho killer targeting strangers is part of a greater cohesive picture. Insanity can be explained through its inexplicable nature. People don't leave messages—not like the one Rhona Clarion left yesterday evening—only to turn up dead overnight. There was a connection. But what?

Lydia accessed old digital yearbooks, her middle and high school years archived electronically. There were plenty of embarrassing pictures and regrettable hairstyles. Several classmates she'd forgotten about. A woman Rhona's age would've graduated long before her. Maybe she was someone's big sister? Nothing sparked. Not to mention, the woman had said, point blank, they didn't know one another.

Grabbing her cell, Lydia called Maureen, who picked up on the first ring. Lydia ran down the night before: the discovery of the body, the restlessness and anxiety, the sixth sense that had kicked in telling her something was off, even before she checked her messages.

"And you're certain you never met anyone by that name?"

"You meet a lot of people in this line of work."

"My point." Maureen's voice softened as she attempted to ease the tension. "I know you're still a baby, especially compared to me." Maureen attempted a laugh. "Trust me, memory doesn't improve with age."

"Even if I did know her, Mo, what the hell? People don't leave messages they want to talk and end up dying before you call them back. That's a movie plotline."

Lydia could hear Maureen acknowledging the same on the other end, if without words.

"Have you called it in yet?"

"No."

"Do you know who's working the case?"

Lydia paused, holding her tongue, hoping Maureen picked up on what she was hinting at, namely that Lydia wanted to wait to notify her supervisors. Lydia had always been inquisitive, her curiosity and independence the qualities that made her so good at her job. She also followed the rules. These were the admirable characteristics Maureen first observed—why she'd gotten her board to offer the scholarship, why Maureen had been with her every step of her career.

"You can't not call it in," Maureen said. "It's not an option."

"I want to assist with the autopsy first."

"Out of the question." Maureen exhaled. This was sitting on evidence. These were the kinds of rash, irresponsible moves a rookie made, the kind that got people fired. "You are now personally involved."

"We don't know it's a murder yet," Lydia said.

"Doesn't matter. The woman *called* you. She is *dead*. There is a log of when she called. You'd be jeopardizing your entire career."

Lydia knew Maureen was right. First place police checked would be phone records, and they'd see she had called. "Can they tell when I played back the message? It's plausible I didn't hear it till tomorrow." Lydia was scrambling. "Please."

"What did it look like at the scene?"

"Body found at bottom of basin. Dawn. Mission Junction. Fully clothed."

"Drowning?"

"Not enough water. No bloat."

"Lydia, this doesn't sound like natural causes."

"No, it doesn't—is her name on your list yet?"

The county liked autopsies performed within the first twenty-four hours. Given the size of Los Angeles, its propensity for violent deaths, that wasn't always possible. Bodies could stay on ice awhile.

Lydia heard Maureen sigh in between clacking keys. "She's not in the system."

"I'm asking to assist."

"Are you working tonight?"

"I don't work again till Saturday. Covered a shift last week. I'll be well rested, promise."

"When you wake up at two this morning, think about it again."

"I've already thought about it."

Maureen, of all people, knew how headstrong Lydia could be. "Okay. But then you report the voicemail. No questions asked. Understood?"

"Yes."

"Say you promise."

"I promise."

"I'll let you know when the vic is slated for the table."

"I owe you, Mo."

"Yes, Lydia, you do."

CHAPTER TEN

THEN, One Month Before the Disappearance, Sunday, February 17, 1991, 1:17 p.m.

Jess and her sister were spending winter break in Santa Barbara with Dad and his new wife, Heather, who was *so* nice and accommodating, it made Jess sick. Heather wasn't much older than Jess. And her father was fifty. Disgusting.

The week had been fine. For Lydia's sake, Jess tried to put on a good face, even though she missed Brad. Her sister was thirteen and the world still seems fair at that age. Jess had less patience for the world of adult bullshit, the "do as I say, not as I do" platitudes and phony goodwill gestures, like your mother telling you not to drink as she pours herself another glassful, lecturing about the dangers of underage sex to the child she had too young; your dad pulling out all the stops to prove who's the better parent, tickets to sold-out shows, every dinner at another new, exclusive restaurant.

Jess hated listening to friends complain about these same things. She recognized how good she had it, which was better than most. Jess would never have to worry about whether she'd have enough to eat or a roof over her head; money would never be an issue.

Still, she hated being caught in Alan and Gloria's games, the gross inequality of it all.

This past week, walking around Santa Barbara, with its gorgeous beaches and overpriced sushi restaurants, Jess would pass the homeless and addicted, the strung-out messes nodding out in the noonday sun, the hobos schlepping past, pushing shopping carts jammed with assorted castoffs, the odds and ends of a wasted life. So many random cords that connected to nothing. That powered nothing. The irony hit Jess hard, how these vagrants carried countless lengths of cable, plugs and adapters, co-axial wires, audio, visual, stereo—white, yellow, and red center conductors to hook up devices that did not exist. Dead batteries to power nonexistent appliances.

She wondered how she'd be feeling if Brad hadn't come into her life. Would she still be spiraling into dark depression? Jess knew that if she'd seen those same bums last year, the sight of such despondency would've ripped her heart out, driven her to tears. It was still sad to see, don't get her wrong. But that light that had gone out at sixteen had begun to reignite after her seventeenth birthday. Around start of senior year. She owed that to Brad. Soon, they wouldn't have to hide their love. They only had a month to go.

The last day of winter break, their father planned a trip to Santa Monica Pier, promising Lydia there would be rides and games, which was too kiddie for Jess. Never mind, they were still rebuilding the Pier from the storms a decade ago. The real reason her father picked the spot was to put the screws to their mother.

Gloria stipulated Alan return the girls closer to Pasa Ardo. Alan, for his part, couldn't resist a counter jab, driving beyond the valley to Santa Monica. The only person screwed in any of this was Richard

Fontaine, mom's middle-aged boy toy slash fix-it man. Jess knew her mother wouldn't be the one to pick them up. She'd send Richard.

Jess didn't want to ruin the day for Lydia. Big sis maintained her smile and good cheer, even after they started walking, shivering along the water because temps refused to crack sixty degrees. There wasn't much happening on the Pier on a cold and damp Sunday afternoon. Options limited, they stopped at a café, sitting on the patio beneath dim skies and heat lamps, and ordered clams on the half shell.

Afterward, Jess excused herself to go for a walk. Richard would be there soon. Jess needed a moment to decompress, shift into Gloria mode. Dad might've been a cheating dog but being around him was easier. Alan never probed too deep, had no desire to go beyond a surface connection.

While Dad and Heather took Lydia to buy overpriced souvenirs to show Mom how much fun they had, Jess climbed down the landing, descending tumbling rock, making for the beach. An arctic blast gusted off the sea. A lone freighter hovered in the distance. Down by the water, it had to be ten degrees colder.

Jess watched the surfers and boogie boarders riding waves, unable to fathom how anyone got in the water when it was this cold. When you spend your life in Southern California, anything below sixty feels like the North Pole.

Our lives comprise tiny moments. Most of these are fleeting. You won't remember what you had for lunch on a random Wednesday any more than you'll grow up and recall sitting in traffic on your way to work sometime in October. There also exists, conversely, wrinkles in time, instances, events, and occurrences that stamp themselves as they're happening, so hard you know you'll never forget them.

There was nothing special about what Jess was doing now, trudging slowly over wet sand, gazing over gray seas, hugging herself in an oversized sweatshirt, shivering, humming Morrissey.

She was about done with high school. How did time fly by so fast? It was like the days were long but the years were short. In the big picture, Jess was happy with her life and who she was becoming, this past year, the best so far. At the same time, she couldn't not think about Lydia, who she'd be leaving behind. Her baby sister didn't know about Brad or Jess' plan. Jess wouldn't be far away—UCLA was just over the hill— but Jess would be living with Brad while Lydia was stuck with Gloria. Jess swore as soon as her sister was eighteen, she'd be out of there too. She and Brad would take her in, wherever they were. And Lydia would go to college and Jess would look after her like a real parent should.

Joggers plodded along the walkway, shirtless despite the chill, bicycles peddling past the rolling carts selling mango and elote. Tourists and sightseers, families, kids, moms and dads. For a moment, the moment was comforting.

We can feel when someone is watching us. It's a primal instinct hardwired, origins dating back to long-toothed beasts tracking prey on the savannah. You'd think that as mankind evolved, we'd have lost the inherent awareness to know when we're being clocked. Danger never abates. It evolves too.

Jess could feel the eyes on her as she spun toward the street, hoping to see Richard but knowing she wouldn't.

Whoever was watching Jess through the crowd didn't care if they were seen, making no effort to hide. Then again, they were so far away, Jess couldn't see much. Ballcap pulled down, windbreaker. It was an adult, not someone her age. She based this on little more than posture, a worn disposition weighing shoulders, curving the spine. On the small side, he possessed a vague familiarity in the sense that everyone of a certain age lacks originality. He could've been some guy, some creeper lurking. She couldn't even be sure "he" was a "him." Southern California had such a homeless problem. You couldn't avoid them, but Jess didn't get the impression the person was homeless. The clothes—light jacket, ballcap, sunglasses on a dull winter day without glare—normal. Too normal. When you're surrounded by freaks—and the boardwalk was chockfull—normal sticks out, a bright blue flower blossoming in a field of mud and bone.

Jess knew one thing: whoever they were, they meant to hurt her.

She was all alone on the sands of the boardwalk, exposed. Except not really. There were beachgoers and people within shouting distance. And the person in the ballcap was still up on the rocks, across the road, far enough away that Jess could make it back to the landing. Far enough away that even as Jess narrowed her gaze and focused extra hard, she admitted she'd have a difficult time describing them.

Jess turned away for a moment, returning to the gray sea, distracted by the freighter blowing its horn. When she spun back around, whoever had been spying was gone.

That was the first time she saw her stalker.

The second time she saw her stalker was a couple weeks later, around the time Brad was being fired. The glimpse was even briefer this time. It was at school. The baseball cap gave them away. A lot of kids at school wore ballcaps. This wasn't a kid from school. It was the same ballcap from the beach, black and orange. They stood farther away this time, stuck around shorter.

Jess thought about reporting this sighting, which was more unsettling than the first because it was closer to home. But with all that was going on with Brad, Cam, and the Rider, she never got around to it.

Then her stalker returned.

Only this time she couldn't holler to passersby or scramble for help, flag down a teacher, lifeguard, or cop. She couldn't file a report or make a telephone call. It would be too late.

By the time she recognized what was happening the third time, Jess would be on top of Cripple Creek Ridge, drunk, high, and disoriented, and the hands would already be wrapped around her throat, choking the life out of her.

CHAPTER ELEVEN

When Lydia woke at two in the morning, as she did every night
she didn't work, she turned on the rest of the lights. She'd gotten a
solid four hours, if interrupted, which was as good as she ever got.
Sometimes she could coax herself back to sleep. Tonight was not one of
those times.

The symptoms of her condition, however mild, made the process
of regaining consciousness painful. The rational, sane part of Lydia's
brain told her that the nyctophobia was responsible for the unease,
the quickening pulse, the anxiety, fear, and dread. But knowing
something in our head doesn't always translate to knowing it in our
heart.

The morning Lydia woke to discover her sister gone, the first
thing she noticed was the silence, the stillness of night. Then she
heard the ticking of every appliance, the hum of fixtures, the drone
of machines powered low. Because she hadn't roused her mother
or done anything to find Jess, Lydia succeeding in assuring that
moment remained stamped. Each morning she woke at two. And
each morning she experienced the loss all over again.

When the debilitating wave passed, Lydia made for the kitchen to brew a fresh pot of coffee. That simple act of movement was enough to shake her free from the malaise.

Hot mug in hand, Lydia fired up a browser, hitting social media sites. Of the four hundred and thirty-six friends she had online, none were named Rhona. She personally knew maybe a couple dozen of these people. The rest were friends of friends or outright strangers. Clicking on this odd consortium of peripheral acquaintances, she found no common denominator, no missing link. She perused random photographs of framed meals and duck-faced selfies. Lydia scrolled mindlessly, thoughts drifting. She could waste hours reading updates on strangers, sifting through countless dark humor memes, because it was true: what doesn't kill you gives you a twisted sense of humor.

At some point, dark surrendered to light, and the sun rose on another day. Lydia typed in her dead sister's name, as she had done so many times before. There was never going to be a breakthrough or new discovery because there was no mystery. Her sister's death wasn't the result of foul play. Jess partied too hard, fell, fractured her neck. Her death was ruled an accident by police following an investigation. The cops *wished* they could prove malfeasance.

Everyone wanted to pin a crime on Brad Pearce, the pervy English teacher who'd molested students—and that's what it's called when adults have sex with girls under eighteen, regardless of how close to legal adulthood those girls may be. Pearce had had sexual relations with at least three high school seniors, including Jess, over several years, at different high schools. Or was rumored to have had. The other girls were never publicly identified, refusing to corroborate allegations. That, or Pearce's lawyers were too damned good at their job. Maybe Lydia could hunt them down, these girls? Women now. Talk to them? Brad Pearce came from money, retained the best defense money could buy. He didn't teach for the paycheck. He taught to prey. Every time the police poked a hole in his alibis and excuses, his legal team filed motions and slapped injunctions to prevent further disclosure. This was all hearsay to Lydia, who had followed the story best she could from boarding school. Everyone knew what Brad had done. No one could prove it. Then again, what was the point now? Brad Pearce was dead. The disgraced former English teacher had succumbed to shame, not long after Jess' body was found. He'd hung himself inside his big San Francisco home. What would these women—even if Lydia were able to find them—be able to tell her? What if one of them loved Brad too, was jealous of her sister? What if Brad Pearce gave orders to shut Jess up? What if he followed her that night at the water tower, hired someone to do it for him, drug her, push her down the ravine? Maybe Jess' death wasn't an accident…

Desperation crept in Lydia's mind, this need to see someone pay.

Except, there'd been an autopsy. Neck broken, sustained during a fatal fall. Open, shut. An accident.

Then why would this Rhona want to talk about Jess? After twenty-five years?

Rhona Clarion had been fifty-one, had never attended Pasa Ardo High. She obviously wasn't one of the rumored "other girls." Lydia had lost touch with most everyone from her hometown. Even if she did remember a few of them, what could she do? Drop a casual email or DM? *Hey! What have you been up to for the last quarter century? Was wondering if you wanted to talk about my dead sister?*

This is what you do, Lydia reminded herself. *This is your job.* Rhona Clarion had not phoned Lydia by mistake. Unlike many careers, Lydia's work didn't always adhere to a linear order. Her job comprised isolated instances, bits and pieces of the discarded, cast off, thrown out, forgotten, strewn about, today, yesterday, two weeks from now, six years ago, last month, scattered fragments for Lydia to reassemble and put back in their rightful place. In some ways being an investigator was like reconstructing a jigsaw puzzle, though she hated that analogy because it implied that with enough time and evidence a complete picture was possible. Which wasn't always the case. Not when your main witness, the one with all the answers, was dead.

After she hit return on her dead sister's name tonight, the top result wasn't some old newspaper story about Jess or the accident.

It was for a YouTube channel called *Night Shade*. Hosted by one Shane Ellet, formerly known as the Rider on the Plain, the lone wolf weirdo acting out a Hollywood fantasy.

That guy?

Lydia cracked the window. A little cool fresh air. On the edge of the Palm Desert, San Perdida this time of year invited all kinds of pleasant aromas—sweet scents of pollen and tart citrus orchards mingling with the tarry aftertaste of creosote. The sun shone, but in the still-chilled air, Lydia only smelled the distant odor of things set afire.

She clicked on the link. Shane's channel loaded. There was an overwritten, adverb-laden introduction about the origins of his love of true crime and unsolved mysteries. Nothing about Jess. He had almost ten thousand subscribers. Hardly viral but still a substantial following. Wanting to be sure she had the same Shane Ellet, Lydia read the entire bio, and, yes, it was him. With a thumbnail profile picture to prove it. The current version. Older, doughier, less hair. Shane had ditched the cheesy name "Rider on the Plain." These days he went by the gentler, if equally cringe-worthy handle "the Moth."

Lydia hadn't known Shane. She remembered he'd been apprehended at the water tower protest. Everyone said the guy was going to prison. Except that Shane, like ninety-two percent of Pasa Ardo, was well off and white. They don't send kids like that to prison. She couldn't believe he'd be this easy to find. Right there on the internet. Different decade, different century, same gimmick. Over the years, she'd never thought of looking him up. Why would she? Police had not only cleared the guy of possible involvement in Jess' death; they'd wiped his record clean, sweeping away all FCC violations. Still, she would've thought he'd be tougher to track down. All she'd had to do was put a name in a search engine. Except she'd typed in Jess' name, not Shane's.

Lydia scrolled down to the hyperlinks. The show he hosted, *Night Shade*, was composed of short episodes, fifteen to twenty minutes— over a hundred of them. Even though she'd shut the bedroom window, the charred remains lingered, singed scent stuck in nasal membranes. Lydia waved at the air before settling on a random broadcast. This one about some missing persons case back east. She paused and un-paused the recording, less interested in the subject matter—the story about a sleazy motel and a mentally handicapped handyman who'd murdered a girl? Lydia wasn't clear, more engrossed by the man hosting the show.

Of course, Lydia had *seen* Shane Ellet in the aftermath, his face all over the papers. At the time, she remembered thinking he was kinda cute, shaggy, skinny, like an indie rocker. Lydia often crushed on boys like that. That wasn't the guy on the screen. No longer anonymous, invisible, and speaking through a modulator, Shane, AKA the Moth, sat behind a tiny desk, front and center, facing the camera, using his real voice, which sounded more gravelly than she'd have thought. Shane wasn't fat. He'd filled out. Or maybe the camera did add ten pounds. He wasn't unattractive, but he still came off as creepy, eyes too intense, buggy. Reminiscent of a heavier Jake Gyllenhaal in *Nightcrawler*, one of the few movies Lydia had caught in the theater because the story took place in her postmortem universe.

It would be easy to dismiss *Night Shade*, this self-produced YouTube exposé. Shane, the Moth, had an agenda. He'd recorded dozens and dozens of episodes over the years, inviting sponsors and increasing ad revenue.

She clicked on different links, each dedicated to another crime or unsolved mystery. There was an episode about Elisa Lam, the foreign student found in a water tank at the Cecil Hotel downtown. She didn't click on that link. That story always freaked her out, the footage of the distraught woman trapped in an elevator. Lydia had been involved in that case.

Lydia watched other recordings. She grew used to Shane's wild-eyed appearance, which with time and familiarity ceased being "creepy," landing him in the broader, more forgivable territory of socially awkward. As for *Night Shade?* All in all, for a homemade show, the production value wasn't awful, video definition improving each year. The content was entertaining. Enough to hold her attention. Which was the only reason she saw it. A more recent episode. A few years back.

"Episode 88: The Mysterious Fate of Jessica Barrett."

Mysterious Fate?

She opened the link, film started to roll, and she hit pause.

Like every episode Lydia had viewed thus far, Shane, the Moth, sat in all black, in a darkened room, at his desk, offering little by way of facial expression. Outside of his lips, there wasn't much movement. Even his hands remained stationary, folded, one over the other. There was so little physical or demonstrative behavior, Lydia wondered why this wasn't a podcast since all he did was talk. And he wasn't that interesting to look at. The voice though… The more she listened, the more Lydia recognized it. Even when he was disguising his voice, there was a certain diction he employed, a stuttering enunciation, cadence, a cross between Christopher Walken and, well, Christian Slater.

Lydia hit play.

CHAPTER TWELVE

Night Shade, *Episode 88, "The Mysterious Fate of Jessica Barrett" with Your Host, the Moth, Pt. I*

They say as a reporter you're not supposed to make yourself part of the story. I wish I could do that here. I can't. Because I was there that night. This was nineteen ninety-one. I knew Jess Barrett. Not well. We had a couple classes together. We knew each other enough to say hi in the hall. Jess was a pretty girl, and, hey, what high school guy doesn't like pretty girls? I'm not saying I had a crush on her. Not saying I didn't. But, yeah, I noticed her.

Jess Barrett was cool. Just … fucking … cool. The kind of girl who was reading Camus, artsy, but popular too. Jess wasn't a girl who fit into convenient labels, y'know? They got that thing now, that Hollywood trope, the manic pixie dream girl. I'm not saying she was like that either. She was quirky though, dressed funky, danced to her own beat, or whatever other cliché you want to lob out there. But she was original, and the older I get the more I appreciate that particular quality. Especially in those days, where it's hard as hell to be original and give zero fucks what others think about you. I wish I could say I was like that then. I wish I could say I was like that now. I keep to myself, don't have much of a social life—I've never been much of a people person, if we're being honest—which should add up to me being more like Jess Barrett, someone who doesn't care what others think about them. I'm not that guy. I check my subscriber list daily. I can tell when I have new subscribers. More importantly, I can tell if someone's left.

Which reminds me. If you haven't already done so, please click the link down below and hit the subscribe button. It helps me out a lot.

So, yeah, let's talk about the night Jess Barrett disappeared. The cops said it was an accident. Now you know me. I'm not some conspiracy whacko. If you watch this show, you know I pride myself on presenting facts, and trying to keep my emotions out of it. But like I said, this is a tough one because I knew the victim. And, yeah, I said victim. Because I'm going to make an exception to my usual rule where I don't pretend to know more than the authorities.

I want to take you back to the night Jess Barrett was murdered.

Yeah, I said murdered.

And there's irrefutable fucking proof.

CHAPTER THIRTEEN

**THEN, A Few Weeks Before the Disappearance,
End of Third Period, 1991, 10:09 a.m.**

Jess Barrett was in love. Okay, maybe it was an attraction. Not a purely physical one though—even if there was no denying Brad Pearce *was* hot. More movie star handsome than English teacher good looking, with that just-woken-up hair and scruff. Smooth but rough. And those arms! Like an old-time Greek sculpture. No, what Jess felt toward Brad was more cerebral allure, intellectual appreciation. Brad was the first teacher who treated his students like equals. Part of that owed, no doubt, to the fact he was so young. Twenty-five wasn't much older than eighteen, and everyone knew girls matured faster than boys. Jess wasn't alone in her feelings for the English teacher. There wasn't a girl in class who hadn't noticed Brad—and that's what he wanted them to call him, Brad, not Mr. Pearce. "Mr. Pearce," he'd said that first day, "is my dad's name." Which was funny because her mom's sometimes boyfriend Richard had said the *same* thing when she and Lydia tried to call him "Mr. Fontaine." Except Richard *was* old, like grandpa old, with wrinkled, leathery skin and moles that had long hairs poking out of them. But Brad... When he said to call him "Brad," students did because he *was* one of them.

You'd think that would be a small ask, requesting students call you by your first name, but it turned into a big deal, so much so that their principal, Mrs. Sheinbaum, addressed the issue, sending out a school-wide letter that all teachers were to be addressed as either Mr., Mrs., Ms., or whatever their preferred prefix. The principal's letter didn't single out any specific teacher, but everyone at school knew who they were talking about. After the letter went out and everyone's parents had the chance to read it, students were talking, rumoring in the halls, and Jess could tell classmates were conflicted. No one wanted to get their favorite teacher in trouble.

Brad didn't say a word about the letter. What he *did* say was far more profound.

He'd sat on his desk, rolled-up sleeves, toned forearm draped over tight thighs, the way he often sat, whether he was teaching Shakespeare or *The Scarlet Letter* as part of the curriculum, or sharing his own personal tastes in literature, the books most high school English teachers weren't touching—*Zen and the Art of Motorcycle Maintenance*, *Lady Chatterley's Lover*—Nietzsche!

Without even *mentioning* the letter, he said, "You're going to face some daunting challenges." He was talking about how they would all be graduating soon, getting ready for college, picking majors, deciding on careers, but he meant more than that. "People will issue all sorts of ultimatums in this life. Some of these will be big, like, if say, this war in Iraq continues and the draft is reinstated."

A few guys groaned. Jess wasn't worried about Iraq. Women didn't get drafted, and the idea that they could make someone go to war seemed so, like, 1967. Plus, it was rotten to admit, but if they *did* reinstate the draft, Pasa Ardo kids didn't have to worry. Their parents could buy their way out.

"Sometimes," Brad added, "it'll seem smaller than that. They'll try to tell you what you can and can't say. It's all a means to control you, get you to think the way *they* do." He stopped, looking students in the eye. "You are going to need to decide what is right for *you*."

After that, everyone in class called him Brad.

Over the course of the school year, he and the class bonded. The boys wanted to be him. The girls wanted to be with him. They formed a team, Brad their coach. Whatever challenge they faced, they'd face together. And when the Rider on the Plain came on the scene, broadcasting weekly, real change in Pasa Ardo not only felt possible; it was a certainty.

As for Brad and Jess, they started as teacher and student. Then they became friends, spending more time together alone after class, talking literature, philosophy, and deep stuff like that. It wasn't until recently they'd taken their relationship to the next level. Jess wasn't a virgin. She'd been with boys. But Brad was a man. He did things to her body that boys couldn't.

Today, Brad had asked Jess to stay after class. Casually. She had study hall fourth period, which was easy to ditch. Brad didn't teach for another hour. No one would know.

Jess had slipped into the supply closet, waiting for him to show up. If someone were to open the closet, someone *not* Brad, she'd say she was looking for pens, which was what Brad instructed her to say. The perfect cover story. Brad was the only one to ever open the door. Part of the thrill was getting caught, forbidden fruit always tasting sweetest. Jess knew enough to keep her mouth shut. She wasn't officially eighteen—that was less than a month away—and even if she were, the school wouldn't understand the depth of their connection. To them, it would be a teacher taking advantage of a student, even though Jess had been the one to seduce him. She loved that word. Seduce. Like *Lolita,* another book she never would've read without Brad's recommendation. When he slipped her a copy months ago, he told her most people misunderstood what the story was about.

He'd said, "People think it's about an inappropriate sexual relationship. But you're smarter than that, Jess. You'll see it's the exact opposite. It's about these constrictions society places upon us, these arbitrary numbers they assign." He touched her shoulder, in a totally appropriate manner. "You will be eighteen soon. That's legally an adult. Which means you can serve in the military, risk your freedom, give up your life for your country. They'll trust you with a gun. But not a beer. Think about that!"

Jess thought about that. She thought about a lot of stuff Brad said. The first time she'd gone down on him in the parking lot, he tried to stop her. But she wanted to. She had to have him, taste him, and she would not be denied.

Sometimes she'd feel bad. But it's not like Cam was her *boyfriend.* They'd gone on a few dates, hooked up—and she liked him. But Cam was a boy. When Jess was with Cam, it was fun, the sex was good, fine, okay. But Brad… He'd become an itch she couldn't satisfy, wanting it so bad she burned for him, and the relief from giving in, submitting, was itself a turn on. Thinking about Brad during class, it was all Jess could do not to squirm, wriggle out of her seat, so aroused, shivering with anticipation.

On cue, the door opened and Brad entered the supply closet, closing it behind him. Jess had been getting excited, wanting to blow his mind. She started to drop to her knees, but he stopped her.

"Ladies first," he said, unbuttoning her jeans. Even the pop sounded erotic. The way he slipped them off, his lack of urgency, how he kept his stare focused on her eyes as he did so, locked, smoldering, intense, it made Jess quiver, the buildup.

She couldn't stop shaking…

A week later, he'd be fired.

CHAPTER FOURTEEN

NOW, Thursday, July 21, 2016, 8:12 a.m.

Cam Rawls walked through the precinct doors whistling, pointing a finger at Juan, before tipping his hat to Caroline. The old habit was hard to break, this divide in how he treated men and women. Today was going to be a good day; he could feel it.

As chief of police in Pasa Ardo, Cam had big shoes to fill, stepping into those once worn by his father, Delmar Rawls, a beloved cop and husband who left an indelible impression on this town and world before he went gently into the good night. Dell taught his son a great deal—about being a cop, about being a man. He could be old fashioned. But so what? Nothing wrong with preserving a tradition when that tradition is rooted in manners, respect, and chivalry. The glow on Caroline's cheeks told Cam she didn't mind. It was hard these days, not knowing where lines were, not wanting to cross them and make a female coworker, especially one he supervised, feel uncomfortable, but to hell with political correctness. Nothing wrong with being kind and making someone smile.

The precinct television played, sound off. On the screen, more wreckage from another wildfire. Every goddamn year…

Cam didn't bother putting on his glasses, instead stepping closer to read the feed along the bottom. Nowhere near them. Nothing to worry about. Old footage. Another year's disaster. Not his problem.

Cam had turned toward his office, thankful to be escaping the heat, when Caroline called after him.

"Got a message for you," she said. "A woman called."

Cam made for her desk, waiting while Caroline shuffled papers. She plucked a pink while-you-were-out notepad, tore off the top sheet, and passed along the neat handwriting.

Cameron Rawls hadn't had time to guess who might've called, but if he had, the last person on any list would be Lydia Barrett.

"Thanks for taking the time to meet," Lydia said, as she arrived for their late lunch.

"I'll admit I was a little surprised." Cam, who'd arrived early, sat back down in the booth.

The Paradiso was one of the nicer restaurants in Pasa Ardo. A small, newish café, stylish and charming, Cam had suggested it, doubting Lydia had been there. She'd been sent away to boarding school after Jess. Moved on from there. Not that he kept tabs on her. Pasa Ardo was intimate enough to notice when one of yours left. On some level Cam admitted he still wanted to impress the little sister of Jess Barrett, which was ridiculous, he knew. He'd had such a crush on Jess. Crush? No, he loved her. Over the years, he'd tried to convince himself he hadn't. They messed around. Had sex a few times. But her death was one of those terrible life events that define you. Its effects lingered, etching deeper and harder with the passing years, rendering the moment less a memory and more a scar.

Cam smiled, glancing around, studying the robin blue walls,

adorned with gigantic, framed posters from the movie *Cinema Paradiso*, the eatery's namesake. The owner had been involved with its production or distribution, worked on the film in some capacity. Cam had never seen it. Foreign, Italian—subtitles. Why read a movie screen when you could read a book? Everyone in SoCal could lay claim to a Hollywood connection. A bus boy who worked on the script for *Aliens 4*. The cashier who knew the key grip or best boy for *Goodfellas*. The Uber driver with a cousin who played an extra in *Jungle Fever*.

Cam retained a sense of pride representing their small hometown, even if Lydia, as rumored, had moved on to bigger things in the big city. Last he'd heard she'd earned a scholarship and was going to medical school to become a doctor. Again, not tabs, mild interest in the baby sister of a dear old friend who was gone.

At the same time, Cam felt uneasy sitting across from her. He hadn't seen Jess' little sister in over two decades. If he didn't know he was meeting her, would he have recognized Lydia Barrett? Probably not. Maybe. Yeah. They were sisters, and Jess' image was burned on Cam's brain. A tee shirt and jeans girl who didn't care about the latest fashion styles or trends, Jess sported jangly bracelets and leather ties on her wrists, a girl who'd have a sleeve tattoo by now had she lived. Not that Lydia was uptight or rigid. A grown woman, Lydia dressed for a career that required a modicum of professionalism. He didn't recall the sisters looking much alike, but now that they were across from one another, he saw the parts of Jess he'd never forget. Lydia was pretty like her sister but in different ways. Whereas Jess' features were hard, sharp, angular, Lydia came across as lighter, smoother, gentler. A more sanitized version, long, soft brown curls instead of the ironed-straight, jet-black hair. Unlike Jess, whose deep brown eyes could bore a hole through you, Lydia possessed a softer gaze, lighter brown behind thin-framed glasses. Still, you could tell they shared the same blood.

Cam and Lydia made small talk, filling space without offering much substance. The café was empty. If it was the weekend, they'd have to contend with a dawdling crowd. The weekday left them stuck between lunch and dinner, those weird, idle hours. The waiter ran down a list of the day's specials, assorted sandwiches, prosciutto on focaccia, sun-dried tomato and burrata on bruschetta, fig jam, pesto; soups simmering meats, pepperoni flowers, salami, pastrami, a side of crostini. Lydia watched the waiter. Cam watched Lydia, trying to reconcile place and time, how they'd traveled this far into the future. Because no matter how old Cam got, no matter how much responsibility he accepted, there was a part of him forever rooted in 1991. Like a time-traveler, he existed in both places simultaneously. That's what it felt like, especially when he was confronted by the past.

When it came time to order, Cam said to bring a white pizzetta with olive oil and nettles for the table, before ordering himself a roasted chicken salad, dressing on the side, which wasn't a meal to get excited over as much as it was the restrained healthy option of a forty-two-year-old man battling the bulge. Cam was currently scoring a draw in that department.

Lydia said the pizzetta was enough, adding an iced tea.

"You look uncomfortable," she said after the waiter left.

Cam choked back a laugh, hoping not to come across as smarmy or inhospitable. But, yeah, sitting there, he felt he was seeing a ghost, so much of Jess still present.

"It's nice to hear from you." Cam wasn't sure he pulled that off. "Just a surprise." He picked up the tiny salt and pepper shakers, rearranging their order.

Lydia studied him, but not in a way that said she was curious about what he'd been doing for the past twenty years. He wished she would ask. That he could reel off, switch to autopilot. Didn't end up going to

UC Berkeley. Stuck closer to home, wanted to be near his father, which felt important after that night. Then Dad got sick. Occidental was as good a school. Probably better. Good enough for the president, he'd joke. Cam often recounted this history. It was cocktail fodder, banal conversation for social situations, a rehearsed bit he could perform without needing to be present: how he'd ended up taking over from his revered father after Dell passed. He'd tell this story with the deference of an excuse, adding a hint of honor at his sacrifice. Cameron Rawls always seemed destined for the big time. An NFL superstar. Business owner. No one ever said these things to his face, but he could tell they were thinking it all the same. So that was the story he told, infusing an understated heroism in his decision to stay behind and protect the county, passing up a more glamorous gig that didn't exist. He'd told this version so often that he'd almost begun to believe it. How Pasa Ardo was a part of him, its community his family, and there's nothing more important than family. He'd deliver that parting line like Vin Diesel in one of those fast car movies. But Lydia didn't seem the least bit interested in Cam's history. A cop, he recognized the look of suspicion.

The longer they sat there, the less Cam could deny it. Suspicion is a two-way street, and it feeds on itself. Cam couldn't stop fidgeting, fiddling with condiments and sugar packets, mannerisms to betray a guilty man. He thought about all the drivers he pulled over, asking why they were so nervous. No reason to be nervous unless you have something to hide, right?

"Do you want wine?" Cam wasn't a big drinker, but at that moment he could use some social lubrication. "Do you drink?"

"Not at this hour."

"Right," Cam said, chuckling to himself. "And I'm working." He looked down at his uniform, which felt foreign, too tight fitting, like a different skin belonging to someone else.

Sunlight beamed in, splattering those humungous gilded posters. Traffic buzzed on the old country road. Crows perched on telephone wires.

"It's hard not to think about your sister," he blurted.

"Do you try not to think about her?"

"Honestly?" Cam said, jumping the pepper shaker over the salt, a makeshift game of checkers. "Yeah, I do."

Lydia reached in her purse, retrieving her phone. Cam worried she was going to share some old picture she'd unearthed, and he wasn't sure his battered old heart could take it. Thankfully, she read from notes she'd collected.

"Do you remember Shane Ellet?"

Cam bit his tongue, rolling his eyes.

"I'll take that as a yes."

"That guy. The Rider on the Plain." Groan. "Yeah, I remember him."

"Not a fan?"

Cam stalled, fumbling for the right words. "He caused a lot of problems back in the day. Because of Dad, I had a front row seat to that circus."

Lydia attempted a smile. "Mr.—Dell. He was a good man."

"Yes. He was." Cam waited. "Why are you asking about Shane Ellet?"

Lydia read from her phone. "He goes by 'the Moth' now."

"The … Moth?"

"Shane Ellet's handle. On the internet. He has a YouTube channel."

Cam rolled his eyes again, this time so hard it hurt, like one more millimeter and he'd rip ligaments, tear nerve endings, pop eyeballs from their sockets, leave them dangling out his skull like a pair of gag glasses. It came across like an act. Part of it was. But most of his disdain was legitimate, rooted in firsthand knowledge. Shane Ellet was a user who'd seized tragedy to catapult from wallflower to popularity. Before he was "Rider," dude was just another trust fund baby no one paid attention to. Back when they were seventeen, eighteen, the Hard Harry impersonation was funny, ironic, whatever. But Cam grew up. Guys like Shane never did. There was nothing "ironic" about Shane's fifteen minutes. He'd copied a movie, trying to pass it off as satire, and people got hurt. Truth was, the guy was a poser, a loser. No surprise he'd end up a washout starring in his own internet show.

Lydia didn't need to hear all that. Instead, Cam said, "I didn't realize grown men did that. YouTube channels. I thought it was for kids." Cam wasn't sure why he said that. He knew all kinds of people, young and old, took advantage of YouTube's instant-access platform. There were plenty of useful tutorials on how to play the piano or install a light fixture, cook risotto with a balsamic reduction, which Cam tried once to impress a date. It didn't work out. Cam knew Shane Ellet wasn't using it for that. For Shane, it was another opportunity to exploit.

"The Moth?" Cam repeated.

"He has a true crime show. Like a podcast, only, you know, with video. Calls it…" Lydia looked embarrassed for him. "*Night Shade.*"

"Night Shade? The Moth? Who calls himself that? Dude is my age."

The waiter delivered the pizzetta, which Cam now felt obligated to surrender since Lydia hadn't ordered food, leaving himself the salad, an uninspiring tuft of greens topped by blanched white chicken cubes.

"Shane views himself as a journalist," Lydia said. "A truth-seeker."

"Dude was weird in high school. I can only imagine how weird he is now."

Lydia's face washed sympathetic, and Cam backtracked. He didn't know their relationship or history.

"Are you guys friends?"

"I haven't talked to Shane Ellet in—" Lydia caught herself. "I don't think I ever talked to Shane Ellet. But this show of his—"

"Show?"

"*Night Shade.*"

"Not exactly subtle."

"I know. Moth. *Night Shade.* Rider on the Plain. A bit heavy-handed. But he's not—would you watch an episode? If I sent you the link?"

"You want me to watch … Shane Ellet's podcast?"

"Video. YouTube channel. Yes."

"You could've asked me that over the phone."

"Could I? I haven't seen you in twenty-five years. I'm just the little sister of the girl who had a crush on you."

"On me?"

The way he said it made Lydia laugh. He didn't mind. It was silly, but Cam felt a flutter in his belly. After all these years… He always thought he was more into Jess Barrett than she him. He could remember moments with Jess more vibrantly than he could recall last week. And the strange part? He didn't like high school any more than anyone else. The only people who recall high school fondly are the bullies and bores. Another Hollywood stereotype. "The best years of your life." No one in real life calls high school that. It's hell. And yet… For as uncomfortable and uncertain as that age was, Cam could admit hearing Jess' name retained an allure, evoking the Cameron Rawls of eighteen, whom he held more respect for than he did the current incarnation. Adult life had been predictably … adult. The worst part? He and Jess didn't have to end. They never really had a chance to begin. Because *he* came along. Cam pushed the thought of Brad Pearce back down where it belonged, burying it among the other wreckages and losses. The state title in 1990. His mom and dad. Those were bittersweet. Thinking of Pearce, he just felt … bitter.

Lydia waved a hand, extracting Cam from the reverie.

"Sorry," he said. "Don't think about that time often." Then after a beat: "Why all the questions about Shane Ellet?"

"Like I said, he has a show—or I guess they call them webisodes. Each features a different crime or unsolved mystery." She stopped.

Cam felt his heart seize up.

"There's one about my sister, about Jess. The night she went missing and fell."

Cam tried to shrug it off. "I tried to help her. I ran after her. But she…" He stopped speaking, like it would hurt to say anything more.

Lydia waited for the rest.

Curious, Cam furrowed his brow. "Did Shane say something on this … show … to upset you?"

Lydia adverted her eyes. "You could say that."

Cam waited for Lydia's focus to return across the nettles. Though he wasn't sure he wanted to hear what she had to say.

"According to Shane Ellet, the Moth—Rider—my sister's death wasn't an accident. She didn't slip, Cam. She was murdered."

CHAPTER FIFTEEN

Jess learned Brad had been fired from Sarah, who'd heard it from Renee, who'd gotten the lowdown from Cam Rawls, so they knew it was true. The town cop's son, Cam had direct access to the pipeline. No one had a reason for *why* Brad had been fired. Jess could call Cam, but that invited its own set of problems.

When Brad dropped Jess off after school last week, Cam had been waiting in the driveway (she'd forgotten they were going to a movie). Jess had a good explanation, saying Brad had been helping her with an essay. Cam still acted strange all night. The ironic part? She and Brad hadn't even done more than kiss that day, and not even where Cam could've seen. They'd kissed out by Cripple Creek, concealed by the creosote bushes and blackberry bramble.

The only person Jess wanted to talk to was Brad. But they had a rule: no calls. It was imperative until she turned eighteen. Paper trails and phone records. Couldn't risk it.

At first, she tried to honor that arrangement, staring at the phone, willing it to ring as she played *Heaven or Las Vegas* by the Cocteau Twins on her CD player. "Cherry-coloured Funk" had been stuck on loop the first time she and Brad had sex at his apartment. You couldn't have asked for a more perfect song, and hearing it now filled her with hunger and anguish in the best possible way.

Surely, he'd call from a payphone, get her a message?

Hours passed. Skies grew dim. Nothing. The sweet pangs of bittersweet heartache turned sour and unpalatable. When the music stopped, Jess wallowed in the silence.

Finally, when she couldn't take it anymore, she called him, but he didn't answer. Then, in case she'd gotten the number wrong, she tried again. There was no option to leave a message, which she couldn't do anyway—that would catalogue incontrovertible evidence. But if that familiar, manly voice prompted her to do so after the beep, Jess wasn't sure she'd be able to resist. *I can pretend I'm a regular student reaching out…* No beep came. The phone rang and rang.

Jess sat on her bed. Reaching behind her neck, she unclasped the necklace. Holding the engraved heart in her palm, she opened the locket and reread the inscription, *From Cam to Jess* on one side, *Forever and Always* on the other, trying not to feel guilty. Jess hadn't led Cam on. She'd told him right from the start she wasn't sure she was ready for anything serious. And when he gave her the gift for Valentine's, she'd cautioned against moving too fast. She *tried* to spare his feelings. He couldn't understand. "Weren't they getting on great?" he'd ask. Yes, they were. She did have feelings for him. *But it was complicated. It's not like Jess could tell him about Brad, could she?*

Last week, after Jess told Cam she needed space, she tried giving the necklace and locket back. Cam wouldn't accept it. He said that the necklace was a present and the inscription transcended romantic love. It was a promise. He'd always be her friend. What could she say to that? And the truth was, Jess enjoyed spending time with Cam. He was tough and sensitive, funny and genuine. Smart and ambitious, he had a plan for his future, too. He wasn't your typical meathead jock. They liked the same music, the same bands, movies, and now books. Cam was everything she'd want in a guy. Or he had been until Brad.

This would be easier if Cam had acted like a jerk. Most guys, when you tell them you just want to be friends, turn into dicks. Not Cam. When she told him she needed space, he didn't push or act needy. He was disappointed but mature about it. Cam said he'd be there when she was ready; he cared about her and wanted to see her happy, with or without him. And the worst part? She knew he meant it.

God, she hoped Cam hadn't been the one who got Brad fired. No way. Cam would never rat them out. Not to Sheinbaum and the school board. They were the enemy.

Brad was a *great* teacher. An *amazing* teacher. A once-in-a-lifetime teacher. He'd impacted Cam as much as he had the rest of the senior class. Brad was the one who'd gotten Cam to stop smashing his skull for the glory of the home team, encouraging him to use his strength for more than physically bashing other boys into submission, to use his brain for more than contributing to unfortunate, rising concussion statistics. Cam had become part of the Rider Crew, too, which is what they called themselves, the Class of '91, those who caught Rider's weekly radio show. The Rider Crew was revolting against the tyranny of the school and its rules, the conformity and boxes every teacher (besides Brad) was trying to cram them into. It was a real movement. Peace, love, and understanding. Like Vietnam. Those who don't learn from history, Brad said, are doomed to repeat it. Vietnam. Now Iraq. Bullshit. Lies. Propaganda. And it felt good to be part of something bigger, building, growing, working toward creating a better world—to be on the precipice of making a real difference.

Darkness fell and the night dragged on. Jess' little sister Lydia could tell something was wrong. She kept popping her head into their bedroom, bugging Jess to watch TV or play a game with her. Lydia hated seeing her big sister upset. She was trying to cheer her up, which was sweet. Jess didn't want to inflict her sorrow and misery. She wished she could paint a fake smile and pretend. Jess was too broken right now to try.

Eventually, Lydia gave up and headed down the hall, probably to read one of her big books in the red or yellow room. All the spare guest rooms were referred to by the color of their walls or carpets.

Jess didn't bother getting ready for bed. Didn't wash off her makeup, brush her teeth, or change into a nighttime shirt. She turned out the lights, crawled into bed, and curled into a ball, pulling the covers high over her head.

Last week life had been so great. Now everything was so screwed up.

Jess felt like her heart was breaking in two, and she swore if it cracked any more, it would tear her apart.

CHAPTER SIXTEEN

After meeting with Cam Rawls, Lydia had driven around aimlessly, her faith wavering. Cam's responses to her questions about Shane Ellet should've satiated her concerns, or at least addressed Shane's accusations. Then again, Lydia hadn't been totally forthright, had she? Which wasn't fair to Cam, blindsiding him like that. When she learned Cam hadn't seen *Night Shade*, Lydia wanted to interrogate without prejudice. The element of surprise, catching him off guard. She couldn't help it. That was her job, get to the heart of the matter. She didn't want to give Cam the opportunity to affect an appropriate, rehearsed response. So she'd let him talk. Watching, waiting, seeing if he'd give himself away. We all have tics, tells that betray truthfulness or lack thereof. On the surface, his answers made sense.

Made sense. Didn't suffice.

Cam hadn't contradicted himself. Certain questions made him uncomfortable, which was understandable. He also hadn't "said" much. Yes, he'd seen Jess that night. And, yes, he had a massive crush on her. Cam even admitted, as Shane had maintained in his webisode, that he'd chased after her when the police showed up. Unlike what Shane suggested, however, Cam never admitted catching her. There was no mention of any struggle, no physical altercation. No injuries incurred.

Which left Lydia conflicted. Lydia remembered Cam visiting the house when Jess was alive. He seldom came alone. Jess and her friends often hung out as a group. Cam was always polite, making it a point to converse with Gloria. He had a reputation as a helluva football player, a ferocious wrestler. On the field of battle, smashmouth brutal. Away from the sports, Cameron Rawls landed in gentle giant territory. It couldn't have been easy being the only black student at Pasa Ardo. If that bothered him, Cam never let it show.

Shane could point all the fingers he wanted at Cam Rawls. If Jess *had* been the victim of homicide, Brad Pearce had a greater motive and more to lose. He was the subject of multiple sexual misconduct allegations, deemed a social pariah in the weeks following Jess' death. He wasn't let go by police for their lack of trying to convict him. If they had *any* concrete evidence of murder, you better believe they'd have used it.

Lydia wanted to kick herself for not asking these questions sooner, back when witnesses could be rounded up, called on the phone, hauled in, talked to. Lydia remembered Jess' friends like Renee Brand and Sarah Chou. She didn't know where to find them. Neither was on social media. The world was different then. If Lydia was looking for someone to suffer and pay, Brad Pearce had. Death by hanging is not a pleasant way to go.

That's karma; it's not justice.

Maybe Shane Ellet wasn't lying, maybe Jess didn't "fall," but that didn't implicate Cam in her death. Lydia couldn't accept that Cam Rawls was, in any way, shape, or form, responsible for her sister's untimely passing. She *could* believe Brad Pearce was.

Then how did he get off?

A great lawyer is a terrific asset. When you have the underage girl you've been sleeping with turning up dead? Under those circumstances, with *those* allegations? You better believe the police are pulling out all the stops. But authorities themselves ruled her death accidental. No matter where Lydia's train of thought started out it always returned to the same station: Why would the cops cover for Brad Pearce? Answer: *They* wouldn't.

A father, however, might suppress evidence, to protect his son.

Maybe Chief of Police Dell Rawls knew a small town's prejudice wouldn't allow innocent until proven guilty. Jess, Cam, and Brad formed a love triangle, the fates of each affecting the other.

Lydia had opened the door for Cam to blame Brad Pearce, an easy softball tossed. He had no one to refute whatever he said about the guy. Pin it all on a dead man.

Instead, Cam reserved his harshest criticism for Shane Ellet.

Cam Rawls sounded like he hated Shane. Which made sense. *If Shane was correct.*

Of course Shane Ellet wasn't correct. Shane was a basement-dwelling, cyber weirdo who made up his own nickname. His channel had some subscribers, okay, and Lydia could admit the man possessed a certain charm. This morning when she couldn't sleep, she'd been swayed by some of what he'd said. After a few hours away from the screen, Lydia, if forced to choose between an upstanding officer of the law and a trust fund, conspiracy YouTuber? A no-brainer. Lydia wouldn't be thinking about any of this if not for a phone call from a dead woman she never met. Why had Rhona Clarion reached out before she died? And to talk about Jess?

Cam didn't come across as disingenuous, just apprehensive, restrained. Cool, calm, collected. When Lydia said she was getting in touch with Shane, Cam didn't flinch.

And therein lay the problem. Lydia worked with liars every day, and that was the thing with the best of them: they never said more than they had to.

"Look what the cat dragged in!" Gloria slurred, words more garbled than usual. She was sitting in the same chair, adorned in the same robe as last time Lydia saw her. "Two times in as many days! My only daughter! To what do I owe the pleasure?"

The inflated verbiage and sloppy speech betrayed a woman inebriated. What else was new? The guilt trip fell short. Lydia was tired. She was back in Pasa Ardo, and wanted to see her old room.

"I have the night off, Mom. Thought I'd take you up on your offer."

"And what offer was that, dear?"

"The other night. You invited me to stay?"

Gloria's face soured as she reached for the bottle to find it drained dry. "Would you be a darling and get your mother a glass of wine? I picked one that was empty."

That's what happens when you drink it all, Mom.

Lydia headed to the spacious kitchen and massive refrigerator, stocked with takeout containers and neglected vegetables but devoid of any wine. "You're all out."

Gloria flicked the back of her hand. "The pantry. Put ice in it."

As Lydia delivered the room-temperature chardonnay, ice cubes clinking like hastily tossed dice, Richard Fontaine entered from the back, grubby jeans stained at the knees.

"Dickie! You're tracking in mud—"

"Lydia!" Richard announced, ignoring her mom. Every time he said her name, he rejoiced, as if seeing her was the highlight of his day. This man, who wasn't even dating her mother, demonstrated more parental warmth and fondness than either her biological mother or father. Alan, Dad, called often enough, suggesting dinner or other casual get-togethers. Sometimes they'd meet. Santa Barbara. Laguna Beach. Occasionally he'd make the trek over the hills to San Perdida. The conversations were pleasant, if superficial. If Lydia had to describe her father with one word, it would be "inaccessible," a part of him walled off, impossible to reach. Often, neither father nor daughter could agree on a date, time, or place, or one of them would cancel plans last minute, citing a hectic schedule. Each time Lydia hung up the phone, she felt relieved. She could tell her dad did too. Lydia had taken psych classes during medical school. It wasn't difficult to understand the reason for this. It was easier to forget the shared loss on their own. Lydia loved her dad, and he her. They both loved Jess. But out of sight, out of mind.

Lydia smiled at Richard, before turning to her mother. "Do you remember if I was ever friends with a girl named Rhona?" Lydia wanted to ask if *Jess* had been friends with a girl by that name, but neither she nor her mother spoke her dead sister's name. Ever. That was Mom's coping strategy.

"Who's that?" Gloria asked.

"I'm asking if you remember anyone named 'Rhona'? From the school, maybe?"

"Rhonda?"

"Rhona. Rhona Clarion."

Gloria turned around, eyes glazed. Lydia accepted how futile the question was. Her mother spent her evenings soothed by the soft haze of alcohol and muscle relaxants. Asking her mom to recall two nights ago was pushing it, never mind two decades.

"Forget it," Lydia said.

With great effort, Gloria hoisted herself to her feet, grabbed her nightcap, and kissed her daughter near the cheek. Her lips were cold from the ice in the chardonnay. "Help yourself to whatever you need."

Richard Fontaine stood silent in the living room, as if tonight might be the night Gloria gave in.

Instead, all she said was, "See you tomorrow, Dickie."

Upstairs, in the bedroom she'd shared with her sister, Lydia felt Jess' presence. Lydia didn't buy into ghosts, religion, or spirituality. She also couldn't write off the sensation she experienced stepping into that room. Maybe it was the conversations she still had with her dead sister, where she'd talk to Jess, only now she could say the things she hadn't when Jess was alive, and her sister was allowed to answer, voice as loud and clear as if she were standing right there in the room beside her.

When Jess went missing, Lydia didn't like sleeping alone. For the first couple of weeks, she'd crawl into bed with Gloria, who was never thrilled with sharing space. Lydia remembered the look of disdain on her mother's face when they'd wake in the morning. Soon, her mother started locking her bedroom door at night.

Now, as an adult, when Lydia visited her mother, this old room was all she looked forward to. It was the only time she felt comfortable in this house, like she was welcome and not an intruder. It was the sole evidence Lydia wasn't an only child, and it was the one room with pictures of Jess.

Gloria hadn't moved anything. Didn't even pack up Jess' old clothes, the room rendered a shrine. A way to honor Jess' memory? For some mothers, maybe. Not Gloria.

It was possible for Lydia to both love her mom and recognize her petty, passive-aggressive behavior. Leaving the room as is, with photos of Jess hung between the Nirvana and Smashing Pumpkins posters, was her mother's way of reminding Lydia of how she'd failed them all. *How could you let your sister leave?* Except if that was the intention, her plan backfired. Instead of disturbing, the familiar offered solace, a moment in time forever preserved. Jess' things were still there. Her books, her bracelets, even awards her big sister had won at horse camp when she was a little girl. Clothes in the closet and pictures on the dresser. All untouched. Her essence. A part of her sister lived on.

Lydia set down her things, extracting her laptop, checking work emails, as she'd done all afternoon, still waiting on word from Maureen regarding Rhona Clarion. Specifically, when Rhona's death had been logged into the system and vic was in queue for autopsy. Once they determined a cause of death, Maureen would be the one to write the official report.

There was no email. Not from Maureen. Not from anyone. No news of interest.

Signing into her L.A. County account, Lydia was surprised to find that the Reporting Desk, the department responsible for cataloging deaths, had, in fact, started a file on Rhona. This was how procedure worked. The Reporting Desk would receive notification of death from discovery parties such as law enforcement, nursing homes, the family, etc., and determine whether that death landed within their jurisdiction and if an investigation was necessary. Lydia had been at this long enough to know what happened next. With the answer to both these questions "yes," detectives would have a new case, and Rhona Clarion would be slated for the medical examiner's office.

Maybe Maureen hadn't received the updated list yet? Lydia checked the time—still before ten—early enough that Mo would be awake. More likely, Maureen would, again, try to talk Lydia into backing off. Report the voicemail. Allow detectives to do their job. Maureen might even do the autopsy *before* she spoke to Lydia.

Lydia couldn't let that happen.

Pulling up a search engine, she returned to Shane Ellet's *Night Shade*. She thought it might take more effort to get in touch with the Moth. But, no, his contact information was right there. An email address.

Lydia wrote a succinct message, polite and to the point, requesting to meet. *Don't say anything to scare him off.* She explained who she was, how she'd seen the show and wanted to talk, in person. If he was, as Cam maintained, "still around," she'd leave her contact info and hope he got back to her.

Then she pulled up the old webisode about her sister and watched it again.

CHAPTER SEVENTEEN

Night Shade, *Episode 88, "The Mysterious Fate of Jessica Barrett," with Your Host, the Moth, Part 2*

…[T]he night Jess Barrett went missing and I revealed who I was, the voice behind the character. It was a big deal back then. My radio show was very popular. Everyone wanted to know who I was. I guess I was drawn to this line of work from the beginning. Those things that go creep in the dark. Our vocations seek us out, not the other way around. I know people who get up, shower, climb in their cars, scramble off to jobs they hate. And they do it because they think they don't have any other choice. And maybe they don't. We all need money. I've been lucky in that regard. Maybe that's all they were meant to do, these people. Maybe I'd be right there with them. I don't think so, though. I'd risk it all, be willing to die—I'd rather jam a stake through my temple, watch the blood dribble down my chin, draining my cerebral fluid into a mug, raising a toast to all the soulless bastards stuck in the nine-to-five grind, drinking till I lost my goddamn mind. I don't understand how these people live, or what they do, or why they do it. I don't understand a lot of things.

I don't want to make it seem like I'm some down-on-his-luck sad bastard. I live a good life. I've been blessed by birth and circumstance, and this *is all easy for me to say. And if you want to hate me for saying it, go right ahead. I can't speculate where I'd be without the money. I didn't always have it. And when I didn't, I still wasn't signing up for the conventional. I call myself the Moth because I am drawn to the light in the darkness. Only from the darkness can you see what's really there. Me? I'm a goddamn optimist.*

They always accuse people like me of being negative, pessimistic, a miserable prick. Except here's the thing: what's the point of noticing all that's wrong with the world if the chance for a better one didn't exist? A bigger, brighter world brimming with possibility. This dark globe needs to be spun around so we can see what's on the other side. Hope. Oh, it exists. I believe in the promised land. It's a life few glimpse, let alone enjoy. More than money or fame or ease—it's being true to yourself, who you are, staying on that righteous path. Self-actualization. The pinnacle of Maslow's Hierarchy of Needs. Some call it unattainable. Bullshit. To get it all, you must be willing to risk it all. The ones who don't, who settle for less? Sure, I feel sorry for them. When you're born into poverty in this country, it's hard, nay, impossible to climb out of that hole. They like to tout this guy Bill or Steve or some other shithead who dropped out of college and went on to make billions as evidence you can achieve your dreams if you work hard enough. These people aren't burdened with the truth. Ignorance is bliss. So for them, it's always, "Man, why you got to bring me down?" It's not a lie if you believe it. No one ever got rich off workingman wages.

You remember Slaughterhouse Five? It's a Kurt Vonnegut novel, and if you haven't read it, I want you to shut off your computer and go read it right now. I'll be here when you get back. (Takes long, dramatic drag off cigarette.) Okay. We ready? That scene in the zoo with Billy Pilgrim—he's the hero, or anti-hero—I'm not sure what Billy is supposed to be except a stand-in for the rest of us dreamers who get unstuck in time. See, for most people, this world will go right on spinning, with or without our consent.

They aren't concerned with what we're talking about here tonight, the dark heart of man. Not ol' Billy, though. Billy spoke right up. He wasn't spending his life in a cage, even if the pursuit of understanding drove him mad. We need more Billy Pilgrims. (Stubs out cigarette, smoke drifting.)

It was nineteen ninety-one. Ya dig? A different world back then. I was waking up. A kid still, sure, but I was starting to see. Like emerging from a coma or bad car accident, the view came to me slowly, fuzzy, out of focus, and then my vision sharpened crystal clear and I couldn't avoid the picture if I wanted to. What I saw was a world and existence I wanted no part of. Clearly delineated. Right. Wrong. Black. White. Good. Bad. Pick a side. And the thing is when you're like that, you seek out others who think like you do because like the Boss say, ain't nobody want to be alone. Left alone, not bothered, sure—we don't want headaches—but people need people. It's why solitary confinement in prison is considered such a harsh and severe form of punishment. Without people we go freaking nuts. And what I'm saying to you now is a variation of that; it's nothing earth-shattering or jaw-dropping. One universal truth. Everybody is crazy. We need to find others who are crazy like us. In my tribe, man.

I was a senior at Pasa Ardo High School, slated to graduate in ninety-one. I did. Graduate, that is. Everyone graduates high school except the burnouts with dirt mustaches who drive muscle cars and work at gas stations. The world was changing, man. In a big, big way. There was a war, and now that it's so many years later, we can look back on that first Iraqi War as another skirmish, a minor conflict relegated to the history books, big dick waving by insecure assholes, a smudge in time. What else is new? Back then? We didn't know if they'd reinstate the draft or what. I was supposed to go to college, but I didn't have any desire. It all came back to this idea of purpose: why are we here? And now that I'm over forty, saying that feels trite. Because we stop asking that question the older we get. It's almost like since there is no answer, nothing definitive anyway, provable—the big answers to the big questions: God, the Universe, Everything. It's passé. It's all derivative, man. I don't have an answer any more than you do. Here's the one thing I do have: I'm not full of shit. I don't play at this—it's my job; I work at it. I'm not interested in comedies of manners and/or conducting pleasantries. I'm not filling the space with hot air because I can't stand the silence. I embrace the silence, the darkness.

It's only from the darkness that you can see the light.

And I was there, man. I was the reason they were there. The water tower. Soledad Gorge. Midnight. March fifteenth. The Ides. No one picked up on that. The Ides of March, get it? No one picks up on anything.

So that night of the protest, the big party by the leaning water tower, I knew it was coming to an end, and it broke my heart, to tell the truth. Before I became the Rider, no one noticed me. I was the eggman, they were the eggman. I was the walrus, goo-goo-g'joob. And goddamn I liked mattering. We all want to matter. But the FCC and Feds were on my ass. I couldn't keep running.

It started as a joke. The Rider on the Plain, right? A rant. A rage. A chance to mock the very institutions sent to indoctrinate us.

We lived so close to Hollywood, and they were always trying to sell us something. How to look. How to act. How to be cool. What to think or say and the people who claimed to be most impervious were the most susceptible. So I embraced it, embodied it. A movie had come out. A stupid shit movie, with stupid shit actors and a stupid shit script, even if it did have a kickass soundtrack. That's where I got the idea. It was hilarious to me, to take this spin, this propaganda, and ape it back, use their tropes and clichés against the bastards. I'd employ the same weapons they leveled against us against them. So that's what I did. My father had this ham radio set, and it didn't take much to get it up and running—I've always been a bit of a gearhead. At night I started broadcasting, I didn't think anyone was listening, but then I overheard at school how someone had caught me on the radio. They didn't know it was me—I disguised my voice—it was all part of the act, see? Modulator. You got them at RadioShack back when there were RadioShacks. It caught on from there. People started listening. I knew I had a message worth sharing. We weren't these stupid kids buying into the bullshit. You can't sell out if you never buy in.

Then they fired the one teacher who gave a damn about us. Brad Pearce. What we didn't know at the time—what we couldn't have known at the time—was ol' Brad was like the rest of them. Worse in fact because he'd gotten us to believe people could be different when you got older, that you didn't have to turn into a hypocritical piece of shit. That was his act.

I don't have an act. Not anymore. Which is why I don't have a people. Or maybe I do and you are it. Or maybe, and this hurts to say, I ended up a phony like the rest. I got my money, my payoff, I have my little show, and so I ramble about inequality and injustice, offering my take on horrific crimes, speculating without an ounce of training or expertise, with no concern for how I pay rent. I'm not changing a goddamn thing. The human condition is a disease and growing up is its most severe symptom.

But back then? I was happy to be noticed. I wasn't a loser. No one picked on me. Pretty girls would talk to me, but even then I could see I'd be forgotten. Until … the Rider on the Plain.

Sometimes I shudder at the name. And trust me I know calling myself the Moth isn't much better. But I'm not here to be cool or "with it" or whatever the it-kids say these days. It's been a long, long time since I gave a damn about being cool. I'm a grown-ass man who lives alone. I answer to no one. My only job is to tell the truth. Which I am going to do now. It's up to you whether you believe me.

So, Jessica Barrett. Man, Jess was cool. There was this one time I walked downstairs to the art room and she was dancing by herself, thrashing, all alone. I can't even remember the song. Maybe it was something cool like the Violent Femmes or old R.E.M. or Black Flag—what's it matter? I watched *her through that little glass window, dancing, not giving a shit. God, she was something else. Maybe the one goddamn genuine person at Pasa Ardo High.*

You can't hide who you are forever. When they fired Brad, this was before we learned he was a sexual deviant rapist fuck, we all loved him. We thought they fired him because he spoke out against institutions and oppression. Turns out he was a scumbag pedo. Sex and aggression, right? And he and Jess, well, I won't disparage the dead. But she deserved better. I told a small lie. Said I'd spoken with Brad, said he'd be there, at the water tower. I hadn't spoken with the guy. He maybe knew about my show. He didn't know it was me. I needed an audience. Now I can see my intentions weren't noble. Back then? I thought I was Christ on the cross.

It was time to climb down so someone else could use the wood.

We met at the tower. I drove up, let the police arrest me. Brad never showed, and so of course everyone blamed me.

And now there is no way to tell this next part without contradicting my commitment to complete honesty but, like, fuck it, right? If I contradict myself, I contradict myself. I am large. I contain multitudes.

See, I saw it happen. When they hauled me in. I watched the chief of police hide evidence, conceal the truth.

The first thing the police did when they arrived at the water tower was arrest my ass. They threw me in the back of a squad car, before returning to the party on the hill to scatter a bunch of scared kids. The cop car was parked at the bottom of the ravine. I sat there a while. Then I saw Cam Rawls—town cop Dell's son—the current Pasa Ardo chief of police, that Cam Rawls. And who was he with? Jess Barrett. They were arguing. I saw Cam take a swipe at her. Now I'm not saying he struck her. Just that there was a physical altercation. And I happen to know, for a fact, that evidence was recovered that night—evidence that might have—and I stress might have—implicated Cam. That evidence? What was it? I'm not at liberty to say. As a journalist, I have to respect the code, y'know? Anonymous sources and all.

I can't tell you more than that. This is the internet, man. Do your own research. Nothing is secret.

Till next time, I am the Moth, your light in the darkness.

The comments that followed were brutal. Lydia had read them the last time, knowing better. You never read the comment section, which is where the worst of humanity reveals itself. Most everyone who watched his channel, the ten thousand or so subscribers, did so with the express purpose of mocking Shane Ellet. Why shouldn't they? The Moth was crazy. He rambled, still spouting teenager revolution bullshit but now as a doughy, thinning-haired, middle-aged white man of means. But, oh, the entertainment factor! That was the overarching sentiment. The comments ran from *Hilarious* to *What a loser* to *Totes nutcase* to *This is the FUNNIEST SHIT ON THE INTERNET*. And, sure, Lydia could see their point. Shane was off. His eyes would grow all screwy, he'd jump from topic to topic; he was clearly high on something and thus easy to dismiss.

Except when it came to *this* story, the one about how Jess died, Lydia believed him.

She believed every goddamn word.

CHAPTER EIGHTEEN

Shane was driving home from Vons, trunk of the Camry stuffed with groceries. OJ. Cold cuts. Pint of vanilla ice cream. Those wedges of smelly cheese his mother was hooked on. His mom had sent him shopping. He didn't appreciate the way she'd asked. He also couldn't say no. His mother was almost eighty with cataracts; she shouldn't be driving. Especially at night. What could he do? His mom had a craving for cheese. Shane didn't like how she hollered out the window. Made him feel like one of those losers in his forties who still lives in his parent's basement. They didn't have many basements in California. And Shane didn't live with his mother. There was a separate dwelling on their property—an in-law unit some called it—Shane called it a bungalow. It's where he filmed his popular web series *Night Shade*. He'd lived there since graduating. From high school. Shane never went to college. Started. Didn't finish.

When you're twenty, with the financial resources Shane had, people can't understand why you wouldn't want to go to college. He gave it a shot. End of freshman year at USC, Shane had soured on the concept of higher education. Learning one of your teaching heroes is a kiddy diddler will do that to you. Brad Pearce wasn't totally full of shit. Like what he said about books. Every lesson they teach you in college can be found in a book. Shane convinced his folks he was saving them money by *not* going. And it was true, Shane read a lot of books. He watched more movies.

The persona Shane worked so hard to cultivate on *Night Shade* landed a long way from the real-life incarnation. This dark man of intrigue, cloaked in black, lifting mysterious boulders to uncover what slithers beneath, delivered via a raspy two-pack-a-day habit. An act. The Moth. Your light in the darkness. Bullshit. Problem was, when you work so hard to cultivate an image, it's hard to turn off. Keep at it long enough, you become the character you create.

Back in the day, Shane Ellet used to pretend he was immune to the manipulation tactics deployed by television and film, insusceptible to Hollywood's attempts to shape our personal aesthetics and lifestyles choices. His embrace of all things pop culture and mainstream was his way of mocking the sheep; a one-man revolt against the restless machination that told us what to buy and whom to be. Who was Shane kidding? Shane Ellet was just a dude who loved movies. He'd seen all the classics. Great cinema and storytelling are great cinema and sto-rytelling. *Casablanca. Heat. The Postman Rings Twice* (the original), *Memento, Pulp Fiction*, the collective works of Kurosawa. Shane adored the films set in and around greater Los Angeles—*Chinatown, Reservoir Dogs, LA Confidential.* Even if they never got the geography quite right.

Driving down Main, the Pasa Ardo street quiet, Shane spied the shops lining this central thoroughfare, the independent hardware store, the mom-and-pop grocery markets, the 1950s-era apothecary that had managed not to be swallowed up by Walgreens or CVS and still boasted a vintage "Drugs" sign out front. Pasa Ardo's downtown was a time capsule that served to remind Shane he had been born in the wrong half of the twentieth century.

Shane wished he could go back, invent a time machine, take what he'd learned and start over. Who doesn't, right? To know what we know now then? If Shane ever found one of those magic lanterns, like on TV, that's what he'd wish for. But that was magic. A machine was science. He'd done the research. Time travel was possible. He didn't understand the math, which was beyond his skillset. But it *could* be done. If he could travel back to any era, he'd pick the 1940s. When the world was still black and white and you could smoke cigarettes anywhere and don a fedora and people wouldn't laugh at you and all the librarians were hot, like in *The Big Sleep*. Be a *real* reporter. Like Walter Winchell.

He accepted that this attitude had been shaped by pop culture, which espoused craft coffeehouses not run as part of a greater corporate conglomerate as inherently superior. Hot water poured over crushed beans is the same no matter what decade you drink it in. To tell the truth, Shane didn't feel so great about himself lately.

Shane Ellet didn't relish his reputation around town. He felt like his best years were behind him, like he'd peaked in high school, which was bad enough. But in Shane's case he'd done so anonymously, his fifteen minutes enjoyed behind a mask. Once outed, no mystery remained. Brad Pearce was exposed. Jess Barrett was dead. Everyone hated Shane.

For not knowing Jess that well, her death sure had shaped the course of his life.

Jess was one of the reasons he'd started *Night Shade*. To set the record straight. People used to tell him how original and irreverent he was. Shane had insights, impressions of this world worth sharing, often hilarious takes on the absurd state of existence that not everyone could articulate. People used to tell him he could be a writer. That was when he was younger. Now folks around Pasa Ardo didn't know his name. You can't go door-to-door explaining your side of the story. That's why he liked YouTube's user-friendly platform. No gatekeepers to pitch a series to. He could take his message straight to the streets. Power to the people. *Night Shade* was designed to crack open the eggs of the unknown and get cooking, however ugly the omelet.

Shane found comfort in the darkness. No, not comfort—a challenge. He wanted to confront it, corner it, conquer it. There was more to Shane Ellet than misguided allegiance to a degenerate conman when he was seventeen. There would be no more hiding behind a garbled, disguised voice, broadcasting over alter-ego airwaves. Each episode of *Night Shade* began with Shane in front of the camera, staring straight into the heart of darkness.

"Here I am," he'd say to the ghosts. "Do your worst. I'm not scared of you."

During his time as the Rider on the Plain (yes, the name was cheesy, but also cleverer than people gave him credit for), Shane admitted a life of privilege. His platform was built on unbridled honesty. He had fans. Everyone thought he'd ripped off Christian Slater from that movie *Pump Up the Volume*. And, okay, sure, yes, the renegade pirate radio DJ part, maybe he'd copped. But that was Hollywood glossing over the struggle real teenagers faced every day, watering down and homogenizing what people his age went through and talked about, had to deal with back then. They weren't twenty-two-year-old actors pretending to be sixteen. What did an elite A-lister know about life at that age? That's the part the movies always got wrong about high school. It wasn't gangs or drugs or unwanted teen pregnancies that were the biggest threats. It was you. It was coming into your own and seeing a world where you might not fit. Sure, some guys fit fine. They go to college, get jobs, find wives, sire two point five kids, and live happily ever after in McMansions with white picket fences securing their perfect plots. Wonderful! For them. But if you *didn't* fit in, if there *wasn't* a place for you, where did you go? And it was about more than money. Shane may've been blessed financially. But it didn't make him feel any less alone, any less of an outcast freak. As human beings, we crave a place to belong. There had to be others like him, people who saw and thought and felt the way he did. *Night Shade* was for them. Big game hunting. Glory. If you're not shooting for the stars, what's the point of trying?

That's what the water tower had been about. It wasn't an uprising or an overthrow—they had no weapons; it had never been an armed revolution. At that age, all you want is a seat at the table, man. To be heard and taken seriously; to have an input about your future—for someone to listen when you say, "To thine own self be true" and not have them laugh at you for being naïve. Everyone missed that point, so intent on figuring out his identity. It was *right* there. He'd taken the name Rider on the Plain from Roger Waters' 1984 solo album *The Pros and Cons of Hitchhiking*, which samples a scene from the movie ... *Shane!* How much more obvious could he be?

A wave of nausea hit. Shane was driving super stoned, having inhaled a hearty lungful. Purple Haze, his guy Donnie called it. Examining the bud, you could see why. The thick, violet tracts of the cannabis flower, sticky sweet trichomes. The pungent aroma of skunky earthiness seeped deep in the nasal passage. Enlightenment stuck to the base of his skull like hearty oatmeal to the ribs. Shane thought he was going to throw up. Then it passed. He continued home with the groceries and cheese for mom, feeling transcendent.

Shane! Shane! And mother wants you!

No one picks up on anything.

Shane retrieved the nubbed, extinguished joint from the ashtray and was scrolling through his digital library to find that particular Roger Waters record when the flashing lights appeared in his rearview.

He stubbed out the joint he had yet to re-light. Even though weed was, effectively, legal in California, you didn't want to get caught with a lit roach. That had to be like drinking and driving with an open container, no? Shane wasn't sure. It had been a while since he'd been stopped by the cops.

Fanning the air, Shane pulled to the curb, setting the car in park on the side of a quiet road. Gone was the bustling Pasa Ardo. Having navigated downtown, he was back in the cuts, the outskirts of Old Town where the old Community Center still stood. He heard the desert whistle, *The Good, the Bad and the Ugly* theme signaling a showdown. Such a great if overlooked part of filmmaking: the soundtrack. Shane knew it was all in his head, that eerie echo, an unsung sound engineer's attempt to mimic the lonesome coyote. Perspiration beaded his crown, threatening to roll down and give him away. *Over what?* He'd done nothing wrong. You read all the time about routine traffic stops going sideways. Reach for your ID, they say it was a gun. Except, this was Pasa Ardo. And Shane was white.

There was no reason for Shane to be surprised to see Cam Rawls walking up. One of the only black guys in town, Cam stood out, big and burly. Plus, Shane was aware Cam, an old classmate and former football star, was the chief of police, so the uniform wasn't a shock. Although their paths seldom crossed. Shane tried to think of the last time their paths *did* cross. It had been a while. Shane wouldn't classify himself as a recluse, but he didn't go into town often. Didn't drive much, seldom left the bungalow except to score weed. Last thing he needed right now was a DUI and waiting for his mom to bail him out. But the closer Cam came, the more surreal the moment grew. Cam had gotten so much older. Like a time jump in a movie. Jarring.

Shane had no reason to be nervous but felt anxious anyway. A long time ago, Shane had accused Cam's dad, Dell, of covering up evidence in the Jess Barrett disappearance. He doubted Cam Rawls watched his YouTube channel. That case was ages ago. Besides, Shane hadn't lied. Hammed it up for theater, maybe. Everything he'd said was true. According to his source.

When Cam got to the driver's side window, Shane waited for the "License and registration, please." That's how these things went, wasn't it? Maybe the gonj was making his head foggy. The car wafted smoky, hazy ribbons of lazy blue-gray floating like stratus clouds. Or was that smoke from the wildfires? The news said there was a new one raging. Or was that last year?

"Jesus Christ, Ellet. How stoned are you?"

"Huh?"

Cam stood, hands on hips, shaking his head. "I've been standing at this window five goddamn minutes and this is the first time you glanced my way."

Though they were the same age, Cam might as well have been his dad, way he said it, with his receding hairline and graying temples. Dude was a behemoth. Shane knew his perspective was skewed, looking up from the driver's seat. And you couldn't dismiss the power dynamic. Unsettling. Shane had to stop smoking and driving.

"The inside of your cab smells like a Snoop Dogg concert."

"Oh, yeah, sorry. Um, it's Cam, right?" Shane knew that. "I'm Shane Ellet. We went to school together?" Shane extended a hand.

Cam pulled back to avoid touching him.

"I know who the fuck you are, Rider. Moth. Whatever punk-ass nickname you've given yourself this time."

Shane *must be* stoned because the attitude directed his way felt way harsh. Misguided. No, misdirected. That was the word he was looking for. Precise diction is paramount. Shane had been trying to be polite. People change after high school. Look at Cam. He was, well, not fat, but far from the peak physical specimen he'd been back in the day. He looked like his dad, Dell. Or maybe Ving Rhames. Or that other actor? He always got the two confused. Shane had changed as well, of course. We all do as we get older. That was the weird part, how you go from, like, being kids and friends and playing games together but then you're all grown up and have jobs, acting out new parts but fulfilling the same roles. It was still a game. Only the stakes change.

"What the fuck is wrong with you?" Cam asked.

"Oh, I was, y'know, thinking about school. How we all, well, we're older now, and here I am, sitting in a car, and you're a police officer, but we used to play cops and robbers together—"

"I never played shit with you."

"I meant metaphysically. Er, hypothetically! Adult roles, how we adopt careers, or they adopt us—"

"Shut up, Shane." Cam ground his jaw. "Jesus, man, when are you gonna grow up?"

Shane wasn't sure how to respond to that.

"Your fucking YouTube channel," Cam said.

"You've watched it?" That wasn't the real question Shane wanted to ask. First, he wanted to know why Cam was being such an asshole, although he'd probably word it better. But, yes, he was flattered anytime he met a fan…

"I'm not a fan," Cam said, as if reaching into Shane's head. "I don't go for that weirdo conspiracy shit."

"It's a true crime show—"

"I know what the fuck it is. Listen, man, I'mma make this real easy for you. You're gonna go back online and scrub those episodes about me and Jess Barrett, you got that? I don't need people asking questions about who I dated a quarter century ago."

Shane didn't say anything.

"Is that a problem? *Moth?*"

Shane wanted to say, goddamn right it was. This was America, freedom of speech. Heard of it, Hitler? The younger version of Shane would've stood up for himself. Rider would've told Cam to kiss his ass. Rider would've gotten out of the car, not giving a good goddamn if Cameron Rawls was a cop with a gun, and said, "No, *you* listen! I'll say *what* I want, *when* I want. And you can't stop me!" This current version wasn't as bold. Shane slumped down in his seat.

"You can't accuse me…" Cam leaned in to whisper, which was pointless. No cars were out at midnight in a subdued valley town. "Of… killing someone. Are you out of your ever-flipping mind?"

"I didn't mean… It's a show, y'know? I'm trying to get subscribers—"

"I don't give a flying fuck about your subscriber list or number of likes or advertising dollars. Now you go delete that shit, or next time I see you, I'mma haul your ass in for driving under the influence." Cam narrowed his gaze. "You feel me?"

Shane nodded, suddenly stone-cold sober in the cool July night.

Cam started back to his car. Shane exhaled relief, before the cop spun around. "Another thing. Check your fucking email. Lydia Barrett—Jess' sister—remember her? She wants to talk to you. Ask you some questions. Meet with her. No matter what she asks, you back off your bullshit allegations against me. And you *do not* mention we've had this conversation. To anyone. Got it? Now get out of here, before I kick your ass on principle."

CHAPTER NINETEEN

THEN, Tuesday, March 12, 1991, 10:12 p.m.

Waiting for Rider to come on the air, Jess tugged off her tee shirt, replacing it with the bigger *Bossanova* one she slept in, from the Pixies concert last December at the Palladium. A bunch of friends had gone together, including Sarah, Renee, and Cam, who surprised her with the tee shirt after the show. The merch booth only had XXL left. That was the first night he kissed her.

Before any deeper emotions could sink in, her little sister Lydia cracked the door to their bedroom, poking in her head. "Can I come in yet?"

"No," Jess said. "I told you. *After* the radio show."

"Why can't I listen with you?"

"It's too grown up. Go watch TV."

"I can't. Mom's asleep on the couch. Every time I try to turn the channel, she wakes up and gets mad."

"Then go read a book."

"Can I read it in here? I'll be *super* quiet. You won't even know I'm here."

"Not right now." Jess crouched down eye level. Lydia had yet to hit her growth spurt, which made Jess' five ten feel abnormally tall. She placed her hands gently on her baby sister's shoulders. "Please, Lydia. A little longer. I promise I'll come get you *the second* it ends, okay?"

Lydia rolled her eyes and threw back her head, overselling the drama, before she stomped off toward the green room, where she'd been stockpiling her books. You never saw a girl that young read so many books. And not little kiddie ones like Nancy Drew. The thousand-page, bleak Russian novel kind.

Usually, Jess had patience for Lydia's endless barrage of questions. Tonight, she did not. This was big. They couldn't let Principal Sheinbaum and the rest of those fascist assholes get away with it.

Tonight, Rider was announcing their plan of action, a meeting place and time where they would take down the school and force them to reinstate Brad. They had a list of demands, and they *would* be met.

Rider was never this late. Where was he? *They didn't catch him, did they?*

Burning a hole in the carpet, from one end to the other, Nirvana to Smashing Pumpkins, Jess stalked and watched the time, feeling her pulse quicken, growing agitated and increasingly concerned.

But not about Brad.

It had been twelve days since they'd last spoken. At first Jess was worried, reading too much into it. Now she knew it was a test. Their connection was too strong, their bond too powerful for a week and a half of radio silence to mean anything. Jess was not going to fail him. Brad needed her—and the Class of '91—now more than ever. He'd reach out to her soon. She could feel it in her heart and soul.

Why was any of this even necessary? The establishment viewed Brad as a threat. They were wrong. Brad Pearce was the reason so many classmates were inspired to continue their education. Sure, most were going to college regardless, because that's what their parents expected; that's what you did when you lived in Pasa Ardo. But now they were *excited* to go. During their private meetings, Brad encouraged Jess to seize the opportunity. He'd say, "School is the one time in your life where you can dedicate all your time to being the best version of yourself."

Alongside the rock posters on her wall, Jess' assorted awards hung. Mostly from when she was a little kid. Her mom had even framed her "Most Improved Swimmer Award" from summer camp a million years ago. Why had Jess kept it? Why hadn't she taken it down? It was meaningless. Like the diploma she was about to receive.

High school was a diploma mill. Roll 'em in, roll 'em out. Everyone graduated high school in Pasa Ardo unless they were a total burnout loser. They'd have a big ceremony where everyone would congratulate and fawn and make like it was some grand accomplishment. Didn't mean jack. Life was out there, waiting for each of them to stamp their mark; the real world was way bigger than this insignificant town.

Before Brad's class, Jess (unlike her baby sister) never read *any* book. She'd skim the bare minimum to pass a test, mail in a report, but she never cared about words. No author spoke to her. In the past year, Jess had read almost fifty books—fifty! She had a journal where she kept track, challenging herself. Books used to seem boring. Brad got her to understand they were the key to life.

One time, when they were meeting at his apartment, after class, before their relationship got physical, Brad held up a copy of Céline (which blew her mind when she started reading it). He said, "I'm happy you're going to college." He'd helped Jess apply to several schools, and with the improvement in her grades, she now had a chance to get accepted somewhere good. He thumped the book. "Just know, everything they are going to teach you is between these pages."

Jess thought he meant the Céline book, but he corrected her.

"It's a good book. But not *that* good." Then he laughed. The way Brad laughed was so authentic, so vibrant. His eyes would crinkle and you could feel the joy radiating. "I'm talking libraries, bookstores. *All the books.* Your professors are going to be invaluable, and if you find the right one—like I did—it'll change your life. But the thirst, passion—the desire—" He pointed between her breasts, at her heart "—must come from there." Her entire body tingled.

Jess wanted to tell Brad she *had* found that one influential professor. No, he wasn't a college professor, but he could be one if he wanted. Brad Pearce was the smartest person she'd ever met. She couldn't find the right words in time.

The phone rang, and Brad sprang to answer it. It was not a friendly conversation. She'd never seen Brad get angry like that. She had to admit it was a turn on, how indignant his voice rose. Whoever had called was getting an earful.

"Are we still doing this?" he said. "You signed the goddamn papers. What do you want? Me to bleed out of my eyes?!"

Jess had to get going or she'd miss her ride with Renee. Jess tried to say goodbye, but Brad didn't notice, too engaged in his righteous fight.

She thought about that afternoon a lot.

She was thinking about that afternoon now, that moment when she knew there was more between them. She could still feel him, in her heart, her soul, their connection unbreakable. Brad had impacted *all* their lives. Now it was their turn to repay the favor.

The Rider on the Plain came crackling over the airwaves.

Good evening, Rider Crew. It's on! Water tower. Soledad Gorge. This Friday, midnight. Oh, and I have a surprise for you. I talked to Brad. He's going to be there!

And so am I! It's my coming out party. We are going to do this together, face to face, get Brad reinstated, and we won't take no for an answer. You won't want to miss this. The revolution will not be televised. This town won't know what hit 'em!

Rider out!

And like that, all was right with the world again.

CHAPTER TWENTY

NOW, Friday, July 22, 2016, 1:03 a.m.

Shane's run-in with Cam aggravated him. That's what he'd call it, right? A run-in. A confrontation. Wasn't pleasant, that was for sure. For a second there he thought the guy might slug him, or worse, haul him in. Not that Shane was blameless.

Forget driving under the influence, Shane had put rumor and conjecture on the web without first vetting any of his information, taking two lowlifes like Ricky and Donnie Simmons' word for it. A rookie reporter's mistake. Shane wasn't backtracking. Not all the way. He didn't appreciate being pushed around, and he didn't like being told what to do. Cam also hadn't been totally wrong about Shane's motivations.

Shane *was* jealous of him. Or had been. He'd been envious of all the popular students in high school, the jocks, the winners, the cool kids. Shane didn't consciously carry this envy. It's not like he trench-coated glum down halls conjuring mass revenge fantasies with assault rifles. Still, jealousy is a hard emotion to holster. Shane resented Cam, football star and all-around winner. Shane hated wondering if he might be racist.

Shane wasn't racist. Was he? A lot of guys in high school bugged Shane. Why did Cam get under his skin worse than the others?

When twenty-five years taps you on the shoulder and tells you to turn around, take a good, hard look, it's not an easy challenge to rise up to. Once upon a time, Shane Ellet wanted to be a writer. A legit journalist. An investigative reporter. When he was younger, he raged against the gross injustices tilted to favor those of his ilk; he possessed the skills—and means—to effect change. But he was lazy.

He'd had this schtick in high school, parlaying the popularity of a fictitious creation he'd conjured—mostly by ripping off a stupid movie—and he'd managed to delude himself into thinking he mattered. Shane Ellet was a joke. Which was why this entire town laughed at him. That wasn't on Cam Rawls. Shane got off on the attention. Each week, all those students tuning in to hear what *he* had to say. Then again, Shane *had* done *some* research. He knew, for a fact, Dell Rawls covered up evidence. He was pretty sure, anyway. Why would Donnie lie?

Stalking the bungalow, that's the question he kept returning to: how much "investigating" had Shane, the Moth, put into those incendiary claims leveled against Cam? He'd never viewed the documents he'd been told existed, taking the word of a drug-dealing dirtbag like Donnie. And wasn't there some other piece of physical evidence? A bracelet or something? Shane should get his medical marijuana card. Make life easier. Or maybe ease up on the weed. It sure wasn't helping him think clearly right now.

Had Shane allowed his jealousy of Cam Rawls to cloud his judgment? Keep him blind to the truth? A stiffer finger could also be pointed at another man: Brad Pearce, heartthrob teacher and all-around phony degenerate. The guy was almost thirty, macking on seventeen-year-old girls. And he'd gotten away with it. How? Same way people like Shane got away with their crimes: by throwing money at the problem. *Or maybe Jess really did fall. Or maybe Brad—or Cam— pushed her?* These were questions probably better asked *before* going to air. What had Cam said when he pulled him over? *When are you going to grow up?*

Whenever these self-loathing moods hit Shane, he could wallow, growing increasingly disgusted with himself. No, Shane wasn't going to beat himself up. Not tonight. What Shane had done was slanderous and irresponsible. Cam Rawls had a right to be pissed. Or not. Answering that would require extra effort. Which Shane could put in. He could make good on being a real reporter. He could finish writing this story decades in the making, delivering satisfying closure.

To achieve that, Shane would need to do something he'd seldom done his whole life: work.

Put down the blunt and focus.

Being a real reporter means trusting your gut. That run-in with Cam wasn't sitting right. *You already said that.* Shane wasn't letting the guy off the hook. Even if Cam let him get away with driving stoned, he didn't appreciate having his First Amendment rights violated. Shane also didn't want to be stupid—and going after the chief of police with so little proof was the very definition of. He had no intention of abandoning his pursuit of the truth. He did, however, have to start being smarter about it.

After he finished taking down the webisode about Jess Barrett, Shane prepared to make good on a pledge long overdue.

Shane Ellet was finally ready to take accountability.

He checked his email. Like Cam said, there was Lydia Barrett's message, requesting a sit-down. Lydia, a coroner's investigator in L.A., had questions. Shane had answers. Moreover, the baby sister of Jess Barrett, she might prove an asset.

Shane started crafting a response, suggesting they meet at this cool retro diner in Downey where they filmed the big showdown scene between Pacino and DeNiro in Michael Mann's masterpiece, *Heat*. Great, great heist film.

Shane didn't like the way the email read. Too needy. He saved the draft. Finish in the morning. No point belaboring now. Few people had insomnia as bad as he did.

In the meantime, Shane would do a little electronic investigating, starting with Brad Pearce. Dell Rawls covering up evidence didn't exonerate the sleazeball. True, Pearce was dead. But everyone knew he and Jess were more than teacher and student. Jess wasn't the first. Pasa Ardo wasn't the only high school where Brad Pearce taught. Pearce's transgressions traveled far and wide, casting a huge net. Lots of fish in that dirty sea.

Shane packed another bowl of weed.

How had Pearce dodged all those sexual abuse charges? Same way Shane got out of his jam: through the high-powered services of Carlson & Associates, SoCal's go-to attorneys for when shit got real.

Was Shane any better than Brad Pearce? *What kind of stupid question is that?* Having money isn't a sin. Sure, if Shane's parents didn't hire that law firm, he's in more trouble. Carlson & Associates were the best there was. That's what Shane had been told anyway. All he knew for certain: once his lawyer entered the conversation, Shane walked out of that jail cell.

Lawyer/client privilege was a real thing. Did it last forever? Shane typed the firm's name into the search engine. They'd repped him so long ago, law offices didn't even *have* websites back then, the internet in its infancy. How times had changed. The Carlson & Associates website was sick, slick, with a tan backdrop, navy blue headers, and an ivory font. Classy.

Shane couldn't remember the name of the lawyer who'd come to the station on his behalf. It wasn't the woman who owned the firm, Susan. It was a dude. Young, brazen, with a big pair of brass balls. Shane snorted recalling how fast the FCC backed off, all charges dismissed. Christ, why had he said that to Dell as he was walking out? Shane recoiled thinking how big an asshole he used to be. Maybe he still was an asshole. Do assholes know they're assholes?

Not the point.

Right. Write. Email. Too late to call.

Shane composed a message to the firm, implementing inflated, erudite turns of phrases like "heretofore" and "as it pertains to." If he couldn't recall his lawyer's name, maybe the lawyer would recall Shane's.

Shane wasn't scared of Cam Rawls or the ghost of Brad Pearce. The bigger problem was Shane himself. Sometimes it was hard to separate from the Rider or Moth persona, and times like these, when he was high as fuck, Shane could get confused, sidetracked, like a hall of mirrors reflected forever on itself, snatching pop culture references out of the ether. *Leave the bowl, take the cannoli.*

He wasn't sure what he was looking for. Regarding Cam, that was easy. He'd enlist Donnie's help, however unwitting- or unwillingly. Brad? He'd start by reaching out to the attorneys who'd gotten them both off.

Where's my lighter?

Shane told himself it was okay if he didn't have all the answers. For now, he only needed to see a few seconds into the future.

CHAPTER TWENTY-ONE

Jess Barrett saw Cam Rawls right away. He was hard to miss. In a crowd of at least a hundred kids, maybe more, all these small groups cliquing in the dark shadows of the leaning water tower—which tilted so much you'd swear one day it would lose its battle with gravity and come crashing to the ground, flooding the valley floor—in an endless sea of faces, Cam's shone brighter than the rest. How had it hit like this? Jess and Cam had been in the same classes since they started school together in pigtails and bowl cuts. She had pictures of them from kindergarten through graduating year (Jess was particularly proud of this final effort. Like getting it right on your driver's license, sticking the landing in a yearbook photo was not easily done). She'd never viewed Cam this way before. He'd always been cute. A lot of boys in her class were cute. Cam had been an athlete, a superstar. Jess didn't care about sports. Then the start of the year, something changed. Some boys you looked at and the way your heart, head, and stomach responded made you want to sit near them. Many evoked that sensation for Jess. Cam never had. Until he did. And then the feeling came on stronger than it had with any other boy. When she noticed him, she recognized the same look of attraction in his eyes.

Now emotions tugged in another direction, like she was cheating. But Brad was gone. She couldn't reach him by phone, which was deliberate on his end, number cut off. It had been a couple weeks. Pretty clear he wanted nothing to do with her, which made her feel like her guts had been kicked out. Cam was her age. What was that anyway? Age. What she and Brad felt for one another wasn't wrong. Seven years? Arbitrary. Her dad was ten years older than her mother, and Mom's new boyfriend, fix-it man Richard, ten years older than that. Jess would be eighteen in a couple days. For all intents and purposes, she was eighteen, their relationship legal.

Except where was Brad? How could she have been so stupid to think this was a test? He used her, got what he wanted, and then threw her away. Cam was here, right in front of her.

"What are you staring at?" Sarah asked Jess, who was slow to respond.

"The cop's son," Renee teased.

"No, I'm not."

"Well, he's staring at you."

"It's kinda obvious, Jess."

More cars and trucks pulled in, music blasting out of tiny speakers. Kids parked against rock and brush, huddled together to smoke weed beneath overhangs, the air pungent and skunky, everyone hooting and hollering drunk.

"Talk to him," Sarah said, nudging Jess' shoulder.

Jess held up her hands, a plea not to be so obvious. But it was already painfully obvious to anyone paying attention. "We're not seeing each other right now."

"You're staring at each other. Like, literally."

Having crushes on boys was nothing new. Jess could run down the list of boys she liked, grade to grade, starting in first and sharing blackboard duty with Raj Patel, on up through fifth and the last year of co-ed soccer with Brian Morrell. Cam was the first time her heart yearned. If Brad Pearce hadn't entered the picture, maybe things would've been different between them. Why did life have to be so complicated?

Perhaps it was the night, how big the moment was shaping up to be—the sound system plugged in and ready to go for the Rider, who'd arrive soon. What if Brad *did* show up with him?

Was Jess scared to be alone? Was that why she felt so attracted to Cam right now? *No!* She relished her solitude. Jess didn't *need* anyone. It was Cam. In the past year, he *had* undergone a change. He'd grown his hair longer, bulked up, had a swagger but didn't lose the best parts of himself: the sensitivity, the decency. Until senior year started, Cam was just another jock in Jess' eyes. She preferred the artsier kids, the ones who listened to R.E.M. before they were big label, who knew about bands like the Replacements and Siouxsie and the Banshees. Cameron Rawls was another popular kid who, despite his mellower disposition, would probably be one of those assholes who go on to refer to high school as the "best years of their life." But then…

"What is she doing?" Sarah asked.

"Going all dreamy over Cameron Rawls," Renee answered. "Either that or she's drunk."

"How about neither?" Jess said, unable to convince herself. She *had* drunk more than usual. And when it came to Cam, she *did* still have feelings for him, every thought a looping circle back to the same unanswerable question, a Clash conundrum. *Which one should I choose?* One invited trouble. The other, double.

Renee waved both arms in the air, like she was flagging down a plane, catching Cam's attention and making it impossible for him to look away.

"Seriously?" Jess said.

"You can thank us later," Renee said, taking Sarah's hand, and making for the keg, as Cam weaved through the crowd.

When he got to Jess, he shuffled his feet, uncertain. Or maybe it was an act. Maybe all guys were great pretenders.

"What happened to Renee and Sarah?" he asked.

Jess pointed toward a row of cars. At an open trunk, the pair giggled, topping off red plastic cups with beer, hose spitting froth and foam.

"So, uh, um," Cam said. "How you been?" He couldn't help but break into a grin, averting his eyes. They'd seen each other naked.

"Your dad know you're here?" she asked, bourbon and beer sloshing in her belly, heartburn churning. Not the greatest sensation.

"He told me not to come. Yeah, he knows." Cam touched her arm. "You okay? You look like you're going to be sick."

"I'm fine," Jess said, stepping back, returning to big picture. "They can't stop us from hanging out. We're on public property."

Cam pointed over her shoulder. A sea of discarded red plastic cups littered the ground. He gestured across the crowd to the truck beds with big, barreled kegs, the orange sparks of joints glowing like fireflies in the night. "They'll use some bullshit charge like underage drinking or whatever to break it up. They'd be here by now, the cops. They're waiting for Rider."

"Any idea who it is?"

"Rider?" Cam shook his head. "Some guy who started this riff on a movie and didn't know it would blow up."

"Nobody from the football or wrestling team?"

"Those guys? They don't have that ambition."

"What about you?"

"Me?" Cam laughed. "The Rider?"

"I was talking about the ambition part."

"I've got plenty of that."

Jess wanted to make a meaningful comment about shared passions, new beliefs, and the open road awaiting both. Or land a lighthearted jab about time and place, the stars lining up. They'd flirted before. They were flirting now. It felt good. She resisted the urge to reach over and kiss him.

Then he said, "He doesn't love you, y'know."

Total buzzkill.

"Excuse me?" *Excuse me?* Like an actress on a TV show.

"I know about you and Mr. Pearce."

"You don't know shit. *Brad* was giving me a ride home…"

"I saw you come out of the supply closet. Buttoning your pants."

"He was … helping me get a pen."

"Please," Cam said. "Don't treat me like I'm stupid." He glanced around, making sure no one was listening. "You should know. I overheard my dad talking. Pearce is in trouble."

"Did you…?"

"No, Jess, I didn't rat you two out, if that's what you're going to ask. But you weren't the only one."

Jess froze, insides knifed, gutted.

"They fired him because he did this at other schools too."

"You're lying."

Cam took a deep breath, gathered himself. "You hurt me, Jess."

"Now you want to hurt me back, that it?"

"I care about you."

"You have a funny way of showing it."

Jess peeled off, blowing past hyperactive kids hurling small stones at tall trees, past Renee and Sarah, who ran after her.

"Whoa," Renee said.

Sarah grabbed her arm. "What did he say?"

Jess scanned the grounds. "I feel like getting wasted."

Sarah pulled out the bottle of Bulleit, passing it to Jess, who took a long swig. Then a longer one.

Drunk wasn't going to cut it. Not tonight. Jess surveyed the grounds, till her eyes landed on Bobby Geremia, Pasa Ardo's very own John Bender, who was on his second tour of senior year. Geremia would have stronger medication. Right now, Jess wanted to go full Ramone. Twenty, twenty, twenty-four hours to go—she wanted to be obliterated.

She hated Cam for telling her that. And the fact she knew he was telling the truth only made her hate him more.

CHAPTER TWENTY-TWO

Lydia hadn't had a chance to make a single incision before the door threw open wide.

"Lydia!"

What could she do but shrug? She'd been caught.

There she stood at the table, gloves and goggles on, looming over the dead body of Rhona Clarion, the cold corpse already prepped for dissection on the cutting table, ungodly odor drifting, which Lydia, thankfully, didn't have to smell, nose plugged. She'd snuck in early, hoping to be finished before Maureen arrived. Only to have Mo show up two hours too soon.

Maureen seethed over the betrayal.

Yes, Maureen had agreed to let Lydia assist. Yes, it was a gray area, one closer to black than it was white—and it was a bad plan, one that left Mo exposed. Lydia knew Maureen would bend rules as much as possible to help her out. Lydia couldn't let her friend suffer the repercussions of her impudence.

Lydia watched as Maureen checked behind her, down the hall, making sure the coast was clear, before locking the door and turning back around, expression livid, cheeks colored crimson. Lydia felt like she'd never disappointed anyone more.

"You can't be doing this." Maureen took a step toward the slab of dead meat, shiny, sharp objects laid out in a neat row, the instruments to excavate, extract, take apart this vessel of bone and muscle and learn what had made it stop working. "I shouldn't have agreed to let you observe!" Mo lowered her voice, even though they were the only two in the room. "This woman called *you*! You are *personally* involved. If anyone checks that log—"

Lydia removed her goggles, nudging aside the metal tray, blades pointing at the wall where the log-in sheet hung. "They'll see I signed in, on my own. Before you got here."

"And what are you hoping to accomplish?"

"Keeping you out of trouble, for one."

"No, Lydia. You don't get to do that. You're not throwing yourself on a grenade and playing hero. This is a serious violation of trust."

"I'll face the repercussions on my own."

"Damn right you will!"

"I appreciate the help. But I couldn't let you sign me in. You're right. It's personal now. I'm connected. Detectives will have Rhona's phone records soon. I needed to make sure you have plausible deniability."

"I told you that you could assist—"

"When? I don't remember that."

Maureen threw back her head, accepting she had no influence over Lydia's actions. By signing in on her own, removing the body from the freezer, Lydia had taken sole accountability. During any inquisition, Maureen could say she'd given Lydia permission to assist with the autopsy all she wanted. Lydia would deny that and maintain she'd acted alone.

"You are throwing away your career."

"Let me worry about my career."

"I've been preparing you since college."

"I know. And I appreciate all you've done." Lydia caught her old instructor's eye. "But I need this."

Maureen pulled her hands over her face, dragging down fingernails so hard she left behind raised pink streaks. Lydia regretted lying to and taking advantage of Maureen, who was the one person in her life who'd always been upfront, who'd given it to her straight, who'd been nothing but an advocate. Which was why Lydia had done it. If she was going down, she wasn't dragging Maureen with her.

"Go get some coffee," Lydia said. "I'll be finished in a couple hours. You won't even know I was here."

Maureen composed herself. On some level, Lydia knew what she'd say next. Maureen Gearon had never shied away from a fight, and she'd never abandon Lydia's side in a time of need.

"I'm not going anywhere," Maureen said.

"You don't have to stay."

"I know. But I am. That's *my* decision. Now let's get to work."

Half an hour later, they had their answer.

Blunt force trauma. Rhona Clarion had hit her head so hard it caused her brain to crash against the side of her skull, instantly killing her. There was no gash or blood because no weapon had penetrated the skin; the fatal injury was internal. You saw it all the time in car crashes. How had Lydia missed this during the visual examination? There was a reason Maureen excelled at her job. She'd known just where to look. Of course this didn't answer who—or what—was responsible for the blow.

Maureen shaved a patch of hair and passed Lydia the magnifier. There it was. A thin gray line, like a faint No. 3 pencil sketch. The other morning, in the dawn's early light, Lydia couldn't deduce the cause of death; she'd been unable to see any obvious wounds. It was only due to Maureen's expertise that they were able to find the hairline fracture.

The next part wasn't pretty. The human cranium comprises several layers of bone. When blunt force trauma occurs, the thinner layers inside the skull will crack off. You can only see this by sawing through the outer surface, through the diploe and squishier membranes, until you reached the inner dome. Once there, Lydia bore witness with her own two eyes: tiny chips of calcium phosphate, the mineral that gives bones its durability, a hardboiled egg peeled from the inside, chips of shell stuck to the pot.

"Someone had to hit her pretty hard," Lydia said.

"I don't think so. Where's the point of contact?"

Maureen was right. There was no crater from a baseball bat, no dent from a hammer. No splatter had been found at the crime scene.

"So someone pushed her, and she fell, hit her head."

"Whiplash would do it. If the brain is rattled hard enough, maybe."

"Unless you think this was an accident?"

"Toxicology report returned nothing of significance. Trace amounts of alcohol. Nothing to explain a woman walking over the edge of a barrier..."

"Then we're dealing with a homicide. Someone killed her."

"Probable. Or she slipped, hit her head on a rock—"

"Why?" Lydia asked. "Why would someone kill her?"

"You've been at this job how long? Why do people do any of the other horrible things they do? There doesn't need to be a motive. Mission Junction is not anywhere a woman wants to be walking alone. Not at that hour."

"Then why was she?"

Maureen couldn't answer that.

"What do we do next?"

"*We* don't do anything. Except step aside and let the homicide detectives do their job. We did ours."

Lydia shoved the metal tray, the small saws and razors, slim, sharp knives that could cut through thick cartilage like soft butter, clanging, rattling, reverberating. Staring at Rhona's thin, dehydrated body was more than Lydia could bear, so she turned away, spun toward the far wall, packed with training aids for new residents. She fixated on the hanging, vivisected skeleton, artificial organs wedged and labeled, replicas to teach the next wave of recruits anatomy. As Lydia had once done under Maureen's tutelage, these students would study facsimiles. Plastic liver, lungs, and kidneys. Intersecting rubber tubes substituted for veins, arteries, and nerves. Latex skin peeled to show the muscles and sinew underneath. This was the easy part to teach. The tactile, the functional. Like a mechanic taking apart car engines and transmissions, revealing fuel valves and gauges, the human body was a machine. The rest was harder to convey, and in times like these, accept: the cruelty man was capable of.

Approaching the skeleton dangling from a hook, an emaciated puppet on a coat rack, Lydia glanced over the synthetic skin that covered half the dummy, studying the framework, that internal structure of bone, all two hundred plus, from the big, thick ones like the femur, to the smallest of the small, the ones so tiny you almost didn't know they existed…

"I can handle the rest," Maureen said. "I'll weigh everything and then write up—"

"Hold on," Lydia said, coming back.

"What are you—"

Lydia motioned to be patient.

Tapping below the cadaver's mandible, she felt for the greater and lesser horn, the horseshoe attached to nothing, palpating the free-floating, U-shaped bone, jiggling the tiny broken remnants.

There was only one way to find out if her hunch was right.

"Hand me that penlight," Lydia said. "And a scalpel."

When they'd wrapped up the autopsy, the two women retreated to the doctor's mess. Maureen couldn't hide the worry and concern, even if her interest had been piqued—she was as invested in understanding what this mystery meant—Rhona's death wasn't random, wasn't the by-product of happenstance—Lydia could still see Maureen's wheels spinning, trying to come up with ways to keep Lydia out of harm's reach.

When Lydia discovered the broken hyoid bone, the true cause of death had been established. There was no doubt now: Rhona Clarion had been murdered. Strangled, to be exact. But that only invited more questions. Had Rhona been strangled first? Or struck? Were they looking at a cover-up? Or had the tiny bones inside her skull broken when someone dropped Rhona in that ravine, tossing her away like trash?

"Why didn't we see ligature marks?" Lydia asked.

"Rhona Clarion was a small woman. I don't think it took much." Maureen appeared to think. "Could've used a scarf to minimize bruising." Mo shrugged. "You know as well as I do. Fifty percent of strangulation cases leave no visible evidence."

"This changes everything."

This wasn't a botched robbery, a panicked thief shoulder-checking a woman as he made his hurried getaway. Someone had placed their hands around Rhona's throat, choking the life out of her, before carrying her body to the dry river's edge.

Sitting in the on-call room, surrounded by shed clothes and vending machine wrappers, Lydia realized her efforts to spare Maureen from having to lie had backfired in a big way.

"How long do you need me to sit on this?" Maureen asked.

"Don't. Report it. I'll deal with it."

"Don't be ridiculous. We both know that is no longer an option."

Maureen was right, of course. Once superiors became involved, the game would change. Lydia would be pulled off the case. Best-case scenario, she'd be placed on administrative leave while governing boards determined the severity of misconduct. Suspension and termination were realistic outcomes. And that was if Lydia confessed now, threw herself on the court's mercy. Waiting any longer to report the voicemail was out of the question. Doing so impeded an ongoing criminal investigation, a serious charge. Lydia was already in enough trouble. With sympathetic supervisors and Maureen leveraging her career and reputation, Lydia might keep her job. Regardless, she'd be on the outside looking in, unable to investigate anything deemed remotely tangential to the case. That included talking to Cam Rawls or Shane Ellet, or working any angle related to her sister's death. Forget proving Brad Pearce had killed Jess, once and for all.

Lydia had to move fast.

"File the report, Mo. Voicemail included. I have tonight off. It'll take twenty-four hours for cause of death to wind through the system and everyone is up to speed."

"When do you plan on sleeping?"

"When this is over."

"And what good does twenty-four hours do you?"

"Gives me time."

"For what?"

"First, I go back to talk to the husband."

"Without mentioning cause of death?"

Lydia had no other choice but to share Shane Ellet's claims, his suspicions regarding Cam Rawls and the possibility Dell Rawls had covered up evidence to protect his son.

"Take a seat, Mo."

Lydia couldn't deny it any longer.

Two cases, twenty-five years apart—her sister's and Rhona Clarion's deaths—had become inextricably linked.

CHAPTER TWENTY-THREE

**THEN, Night of the Protest,
Thursday, March 14, 1991, 10:59 p.m.**

Whatever Bobby Geremia gave Jess made her loopy. Not at first. At
first, she chewed, ground, dry swallowed the pill dust with vengeful
spite, waiting for something to kick in. Nothing happened. She stared
up at the big valley stars, wrapped in the cool breezes blowing down
the mountainside, feeling hollow and empty inside. Then Renee and
Sarah found her. Impatient, Jess guzzled more bourbon with beer
chasers, and whatever she'd taken hit hard. Jess had never blacked out
in her life—she didn't party like that—and she wasn't unconscious
now. She also wasn't on a linear timeline. Like a CD skipping. One
second, she was in the verse, climbing rocks and laughing unsteady
with friends, then it was the bridge and she was in the forest crying
alone. A snippet of chorus later, she was sitting around a campfire,
trading hits off the blunt being passed. *Fuck Cam. Fuck Brad. Fuck
every goddamn guy...*

The music sounded sweet, chubby bass rolling over shimmering gui-
tars, layered waves of flange. If silver could speak, this was the sound it
would make.

She felt good. Light. Happy. Or rather unburdened. Weight of the world lifted, a universe of possibility exchanged, like dancing with a hula hoop in a sun shower.

With the pressure of an uncertain future laid to rest, Jess laughed harder. The anger she felt toward Brad and Cam was still there, but pushed further down, it had been wrapped in an extra soft blanket, plush edges tucked and folded, harshest effects smothered.

The discomfort came when Jess found herself unstuck in time. *Where did she hear that? Unstuck in time?* It was a book. Yes, a book she'd read. Brad gave it to her. He gave her books and purpose and so much more but she wasn't thinking about him anymore, was she? No, she was sitting with the stoners, smoking weed on a rock, laughing her ass off, laughing so hard she couldn't breathe. *Someone pass that vodka!* Then she was at the base of the leaning water tower, by herself again, feeling like she might cry. Why wasn't time in a straight line anymore? Music still played but it had grown grating. She recognized the melody, knew the tune, but its arrangement was out of order. All flow was gone, no groove, no pocket. Pretty parts shifted to the wrong key, rhythm lost, leaving only jarring bits of discordant noise jumping all over the place, notes that abandoned scale, reckless and without melody, like jazz. Why did she feel like she was in two places at once? She heard voices calling her name but didn't see anyone. That's because her eyes were shut tight. *You can't see when your eyes are closed!* When she opened them, she was back around the bonfire, which blazed high, crackling oranges, cackling yellows, crinkling reds, and Jess was dancing, spinning in circles, faster and faster, higher and higher. *Nothing will be the same after tonight.*

The rest happened quickly. Someone shouted, "He's here!" Then came that familiar voice blasted over the loudspeakers. Only this time, the voice sounded natural, the modulator that had been masking true identity stripped away.

The Rider on the Plain.

"All right you sonsofbitches! You ready to do this?"

Nobody got the chance to do this or even to figure out what this was.

The crowd mashed together. Jess couldn't see who was talking. People stood on tiptoes, peering over each other's shoulders and heads, shoving, everyone trying to catch a glimpse.

A few "No ways!" rose above the din, before the crowd grew deathly silent.

A solitary: "You gotta be shittin' me. *That* guy?"

Then came the loud burst of a police horn, followed by whirling lights and sirens. A gun fired into the air. Coyotes howled. Footsteps stampeded. Classmates shrieked. Cam let go of Jess' hand. Since when had he been holding her hand? How had she ended up next to that lying asshole? Jess was outraged, furious, ready to fight. She was also having difficulty standing and couldn't see straight.

What did he want? He was asking for something, pointing, yelling, screaming, swiping at her neck, swishing air. She slapped his arms, punched with fists, but he still caught her by the throat. Jess clasped her hand over his and tried to fight, kick, break free. Asphyxiated, she couldn't breathe. Jess felt the snap.

She lost her footing, tripping, stumbling backwards, falling further into the abyss.

CHAPTER TWENTY-FOUR

NOW, Friday, July 22, 2016, 10 a.m. – 1 p.m. (approx.)

It wasn't easy calling Dan Clarion, still grieving over the loss of his wife. Lydia had seen—and grilled—him the other day, pressing so hard she'd left the little man in tears. But Dan Clarion didn't harbor a grudge. He sat on the phone with Lydia, patiently answering her questions. She wished she could return the favor and answer his. His daughters, he said, were with his brother's family in Joshua Tree. They were all taking this hard. Lydia listened sympathetically. She'd played the heavy earlier. Face to face, she'd had to see if she was dealing with a domestic abuse case. Once she determined she was not, she moved into counselor mode, aiming to help. The tears that fell were genuine. Not that her opinion of Dan was end all. Detectives would be the ones who ultimately determined his fate.

Lydia had been in this situation many times, and it never got easier. There were no words to console. It's a cold, uncaring world. Sorry for your loss. Shit happens. Empty platitudes.

Sitting in her San Perdida apartment, tall grandfather clock looming in the background, Lydia listened to the grieving widower, questioning who could've done this, syncopated ticks enough to drive anyone mad. Lydia felt like the narrator in Poe's short story, wondering if Dan could hear the guilt she felt, betrayed by the thumping heart she hadn't buried deep enough.

"Dan, can you think of any reason why your wife might've been in Mission Junction?"

This was the one area where Maureen and Lydia's findings differed. To Lydia, Rhona Clarion was moved after she was killed, deposited, dumped, carried and set down gently. Lydia pointed to the lack of scuff marks or rips in her clothing, which would be present if she were thrown down the rocky banks. Maureen agreed but countered the woman could've been killed where she was found. Of course, this didn't answer why would Rhona Clarion was in Mission Junction in the first place. If Lydia had to choose between her hypothesis and Maureen's proficiency, she was going with the expert's diagnosis.

"None at all," the widower said, before another earnest plea. "They still don't know how she died?"

Lydia didn't respond. She hated lying. Omission wasn't much better. She could put his mind at ease with the truth, but once she did that, the clock sped up. Detectives had been in touch with Dan Clarion, the same detectives awaiting Maureen's report. They would be the ones to delve deeper into personal questions, like whether Rhona could've been having an affair. Lydia's interests were more selfish. If Lydia told Dan his wife had been strangled, any closure he might gain wouldn't offset the price she'd pay. And it wouldn't bring back his wife. She couldn't risk Dan talking to detectives, saying he'd spoken with the coroner's investigator who'd confirmed cause of death. Nor could she ask Dan *not* to speak with them, which was twice as fishy. Then Lydia couldn't do her job, which she rationalized, in the big picture, benefited Dan Clarion and his daughters more. That's how she justified it to herself, anyway. Arguing with oneself defines the can't-win battle.

"She did social work?" Lydia asked, referencing Rhona's profession, which Dan had confirmed during their first conversation.

"The detectives already asked me all these questions," the meek man replied, growing agitated. "She worked for the state. Helping find housing for the homeless."

"Did she ever visit rougher sections of the city?"

"Rhona worked from an office. Downtown. A *nice* office. I never would've allowed her to walk alone along Spring Street. The detectives asked this too. I don't understand. Don't your departments talk to one another?"

Normally, Dan. This is anything but. Normal cases don't involve a voicemail left by the deceased, evoking a twenty-five-year-old case concerning the recipient's dead sister.

"I don't know what else I can tell you," he said.

Though she knew detectives would've asked this as well, Lydia had to try. "Can I get a list of friends, associates, coworkers—others who might offer additional perspectives?"

"There is no additional perspective!" the little man shouted. "We're parents. Were. We didn't get out much. We seldom ventured from home. Unless I had a business trip. I told her to quit, retire. We didn't need the pension."

Dan wasn't lying. Lydia had been in their house. The family was well off. Fairfax screamed financially solvent. Maybe that was part of what ate away at the little man so much. His money couldn't fix this problem. All the money in the world can't bring back the dead.

Lydia could've told him he'd go crazy trying to make sense of the senseless. Being a sympathetic ear was not a luxury she enjoyed today. "A list of friends, close associates, coworkers," she repeated. "Anyone Rhona might have been in contact with of late."

The little man groaned, disgusted by the process. Lydia was too, but this was the game she'd signed up to play.

"You have her phone," Dan said.

"Police are pulling records. These things take time. Often it's quicker if I ask the family."

"I can send along the contact information I have."

"That would be helpful."

"We had our separate lives, too. I didn't know *everyone* she had dinner or drinks with. We'd reached an age of independence."

Lydia assured him any help would be beneficial, supplied her email address, and got off the phone.

Lydia wanted to tell Dan it would be okay, assure the widower that life would return to normal and the kids wouldn't carry this scar with them for the rest of their lives, but she wasn't adding another lie on top of the ones she'd already told.

Within ten minutes, Lydia had her list. She began reaching out, sending emails, making calls.

By noon, Lydia had nothing. Rhona's friends, all devastated, recited the same spiel. Rhona was a wonderful woman, wife, and mother; the type that would give you the shirt off her back, the sort who'd devoted her life to helping others. In death, basic human kindness gets elevated to sainthood. Lydia hated thinking that was something her mother might say.

Through all the years working this job, Lydia had avoided growing numb. She'd seen her partner Ward point at signs of sexual abuse while eating a gas station hot dog; she'd listened to detectives crack dirty jokes as EMTs zipped up kids in body bags. Lydia wanted to believe she was better than that.

Window open, Lydia overheard the cars on the freeway, inhaled the faint aroma of gasoline drifting with the charred smoke lingering in the distance. She fought against the negativity knocking at her door. Enduring each of Rhona's friends recite her virtuosity, there was that mean-spirited, petty part of Lydia, a mirror of her mother, the one that wanted to scream, "What about me? How's that help me get what *I* want?"

You're better than that.

How many times had Lydia recited this to herself?

Enough times that she'd started answering. *No, I'm not.*

No one is that selfless. Lydia had seen the house the Clarions lived in—whatever Rhona did for social services, it was not charity. The woman had been well compensated. *Or maybe this was her way of giving back to the community?* What did Lydia know about Rhona or her husband and their finances? Other than they lived in a nice house in a good neighborhood with refined furnishings. She hadn't returned to Fairfax to get to know Dan Clarion or understand his pain better. She'd made a phone call. Impersonal. She had an agenda, head lowered, bulling forward, assuming the worst in everyone. *You're projecting.* That's what a therapist would say. Therapy. How long had she thrown money down that hole? What was the endgame? Learning to be kinder to herself, gentler? Get more sleep. How did that help in a world that never stopped fighting? That continued to kick, punch, and beat you even after you were out cold?

Lydia sat at the computer, that word, *therapy*, ping-ponging around her skull. The need to purge, the catharsis. Yes, we're all crazy. To be human, a therapist had once said, is to be mad. Therapy. Talking. Sharing. Talking. Sharing. Therapy. We all need someone we can confide in, no matter how low we get or alone we feel. Lydia had Maureen. Who did Rhona have? More to the point: who had Rhona?

That's when Lydia decided to phone back one of Rhona's coworkers, a woman named Olivia, who had been among the more irritating interviews that morning, chatty with little to say, one of those people who loved the sound of their own voice. But something Olivia had said earlier, a phrase, the "therapeutic aspect of this job," now caught Lydia's attention.

"Hello, Olivia. Lydia Barrett here again."

The woman was still dabbing tears, which managed to anger Lydia more. Yes, we all mourn in our own way, but this Olivia's sorrow felt forced, as if points would be awarded at the end of her performance.

"Are you still there?" Olivia asked.

"Bad connection," Lydia lied. "Did Rhona work one-on-one with clients?"

"Helping find housing, yes. We often partner with BRS."

"BRS?"

"Bureau of Rehabilitation Services. Sometimes people with a history of addiction—a select group—when they complete inpatient treatment, they're sent our way."

"What makes them special?

"Some people don't bounce back. Homelessness and drug addiction take a toll."

"I can imagine." Lydia couldn't imagine. Her only personal experience with addiction was Richard's reclamation projects and watching Gloria imbibe her nightly wine. But wine in suburbia wasn't an addiction; it was an acceptable, even encouraged aperitif. In fact, when at social functions, Lydia often had to explain why she *wasn't* drinking.

"Some clients have more potential," Olivia continued. "If BRS isn't ready to give up on them, they ask for our help. We try to get them into other programs."

"Programs?"

"Educational. Vocational. Technical. Sad to say, it doesn't happen often. Los Angeles has such a severe homeless problem—"

"You're saying, for special cases, Rhona would take a more hands-on approach?"

"Yes."

"More in-depth talking? Like therapy?"

"Rhona wasn't a therapist, but there are areas that overlap, what we do here. We're trying to get people back on their feet—"

"I understand. I'm assuming notes were kept. Detailed summaries taken and recorded? Would you have a list of people Rhona met with? I'm mostly interested in the past few weeks."

"I believe I could find that, yes."

"Could you email me a list?"

"I have to check with my supervisor…"

"Time is of the essence," Lydia said, parroting a line that must've been used in films her father made. She'd heard it somewhere. It wasn't her natural voice.

"I'd need permission. Confidentiality laws. I can ask my supervisor. But she's on vacation, so it's gonna take—"

Lydia thanked Olivia for her time, ringing Maureen, who, higher up the food chain, was able to bypass protocol and get such a list faster, crosscheck, root out commonalities. Maureen didn't answer. Lydia left a detailed message.

Afterwards, Lydia wrestled with what she'd done. Jeopardizing her friend's career. Steamrolling Dan Clarion. Pushing around people like Olivia. Was this crusade about solving who killed Rhona? Or was it purely selfish? Concerned only with what happened to Jess?

Her phone flagged an incoming email.

Only it wasn't from Olivia, Dan, Maureen, or anyone else she'd called this morning.

The email was from Shane Ellet.

The Rider on the Plain.

The Moth.

CHAPTER TWENTY-FIVE

**THEN, Morning of the Disappearance,
Friday, March 15, 1991, 7:04 a.m.**

By the time dawn broke, Shane Ellet had been let go. Dell Rawls was frustrated—for having his time wasted, but also, if he was being honest, there was an indignant outrage over the privilege Pasa Ardo families enjoyed. Change the color of their skin, drop them in South Central, and you have a different story, one that ends with more than slaps on wrists and threats of lawsuits from angry parents.

Dell had been gearing up for big charges against that little shit. The prosecutor had no interest in charging a lily-white suburban punk like Shane, whose parents had the same money as the rest of Pasa Ardo's immoral majority, which afforded the kinds of lawyers with names and reputations that didn't get pushed around. As Pearce had done, the Ellets had gone with the best: Carlson & Associates. Though Shane didn't merit the great and powerful Susan Carlson herself. Instead, he got one of the associates. A greenhorn but good. Once the Feds backed off, they had nothing. Illegal tampering with public airwaves *was* their case. Either way, Ellet was going home.

But not before the little shit fired a parting shot, aimed squarely at Dell's boy.

In the morning light, Dell headed home, big-headed orange sun peeking its crown above the pink horizon. Brilliant beams streamed through creosote and palm. Dell inhaled sage and tried to regain his cool. Ellet had been lying. That punk hadn't seen a goddamn thing. Dell would ask Cam, point blank, and his son would assure him Ellet was lying, and then Dell could get some rest.

Dell entered the kitchen to find Cam standing shirtless by the sink, clutching his side.

Father and son stared at one another, till Dell broke the silence.

"What happened to your ribs?"

"I fell." Cam narrowed his stare. "When you and the rest of the fascists showed up."

Dell Rawls joined his son by the sink, accepting that his boy's rage was misdirected. Dell's anger was too. He could only be so pissed at Shane Ellet, a seventeen-year-old smart ass who, like so many before him, believed he was leading a revolution. Dell came of age in the '60s, in a neighborhood and world where boys really did face the reality of being drafted, flown overseas, and dropped in a jungle, their chances of survival depending on which way the winds were blowing that day. A new war fueled this recent uprising. If Dell had learned one thing about American history: there was always a new war waiting to take the old one's place. Country had been in existence over two hundred years, only a handful of them free from conflict. We spend millions upon millions a day on war. Forget produce or chicken, pork belly futures, gold or God—funding fighting, on both sides of the battlefield, was where the real profits were.

Dell Rawls wasn't a social justice crusader. His first responsibility wasn't even as a cop; it was as a dad.

"There are other ways to effect change," Dell said. "Illegally gathering, drinking and smoking—it's not the best way to get your point across."

"What would you have us do? Sign a petition?"

Dell wasn't getting sucked into another meaningless argument, the two of them taking their frustrations out on each other because they couldn't aim ire where they wanted to. The loss of a mother and wife was a wound that never healed.

"How's Jess?" Dell asked.

"What do you care?"

Dell didn't keep up on his son's love life as much as Rose would've. Dell knew Cam and Jess Barrett were close. He also knew Shane had been incited by Brad Pearce, a snake-oil salesman who had used a skirmish overseas to get into the pants of certain senior girls. Narcissists and their silver tongues. It made sense Shane Ellet would be a vocal proponent of Brad Pearce. That's why he'd said what he had at the station.

If Dell had his way, he'd throw them all behind bars, for the principle of it.

But his hands were tied. With Pearce, Ellet, and the rest of them. Dell Rawls accepted what his job was: to babysit a bunch of spoiled brats. Dell wasn't angry at Cam, whom he'd warned against attending the protest, knowing full well his boy would. Cam was his blood. When he was his son's age, Dell Rawls couldn't be told what to do or say, not by his own father, not by the cops, not by anyone.

Dell didn't make it a habit to drink beer at sunrise, but he sensed the long conversation on tap, and it was one equally overdue. Grabbing a cold one from the fridge, Dell popped the tab, enjoying a long, cool swallow. To hell with it. He snared the spare pack of cigarettes he kept in a junk drawer, cracking the window above the sink.

"Funny," Cam said, gesturing at the Newport Lights. "Thought you said smoking was bad for you. I seem to remember a whole speech about that. Smoking and drinking. Like all of two minutes ago."

"Fascists?" Dell repeated with a chuckle, which disarmed Cam enough that he too had to grin, making him turn away to regain his self-righteous ardor.

"You guys didn't have to cause such a scene," Cam said.

"Maybe not. But that's my job, upholding the law." Dell's words lacked conviction. No one sees through hypocrisy faster than a teenager on a crusade. "You're right." He held up the lit cigarette. "I did tell you not to smoke these things, and here I am doing it, and I know how that must look to you."

"Like you're a fake, a phony, a fraud?"

His son posed so arrogantly, side-eye smoldering, trying to fold his arms, tough-guy stance, while favoring those banged-up ribs. Dell couldn't match the intensity.

Exhausted, resigned, Dell took another swig and a drag, gazing up at the vanishing stars, one more dawn outlasting the onslaught of night, before dropping the butt down the drain.

"Nothing to say?" Cam sneered. "You drive up there, scare away all my friends. We weren't doing anything. Oh, wait. Some kids were drinking and smoking, but *obviously* that's so bad, right, Dad?"

"It's a funny thing, being a father." Dell addressed his boy, but didn't look at him, talking to the cupboard he'd sanded and still needed to stain, paint. "It's like starting over. You can't see it now because you're too young."

"Don't talk to me like I'm twelve. I'm old enough to see—"

"How the world works."

"Goddamn right."

"Do not take the Lord's name in vain." A Baptist upbringing was not easy to shake. "But you're not wrong."

Cam waited for the twist, the wrinkle he knew must be coming because Dell Rawls didn't surrender this easily. His son reserved the right to be skeptical.

"It's the compromise," Dell said. "We all start out young, strong, thinking we can take on the world. When our best efforts come up short, it's bad luck, someone's out to get us, never taking personal responsibility."

"Nobody is trying to 'take on the world.' We're sticking up for the *one* teacher who cared about us. Who treated us like actual human beings—"

"Brad Pearce was fired for sexual misconduct."

"I know."

Dell stared.

"But not because you told me. I had to overhear you talking to other cops."

"It's an ongoing investigation. I'm not supposed to be talking about it, at all. But, hell, if you knew about it, why did you do something so stupid like you did tonight?"

"I didn't do anything besides get together with friends."

"Your friend, Mr. Pearce, English teacher renegade—this isn't the first time he's been accused of this behavior. He did it at other schools. We have a pattern of abuse. Unfortunately, his lawyers have been able to keep records sealed. We're fighting for discovery." Dell paused. "That's the legal term. You don't have to worry about that. Just know these are serious allegations."

Cam scoffed. But not in a way that said he didn't believe his father. There was something else fueling his disdain.

"You're old enough to know what sexual consent is. So, yes, very serious." Dell's face twisted up, betraying his personal conflict. "And you should know, one of the girls he's been accused of having inappropriate relations with is—"

"Jess."

Dell didn't move.

"I know what Mr. Pearce did." Cam couldn't look at his father. "I saw them together."

Cam had known all along. His girl had chosen another man, a teacher, one beloved by all. Cam was taking his frustrations out on his father. Because he was there to take it. Cam hadn't gone to the water tower to save Brad Pearce's job; his son had gone to protect the girl he loved.

And it crushed Dell, watching his boy's heart break all over again.

Later, Dell would wonder about the exact order of events. If he had this insight into Cam's motivations now or did Dell reach this conclusion later? Did he fill in blank spaces, tighten threads, supply the missing pieces to make the picture fit?

Dell never did get around to asking Cam about what Shane said when he was leaving the station. Dell knew Cam couldn't hurt Jess, his boy no more capable of harming a girl than he was sprouting wings and flying to the sun. After that, Dell went to bed. Exhausted, he assumed Cam had as well.

The admission from Cam that he'd fallen, that his boy knew about Jess' affair with her teacher, the confession that Cam had seen Jess— had spoken with her—satisfied Dell's concerns. Nothing Cam said warranted criminal negligence or malfeasance. Or maybe what his son said made inconvenient details easier to excuse, overlook. Ignore. Shane Ellet was a smug punk running off at the mouth in a desperate attempt to save his own hide.

And that point of view would remain in place, unchallenged, for all of four hours.

Until the call came in that Jess Barrett was missing.

CHAPTER TWENTY-SIX

NOW, Friday, July 22, 2016, 8:15 p.m.

It took Lydia a few minutes of sitting in the retro diner booth in Downey to understand why Shane Ellet was so adamant about meeting there. Lydia didn't have much time for movies. Never been a fan, which people had a difficult time understanding. "What do you mean you don't like movies?" Which wasn't true. Lydia liked them fine. She didn't often find herself with two hours to kill. And when she did, watching actors preen across a screen wasn't how she'd choose to spend them.

She had, however, seen this film, the one with *this* diner. Back then the restaurant was called something else. Now it had been rechristened a Bob's Big Boy Broiler, part of a chain, but they'd kept its old-school aesthetic. *What was the name of the movie?* Waiting on Shane Ellet, Lydia had to laugh. The movie, a neo-noir gangster flick, featured two tough guys squaring off over coffee, macho dialogue, cool cinematography, and slick direction—same guy who'd made that old television show, *Miami Vice*. The name would come to her eventually.

What Lydia recollected about Shane—and this was going back a quarter of a century, relying on the recall of a thirteen-year-old girl— his whole schtick revolved around being impervious to pop culture's influence, which he proved by embracing it wholesale.

Bullshit.

Shane Ellet, the Moth, the Rider on the Plain, was as gullible as the rest of the coveted demographic. *He* was the exact kind of person they targeted because he, like the rest of them, lapped it up.

Gazing around the Googie-style restaurant, Lydia had to appreciate the speculative architecture, which had impacted SoCal designers since the Golden Age, an affectation tailor-made for the studios over the hill. Selling cool was a twenty-four-seven, three-sixty-five job. Hollywood never sleeps.

The Streamline Moderne design implemented the final phase of Art Deco evolution, an aspect that fascinated Lydia, the way styles morph, dragging elements from the latest era into the next. Viewing the stylistic choices architects in the '30s made of what the future would look like, Lydia wondered how disappointed they'd be to see their predictions hadn't come true. Instead of flying cars, sleeping pods, and communal living, people had opted for stagnation, comforted by repetition, terrified beyond tradition, motivated by money and little else.

The waitress brought Lydia's coffee. She had a sudden craving for pie, which she seldom ate. Several sat on prominent display along the counter. Red ripe cherries and golden-crusted apple with melted brown sugar and cinnamon bubbling over the edge. You could practically taste the ala mode drizzling its sweet cream. It felt like that type of diner, a place where you ate pie, drank burnt coffee, and talked about movies.

She recognized him as soon as he walked through the doors, fifteen minutes fashionably late, which he blamed on parking. Parking *could* be a problem downtown. They weren't downtown. This was Downey. Out the window plenty of well-lit parking spaces remained unoccupied.

Taking a seat, Shane barked for coffee, like an addict in need of a fix. The guy resembled a disc jockey past his prime, snapping fingers and pointing at his mug. Clothes mismatched, contrasting patterns, striped thrift store bowling shirt complementing plaid corduroys, the helter-skelter ensemble, Lydia suspected, carefully selected. The only thing missing was a fedora or maybe a pea green blazer with tan patches sewn on the elbow. Or perhaps she was projecting. A form of countertransference, as psychiatrists might say. Lydia had a right to be skeptical of Shane Ellet. She hated that she was here. She hated believing he was telling the truth about Cam Rawls. When he was filming his webisodes, he wore all black. That was when he was the Moth. She should've been grateful he'd come out of character. Except Shane Ellet's entire existence revolved around an act. Was "out of character" even possible?

"I remember your sister." Those were Shane's first words after the perfunctory hello, complaints about parking, and his mistreatment of the waitress—one of Lydia's pet peeves.

Shane leaned back, arms spread, affecting the pose of a laid-back dude trying way too hard to come across like a laid-back dude. Why was Lydia studying Shane and his responses so intensely? She'd done the same with Cam. Due to the impact both had on Jess' short life, Cam and Shane—their mere presence—elicited a strong reaction. Lydia felt that sisterly bond severed decades ago. Because it never went away, that sensation, did it? The loss of a sibling, phantom limb pain. Lydia had to choose which one to believe. If Shane was telling the truth—and he'd need to provide hardcore, irrefutable proof—Cam played a role in Jess' death. Maybe it was partly an accident. Maybe in her drunken delirium, her sister *had* slipped on a rocky ledge. Lydia wasn't ready to outright accuse Cam Rawls, chief of police, of murder with intent. But a father covering up evidence? Destroying? Concealing? These were serious abuses of power. And what, if in having done so, a predator like Brad Pearce had been allowed to walk free?

"What?" Shane asked.

Lydia realized she'd been staring.

She apologized, tossing in perfunctory excuses about being tired, overworked. In reality, she was formulating questions, treating Shane Ellet as a potential witness. She hadn't settled on which approach to take. Obtuse. Trusting. Curt. The tack she adopted depended on initial impressions of the subject. And face-to-face, she was having a difficult time getting a read on the man.

"You're an insomniac too?" he asked.

"Wha—?" The question caught Lydia off guard. "No. Sometimes I—"

"I recognize the look." Shane drew attention to his eyes, which had dark circles and bags under them. "Always been a night owl." He held up a hand. "Not saying you don't have nice eyes. I mean, I'm not implying you, I meant, um, y'know." He pointed out the window, into the black night. Streaks of red, white, and yellow traced the main thoroughfare, invisible strangers in shadowy cabs with their own secrets to conceal and carry. "I like being awake when everyone else is asleep. It's peaceful. That's when I film my program."

Program. Not web series or YouTube videos. It was clear how seriously Shane took his job as the Moth. He was so sincere, it made Lydia want to laugh. But there's sincerity, and then there's pride. Lydia wasn't sure which one currently confronted her. Did one negate the other?

The waitress brought Shane's coffee. "And a slice of pie," he said. "Cherry."

That made Lydia break into a grin.

"What?"

"Nothing," she said. This incarnation of Shane wasn't just sensitive; he wore his heart on his sleeve like a badge. Seeing his feelings were hurt, she added, "I was thinking of ordering the same." Then to clarify: "I rarely eat pie."

"Two slices then," Shane said, smiling. "With a scoop of vanilla ice cream." He turned to Lydia. "They get it from a creamery down the road. Hand churned. You can taste the bean. Outstanding." Then to the waitress: "Hey, sorry about demanding coffee earlier."

"Not a problem," said the waitress, a middle-aged woman who looked like she'd dealt with worse.

"No," Shane said. "It was rude. I was running late, anxious. I was out of line. I'm sorry."

The waitress assured him it was fine. When she walked away, Shane seemed to relax, like he could resume normal breathing. Lydia recognized the telltale signs of an introvert. The exertion of having to be social exacted a heavy toll, which caused Shane to act restless and odd, inhibiting her ability to get a read on the guy. Shane Ellet was a difficult man to profile because he embodied a multitude of contradictions.

He wasn't unattractive, the adage about the camera adding ten pounds true. He wasn't good looking either. Take away the funky, sec-ondhand garb and he'd blend in with everyone else down here. Shane was such an everyman he was in danger of disappearing.

"You keep staring at me," Shane said.

"I'm sorry." Lydia was running out of excuses for being rude. And staring *was* rude. She'd been waiting to talk to the guy. Now that he was in front of her, she didn't know where to begin. On one hand, he'd been such a mystical figure back in the day—for a thirteen-year-old girl, he'd been like, well, a celebrity. On the other, she wasn't a kid anymore. Lydia had been ready to hate him, his Rider run ending with his being exposed as a fraud. Yet, Shane Ellet still projected an aura. Intentional or not, he managed to pull it off. *Joie de vivre*, as the French might say, if startlingly awkward.

"I've watched your show," she said. "*Night Shade.*"

"You like it?" Shane added a thick stream of half and half to his coffee before complementing that with enough sugar to make the spoon stand straight up.

"It's … interesting."

"I have over ten thousand subscribers."

Headlights continued to speed past. When vehicles turned left, the lights climbed the walls of glass and steel, refracting off sharp angles, casting peculiar shadows across Shane's nose and face, splitting him in half, as if he were two people.

"Yes," Lydia said. "It's very well done." She didn't know whether it was well done. The webisodes were self-produced with an amateur flair, but she couldn't deny the Moth persona *was* captivating, enough to earn a minor cult following of fellow insomniacs and true-crime aficionados. Even if they were tuning in to mock him, they were still watching.

"The episode with your sister has over four thousand views," Shane boasted. "Not my most popular—that would be the Elisa Lam one— you know about her? The girl they found in the water tank at the Cecil Hotel? That one has, I don't even know, I lost track, maybe eighteen thousand views? But the one with your sister is still one of my more popular exposés."

The pies arrived and Shane dug in. Lydia couldn't make up her mind whether she liked this guy. With most, Lydia could deduce immediately whether they were trustworthy, honest, reliable, or even a decent human. Shane Ellet was *such* a contrarian, an outlier, an anomaly. Unique, in the truest sense of the word.

"What can I do for you?" Shane asked, smiling through a mouthful of mashed cherries, teeth stained red.

An abrupt about face. Straight to the point. Lydia decided right then that, yeah, she did like him. He was strange, quirky, an oddball, offbeat.

He lacked social skills and couldn't hide how needy he was. But he wasn't inauthentic.

"I like you," Shane said. "You're not like your sister."

"You didn't like my sister?"

Shane's face drained of color, before filling with blood, mortified. "Oh, god, no, I didn't mean it like that. Jess was super cool."

"So … I'm not cool?"

Now Shane laughed. "I guess, yeah, that's what I'm saying. Not cool. You're like me. Really, really … *uncool.*"

And they both laughed.

"It's not an insult. My favorite people in the world are uncool. I think people start to get interesting when they stop worrying about being cool." Then as if he'd thought of it for the first time: "Uncool is the new cool!"

Wiping away the cherry juice, he smiled, which brightened his entire face. Lydia was in no way flirting with this guy. And she didn't get the sense he was trying to flirt with her. But he was right about one thing: they were both uncool. Gloriously uncool.

After that, conversation came easy, Shane opening up enough to let Lydia in, allowing the coroner's investigator to witness the subtle distinction between theater and verisimilitude. In the Moth's world, the two weren't mutually exclusive; there existed a thin circle where that Venn diagram intersected.

Lydia asked what she'd come to ask.

"No," he confessed, "I don't believe Cam Rawls meant to hurt your sister."

"But you think he was involved in what happened to her?"

"That I can't say."

"Why did you say it then?"

"Lack of speculative theory for a dull show makes?"

"So you … made up … false allegations? Against the chief of police. For … views? Likes? Subscribers?" Lydia wasn't buying it.

Shane shifted, uncomfortable.

"Want to know what I think? I think you *did* see something that night, and now that I, a person in law enforcement, am making inquiries, you're getting nervous."

"I have…" Shane leaned in. "I have to protect my sources. But, yeah, I'm not too comfortable calling out the chief of police."

"You broadcasted it over the internet. In your hometown."

Shane shrugged a *mea culpa*. Lydia got it, the false sense of empowerment that came from the anonymity of the web. It's why so many trolls were tough guys on the internet, talking a big game. Or like Richard Fontaine once said, "Writing checks with a John Wayne mouth that Don Knotts' fists couldn't cash." Even Lydia knew who those two actors were.

"No," she said. "I need more than that."

"I saw them fighting that night," Shane admitted. "Your sister and Cam. From the backseat of the cruiser. Up on the ridge. They were in plain view so I couldn't have been the only one. She was with her friends. What were their names? Sarah, Renee?"

"I've reached out to every friend of hers I can remember, every one I've been able to track down, that is. So far no one has gotten back to me."

"They'd broken up that night, your sister and Cam. That's what I heard."

"How bad was the fight?"

"Bad." Shane chewed on a cuticle. "You might not believe this, but back then that 'Rider on the Plain' stuff was a big deal. A lot of people were there that night. When the cops were shoving me in the backseat,

I saw Jess and Cam arguing. It was heated. It looked like he took a swipe at her."

"Cam hit my sister?"

"Not exactly. More like he was pulling on something."

"Like what?"

"A necklace?" Shane shrugged, before abandoning the ruse. "I mean, I know it was a necklace." Shane puffed up his cheeks, blowing out a steady stream of hot air. "Okay, here's why I said what I said about evidence being covered up."

Lydia waited.

"It *was* a necklace. And it snapped. Your sister fell on her butt. Cam tried to help her up, but she slapped his hand away."

"And?" Lydia might as well have said, *So what?*

"Cam ran off. Your sister stumbled in the opposite direction."

"Stumbled? Was she hurt?"

Shane hesitated, as if not to besmirch the dead. "She looked fucked up. Like wasted. Pills. Alcohol. Something harder? I never knew your sister to party that hard."

Lydia's pie remained untouched. She couldn't call him a liar but she also got the sense he was holding back.

"Why are you are looking at me like that?"

"I understand why you might backtrack about Cam and Dell Rawls."

"I'm not backtracking. I'm an artist, a performer. I blend truth and fiction."

"And I'm an investigator. And one of the techniques people use when they don't want to lie to law enforcement but can't risk the repercussions of telling the total truth is they share a partial truth." And before Shane could object, Lydia waved him off. "Ninety-nine percent truth."

"I like you," he said. "And I liked your sister. And I was, I'll admit it, an insecure, attention-seeking kid back then."

Who wasn't?

Shane watched as the waitress dropped the check. Lydia slid it her way.

"Maybe I'm still an insecure attention-seeking asshole." Shane panned around the dinette. "I don't want trouble."

"Won't mention your name. We're just talking, right?"

"When I was doing research for the episode… I found a couple … discrepancies."

"Such as?"

"You know Ricky Simmons?"

Lydia shook her head.

"Like ten years older than us. He was the guy who shoved me in the cruiser that night. I don't know if he was officially a 'cop.' Used to work for Pasa Ardo PD, though, I know that. Like an on-call deputy, an extra set of hands for when times got busy. Two things. One, that necklace? It belonged to your sister. Fact. It was logged into evidence. Then it was missing from evidence. Also, fact."

"You know this how?"

"Ricky Simmons has a brother, Donnie. Had. Ricky's dead. Donnie is still around. I don't want to get him in trouble, either." Shane had to think. "Or maybe not. On account of Ricky being dead? But he's a good guy. Donnie. Or maybe not. Ricky was a jerk. That job paid shit."

It hit Lydia what was so off about Shane Ellet. The inability to stay on topic, the spinning and spiraling, the buggy eyes and vacillating moods. The guy was a major pothead.

"Are you stoned?"

"A little. I mean, I smoke. A lot. I'm not lying." Shane started getting animated. "Back in the day, Ricky Simmons worked for Dell Rawls. He's dead."

"You mentioned that—"

"Motorcycle accident years ago."

"On the job?"

"Nah, Ricky was bad news. He got fired. According to Donnie, Ricky took evidence that proved Dell lied about the cause of death or something."

"Or … something?"

Shifting in his seat, Shane confessed: "I know. Ricky was a crook. Donnie is a stoner, like me. Not the most reliable eyewitness. But while researching the show, I remembered him saying—"

"Wait. Who's 'him'?"

"Donnie. Ricky's brother. He said Ricky had proof."

"What kind of proof?"

"Besides the necklace he told me about? Paperwork, I think."

"You … think?"

Shane seemed taken aback by the question, shocked anyone would push the issue that far.

"Wait a second," Lydia said. "You're taking this at face value? You've never actually *seen* anything?"

"When you put it that way, it sounds—"

"Irresponsible? Wrong? Slanderous? Shane, you can't accuse people of homicide without proof."

"There *is* proof. Talk to Donnie. He has *something*. Why would he lie about it?"

Lydia couldn't believe she'd driven out here for this.

Yet here she was.

Lydia jammed her thumbs into her temples and shut her eyes tight to keep from screaming.

CHAPTER TWENTY-SEVEN

Chief Rawls arrived as soon as he heard Jess hadn't come home. Her mom had been on the phone all morning, calling every friend's house or place Jess might've gone. She was nowhere to be found. The town sheriff explained how he'd broken up the party—everyone, including Jess, scattering in several directions. There was one bit of good news, though: they caught the Rider. Chief Rawls said that despite all his tough guy talk while operating as the faceless Rider, Shane Ellet had spent the night in a holding cell, blubbering like a baby.

Gloria Barrett said she could not care less. "How does that help me find my daughter?"

For weeks, Jess and her friends had been listening to Rider's radio show, everyone enraged over the firing of Brad Pearce, the hot, young, new English teacher. Lydia remembered Jess talking about the soul-mate connection she felt with Mr. Pearce, because he was "a truth teller, a beacon in the seas of deception." Those were Jess' words, her exact phrasing. Only she called him by his first name, Brad. Lydia could admit feeling jealous over having at least one adult in your life who told the truth, who didn't pump you full of shallow platitudes, about how you could be anything you wanted if you tried hard enough or how it was what was on the inside that mattered most. Overhearing her sister's conversations with friends on the telephone, Lydia would've thought Jess was in love with Mr. Pearce. Then again, what did Lydia know about love? Jess was boy crazy. Sometimes she sounded like she loved Cam Rawls. Sometimes she sounded like she loved the Rider. Sometimes it sounded like Jess loved every damned boy she'd ever met.

Sitting on the steps, eavesdropping as Chief Rawls summarized last night's events, Lydia felt like she was solving a puzzle.

Lydia knew Jess and the rest of the senior class at Pasa Ardo High adored Mr. Pearce. Chief Rawls did not share their fondness, calling him a "lothario." Most thirteen-year-old girls wouldn't understand what the word meant. Lydia wasn't like most girls her age. She knew the definition because she'd read books like *Don Quixote* and Goethe's *Wilhelm Meister's Apprenticeship*, which were hardly age appropriate, but having done so proved useful in times like these. Brad Pearce was a player. Chief Rawls said, "He burns through women and wives like a chain-smoker does cigarettes on a jittery day."

Then he talked about something Jess never mentioned, scary details Lydia hadn't considered, and the story took a sharp turn into much darker territory.

"We're hoping to press charges," Chief Rawls said. "For misconduct at his last job, another school." There was a lull in the conversation, as if he were speaking under his breath, sharing information so classified it must be whispered. This of course made Lydia want to hear more. Edging closer to the doorway, Lydia couldn't make out every word, but she was able to deduce these were not charges anyone wanted filed against them. She picked up on the phrases "non-consensual advances" and "relations with minors." Lydia wasn't some sheltered suburbanite. She knew what sexual abuse was. This teacher that Jess idolized, this teacher that was worth last night's rebellion, was a pervert. Gross.

"How does the high school hire a man like that?" Gloria reached for her glass.

"Pearce comes from money. The kind of money that covers up transgressions. But you have my word, that stops now. I don't care if I get taken to court—"

"And how's that help me now?!" her mother screamed.

Lydia didn't understand why her mother was so upset. A teacher being involved with his students was disgusting, but it wasn't like Gloria to care about anyone but herself. She didn't know these other girls. It was a different school.

"When did you know, Dell?"

Lydia peeked her head around the corner.

"It's an ongoing investigation. I'm telling you now—"

"Too late!" Gloria's voice threatened to crack. Lydia had never heard her mother so angry, not even in arguments with her father. "Where is he?" she demanded.

"Up north. San Francisco. Police are talking to him."

"What did he say about Jessica?"

Chief Rawls didn't answer right away, or if he responded it was with a secretive gesture, a nod, an affirmation about something so wicked it caused her mother to wail, pound the table with her fist.

Then Lydia understood.

Mr. Pearce had done it again. To Jess. Her sister was one of the girls he'd touched. The sounds escaping her mother's mouth were not human, more like a demon's wailing from the deepest bowels of hell. It was a sound Lydia would never forget.

Lydia fell back on the stairs, head in her hands. Mr. Pearce had raped Jess too. And Lydia never knew, picking fights about a stupid acceptance letter to college.

Chief Rawls urged Gloria to calm down. Lydia ran into the kitchen to comfort her mom, but her mother was inconsolable, pushing Lydia off. Chief Rawls assured Lydia everything would be fine. Nothing was fine. Nothing would ever be fine again. And none of this answered where her sister was.

After Chief Rawls left, Gloria opened a new bottle of wine, and the situation grew more tense. Lydia again tried to comfort her mother but, once more, was shooed away. Richard had returned inside, his sweaty brow awash with grave concern following a hard morning's work in the field. As always, Richard was the one to console Lydia, like a dad, holding her tight, stroking her hair, warm, affectionate. Why did her mom hate her so much? Even before today, Lydia could feel it. She'd always kept Lydia at a distance. Jess looked like Dad, with her tanned complexion and darker hair. Lydia was fairer, like her mom. It's not like Lydia and Gloria fought. They didn't talk. Jess and their mom butted heads all the time. Of the two sisters, Jess was the troublemaker. Until this past year, Jess' grades yielded a steady stream of C-minuses and guidance counselor interventions. Lydia was a straight-A, no-problem child. But that didn't make Mom love her any more. To Gloria, Lydia might as well have been invisible. Until Jess went missing. When Jess went missing, from that morning on, Gloria started noticing Lydia. But not in a way any child wants to be noticed.

"Did you hear him, Dickie," Gloria said, ignoring Lydia standing there. "Divorced. Underage girls. Multiple allegations from *other* schools. How does a man like that hide such information? How can a school hire him? What kind of … charlatan, lover boy, gigolo is married and divorced before thirty? Run out of multiple schools for dating students, only to be hired by another?"

"A charming and persuasive one?"

"You think this is funny?"

"No," Richard responded. "Nothing funny about it."

"How did I not know about this?" Gloria glowered at Lydia, pointing a crooked finger. "Did you know?"

Lydia shook her head.

"I'm sure. You and your sister talk about everything." Gloria balled her fists. "They sent a sexual predator to prey on young, naïve girls who don't know any better!"

Lydia started crying.

"Don't!" Gloria shouted. "Don't you dare cry! Not when this is all your fault." Her mother refilled her glass to the top. "How could you let your sister go out in the middle of the night? I hope you're proud of yourself."

"Gloria," Richard said. "She's a child. And we don't know anything is wrong—"

"It's after noon, Dickie! Jess either ran off with that man or he's holding her against her will. Either way, my little girl is gone. Gone! We've called everyone she knows. I can *feel* it. In here!" Mom jabbed her own sternum, before tossing back a hearty swallow. "What kind of teenage girl shares a room with her baby sister?"

Her mom was the only one who called Richard "Dickie," and every time she did, his face contorted. Lydia saw it now. When Lydia and Jess once tried to call him "Mr. Fontaine," he'd nipped that in the bud. "Girls," he'd said, "Please, it's Richard." Then he'd chuckled. "Mr. Fontaine is my dad's name." Which was a funny thing to say, since Richard was old enough to be a dad—maybe even a granddad. He was older than Lydia and Jess' father, Alan, that was for sure.

Lydia wanted to say they should call her father. But she knew that would trigger more outrage. There was a phone right on the table. She could pick it up and call her father herself. She didn't dare, terrified of Gloria's temper.

Lydia came to with her mother snapping fingers inches in front of her face.

"This," Gloria said. "*This* is your problem, Lydia. You're always off in La La Land, dreaming."

Lydia wanted to fight back, hurl something sharp, mean but true, like how if her mother wasn't passed out every night with her wine and sleeping pills, she could've stopped Jess herself. A good mother would've known her underage daughter was involved with a teacher. But Lydia remained silent, more concerned about Jess' well-being than winning a battle of words with her drunken mom. A part of Lydia clung to hope her intuition was wrong. Also, Lydia *did* feel guilty.

What if that was the last time she talked to Jess? What if the last thing her sister heard was "I hate you!" and a slammed door?

How would Lydia live with herself?

CHAPTER TWENTY-EIGHT

NOW, Friday, July 22, 2016, 10:11 p.m.

Lydia's cell buzzed with a call when she got in the car. She was surprised to see Gil's name on the screen. During their time dating, the pair communicated mostly via text. After the breakup, they communicated *only* via text. Who talks on a telephone?

"You been watching the news?" he asked, while Lydia searched for a freeway entrance hidden among the endless slew of fast-food restaurants, taquerias, hair-and-nail salons, and gas stations.

"Haven't had much time," she said.

After the bright yellow Shell Station, Lydia hooked a right before the underpass. The on-ramp immediately clogged, a sea of pumping red brakes and wave of bleating horns. *Probably quicker to take backstreets…*

"The fire," he said.

"The one on the TV the other day?"

"No. Another broke out this afternoon."

"And?"

She peered around the glut, up the concrete barrier, past the orange plastic divider. Nowhere to go, freeway jammed. Every hour was rush hour in greater Los Angeles, except maybe three a.m., and even then you could get detained by road work, traffic cones cordoning off seven miles to accommodate driverless dump trucks and idle cranes, flood-lights and never-ending cigarette breaks.

"Remember how I told you not to worry?"

"How bad are we talking?"

"As bad as I've seen."

A vagabond, meandering up the shoulder, weaved through the stalled cars and trucks, grinning a mouthful of rot, holding a tin cup in one hand, a chicken-scratched sign in the other: *Every smile counts.*

"It's gonna hit," Gil said.

"As in…"

"Your hometown. You should get your mom out of there."

"You know Gloria."

When the homeless man reached her, he lingered. Somehow, they knew she was an easy mark. Rolling down her window, Lydia grabbed a fistful of quarters, dimes, nickels, and pennies from the change holder, dumping it all in, metal clinking tin.

"God bless," the man muttered, shuffling down the line. She watched him in her rearview, weaving barefoot and shirtless, silhouetted by downtown lights.

"She's not going to have a choice," Gil said. "They'll be issuing a mandatory evacuation."

"When?"

"Tomorrow afternoon? Evening at the latest. Wanted to give you the heads up so you could start the process. I know how hardheaded she can be."

Finally, the signal turned green, granting permission to move. Lydia thanked Gil for calling, promising she'd talk to Gloria, anything to get off the phone and focus. Right now, she had more pressing concerns.

Staring at the navigation on her GPS, she tried to pick between the squiggly intersecting lines of the 5, 102, and 710, searching for the fastest slowest route to the Mell-O-Dee, the bar where Shane Ellet said she could find Donnie Simmons.

Donnie Simmons sat by the door, two seats from the end, near the jukebox, right where Shane had told Lydia he'd be. Red neon hazed from the sign out front, coloring his face extra ruddy. He had the cracked leather skin of a smoker and the swollen bloat of a drinker, adding twenty years to the thirty-whatever he was supposed to be. Like a chubbier Keith Richards on any given Friday at closing time.

Lydia explained who she was, who she worked for, and what she wanted.

"Fucking Shane," was all Donnie said.

"I didn't mention anyone by that name."

"Do I look stupid?"

"I'm not a cop."

Donnie thumbed over his shoulder. "Dude was in here an hour ago. Bought some weed. He fucking told me he was running late to meet some dead person investigator. I'm not an idiot."

Lydia didn't want to throw Shane under the bus, but it was hard to refute the obvious. How else would Lydia have known where to find him?

"I'm not interested in making an arrest tonight, Donnie. That's not what I do anyway."

He scoffed, nodding at the seat beside him. "You can buy me a drink."

Lydia paid the small price of admission.

"I don't know what you think I can tell you," Donnie said, bringing the freshly tapped beer to his scruffy lips, not waiting for the head to settle, adding a foam mustache on top of the patchwork one he already sported.

"Shane mentioned … evidence?"

Donnie smacked the table, causing the other customers, the few there were, to shift languid gazes in their general direction. "I fucking knew it! Anonymous source, my ass."

"Tell me about the evidence and I'll be out of here."

"Shane already told you. My brother, Ricky." Here, Donnie stopped to go through the station of the cross, the relapsed Catholic. "Ricky worked for the cops. A few months. Had a side hustle lifting shit from evidence." When Lydia didn't respond, Donnie added, "To hock? Y'know, sell?"

"I know what fencing is," Lydia said. "Shane talked about paperwork."

"I don't know nothin' about no paperwork. All my brother's shit was boxed up after he crashed his bike into that tree." Donnie took another swallow of beer. "I wouldn't even know where to look or what I was looking for."

Lydia eyed the door, contemplating how much more time she was willing to waste. *Since she was already here…* "Tell me about this side hustle."

Donnie took a second to consider if there was any angle that would get him into trouble. Then realizing with Ricky dead: "My brother was at the water tower raid—you know about that, right? Fucking Shane's bullshit. So, Ricky's there, finds this half a locket."

"Half a locket? Like a necklace?"

"Yeah. Busted. So just the necklace and half a locket. When they found your sister's body. White gold or some shit. Ricky said it was nice. Got an inscription. 'From Cam to Jess.' He logs it into evidence, keeps his eye on it. Couple weeks later, when things settle down, he goes back. Figure he'll make a few bucks. Gone."

The same logic Lydia used earlier applied here, didn't it? Dell could've just been a father protecting the son he knew was innocent. Takes the necklace and locket instead of taking his chances in court. Unethical? Unprofessional? Sure. Didn't translate to murder.

Like he could hear her thoughts: "Ricky said it had a big ol' fingerprint on it. In blood."

"What did Ricky think it meant?"

"Same thing you're thinking. Dell's kid did something bad, and Dell covered it up. Anyway, that's what I told Shane for his stupid podcast. Under the condition he didn't tell anyone it was me. And you see how well that worked out."

"Where's this locket?"

Donnie shrugged. "They boxed Ricky's shit up when he died. I don't know where that crap is." He chugged the rest of his pint. "Do yourself a favor, lady."

It felt strange to be called "lady" by a man younger than her.

"Stay away from Shane Ellet. He's a prima donna fuck-up. Pretends he's all sensitive and shy. An act. Dude's gotta be the center of attention, always." Donnie shook his head, refocusing his gaze on the television above the bar, where the late innings of a baseball game played.

"Sorry," he said. "Don't mean to be rude. But I got a lot of money riding on this."

CHAPTER TWENTY-NINE

THEN, Night of the Disappearance,
Friday, March 15, 11:29 p.m.

It was close to midnight by the time Dell made it home, wiped out and exhausted, parking his squad car alongside Cam's truck in the driveway. It had been a grueling day, which he'd closed out with a long, fruitless search of Soledad Gorge and its surrounding valley trying to find any trace of Jess Barrett.

Following his emotionally draining morning with her mother Gloria, Dell and his crew spent the afternoon and evening scouring the water tower, canyon, and immediate vicinity. With reports Jess had been severely intoxicated, Dell was hoping they'd get lucky and find the girl incapacitated with a broken leg, perhaps a little dehydrated and embarrassed but none the worse for wear. No such luck.

Now Dell needed his son's help. The process to bring in Pearce had begun.

With Cam's admission that he knew about Jess and Pearce's relationship, Dell wanted insight into the fired English teacher's personal life, his habits, proclivities, weaknesses. Dell hated using his son for this information, which would reopen a wound, Cam still reeling from Jess' rejection. But the small-town cop knew this was his one shot to get it right. Pearce had already lawyered up with high-powered attorney Susan Carlson. Dell needed all the ammunition he could get.

Dell couldn't prove it yet, but he knew Brad Pearce was guilty—guilty of sexual misconduct and abuse of power, and with Jess Barrett nowhere to be found, he feared possibly worse. Had Cam seen them at a motel? A restaurant? Had Jess let any plans slip? Dell didn't want to go into his meeting with the disgraced teacher empty handed.

At the same time, Dell had to fight to stay calm, resist the urge to lash out at his son for buying into the propaganda and lies spewed by a false prophet. Dell nursed an underlying hurt, the better parts of his heart questioning what he'd done wrong. Hadn't he been a good father? An admirable role model? How had Cam allowed himself to be swept up by the lies of a huckster like Pearce?

The door to Cam's room was closed but the lights were on, soft yellow spilling out the cracks. Dell knocked. No answer. The rest of the house was silent, dark.

Maybe Cam had his headphones on, was listening to his stereo? Opening the door, Dell found an empty room. Which wasn't too strange. Yes, Cam's truck was in the driveway, but his boy had plenty of friends with cars. He could've been hanging out with buddies, catching a late movie, though no note had been left on the kitchen table. It wasn't required, but on weekends, if Cam was leaving for extended periods of time, he usually informed his dad, letting him know where he'd gone and what time he could be expected back. An unspoken agreement. Consideration.

Since Brad Pearce had entered their lives, so much had changed.

Dell panned around the room, taking in the framed concert tickets to A Tribe Called Quest, Cam's tacked-up posters of De La Soul and N.W.A., which stood for what Dell knew goddamn well what it stood for. A new generation finds comfort in *their* music. They don't care how much Dad digs Dylan or the Temptations. His boy was on his way to independence.

Though, if the boy craved agency, he could start by doing a better job keeping his room clean. Like a war zone. Cam wasn't always going to have someone picking up his messes for him. College was a few months away.

Dell began collecting dirty clothes spread about the room, tee shirts, boxer shorts, single socks, tossing them in the hamper. Plucking a pair of filthy jeans, the ones Cam had been wearing at the rally, Dell found them stiff and caked in mud—more mud than he'd remembered during their argument in the kitchen earlier. Was it an argument? More like a conversation with a young man whose heart had been broken for good and true the first time. It's a feeling you never forget, never get over. Dell hadn't.

Sixteen, driving around town, past her house, feeling like no one on Earth could hurt as much as he was hurting, playing Dylan's *Blonde on Blonde* on repeat because heartbreak has never known a more poignant soundtrack. Funny part? Dell couldn't even remember the girl's name. That wasn't true. Lisa. Her name was Lisa. But he didn't remember as much about her or their time together as he did this one night, cruising in the pissing rain, struggling to breathe, feeling as if his heart had been ripped from his chest, leaving behind a gaping wound that would never be filled, even as Bob promised that, sooner or later, one of them would learn.

Time went by. Tears were shed.

No one learned a damn thing.

With Dell's mind half in the past, it took a moment to process what he was feeling, the slight bulge in the dirty jeans' front pocket. Reaching inside, Dell extracted … a heart locket. It wasn't attached to anything. No necklace. No chain. Just a locket. Dell didn't want his son to think he was snooping—he trusted the boy—but he was glad the jewelry hadn't gone through the wash. It had heft, quality, white gold or sterling silver.

As Dell went to lay it on the dresser, he noticed that the locket was broken, hinge wrenched, cracked in two. Only half the heart remained. An inscription: Forever and Always…

And on the outside … *was that a dark red stain?*

Dell did a double take, thinking maybe he was seeing something that wasn't there. Dirt or other benign debris. But, no, it was blood— Dell had been a police officer long enough to tell the difference between blood and chocolate. And inside the blood, an impression.

A thumbprint.

Dell felt someone looming in the doorway and spun around, locket in fist, caught red-handed.

"What are you doing in here?"

CHAPTER THIRTY

Since San Perdida was in the foothills of the San Gabriel Mountains, Lydia, as she often did, bypassed the worst traffic, taking the 210 to the 15 to get home. It was almost midnight. Her conversation with Shane and the derelict rebuttal of Donnie Simmons was giving her plenty to think about. Mostly, why was she pursuing the testimony of two questionable witnesses in the first place? Except … the missing necklace and locket.

Lydia remembered it. Not enough to say whether the jewelry came from Cam. But Jess adored it, seldom took it off. Lydia didn't remember seeing it at the viewing. She'd forgotten about it after the funeral. Last week, Lydia never could've believed Cam Rawls played a part in her sister's death. A lot had changed in a week.

Climbing the hillside, you could see the heavy smoke, even this far across the city, drifting a hundred miles to the edge of the desert. Inhaling noxious fumes was nothing new during wildfire season. Between the infernos and controlled burns, the smog and pollution, you didn't get many spring-scented, azure days. Lydia didn't know the source of this smoke, except to say where there's smoke there's fire. She could smell it, see it, taste it, feel its ashy film on her flesh. At the mountaintop, the smoke charcoaled thicker, obfuscating the full waning gibbous moon, turning what should've been a luminous landscape into an orange-tinged, poisoned-planet atmosphere. Like a scene ripped from a science-fiction novel, a post-apocalyptic nightmare. Jules Verne backpacking across the surface of Venus during a gnarly solar storm.

Once she crossed the mountains, the air cleared. She thought of calling Gloria to share Gil's concerns but remembered how late it was. By the time Lydia made it back to San Perdida, the wildfire felt like less of a threat. Smoke hovered in the distance, wisps of a washed-out mushroom cloud, like those posters from afterschool specials she and Jess watched as kids. 1983, '84, her earliest memories, consciousness coming into awareness, synapses forming the connections that would establish lifelong responses to, well, everything. Sometimes she wondered if that's where her fear of the dark and difficulty sleeping began. Can you imagine? Being raised under such a threat. Now that she was almost forty, Lydia didn't often think about TV specials like *The Day After*, which was one of the first major productions her father had been involved in. That's how she grew up, though. As if tomorrow might deliver total nuclear annihilation, atom bombs laying waste to the land, acid rain eating flesh, fallout survivors turned into the walking dead, skin melting off the skull, planet Earth a soundless void save for the scuba tank breathing apparatus of a gas mask.

Lydia was thinking about this, growing up in the valley, with its pastel leg warmers, headbands, and bubble-gum perk, starkly juxtaposed against black clouds looming, when she locked up her car in the underground garage, which remained bright as day regardless the time of night. She gathered her laptop and notes, purse and workout clothes to the yoga class she didn't make, heading for the well. By the time she reached the door, the dread had returned. It was only one flight to the courtyard. One, pitch-black, uncertain flight.

Lydia turned on her iPhone flashlight. The anxiety crept in, making it tougher to breathe, the stairwell musty, suffocating. Doctors offered her pills. What was she going to do? Pop a benzo every time the sun went down or a lightbulb blew out? This was her life, learning to live with the fear, conquering it by not giving in, refusing to surrender. No different than someone with obsessive compulsive disorder ignoring rituals and mental commands to touch a wall three times before exiting a room. She would not allow her phobia to control her. With each step, the distance between stairs felt farther. Lydia focused on her breathing. *There's nothing to be scared of. It's all in your head…*

Reaching the top of the well, she cracked open the door to the landing, an expansive square with a swimming pool for residents and tall lamps illuminating the courtyard. Passageways cleared, sight restored, Lydia was able to breathe again.

Arms filled with personal possessions, she used her foot to nudge open the door, kick it wide. She eyed that final flight of stairs, across the quad, with railings and banisters, which led to the apartment she shared with an ex-boyfriend, knowing as soon as she was inside, she'd be able to switch on all the lights. This thought made her feel safe, comforted, allowing Lydia to gloss over an inability to commit in romantic relationships in order to reinforce the one key lesson she must never forget, the one every psychotherapist had hammered home: the darkness doesn't last forever.

She didn't see the figure rushing toward her until it was too late.

Dressed all in black, shoulder lowered, the big blur drove headfirst, like a football player, knocking her off her feet, sending Lydia spiraling in the air.

She didn't feel the pain right away, flying, floating in slow motion. For a moment the snapshot stilled. Laptop hovering, papers defying gravity, body paused mid-air.

Then time returned to its normal speed and Lydia felt everything, a searing, burning pain radiating off the back of her skull from where her head hit, arms and legs flailing, bone smacking stone, as she tumbled down the well.

Her neighbor had called 911 after discovering Lydia sprawled at the bottom of the stairs, splayed out and disoriented, dazed but conscious. Despite insistences she was fine, Lydia was unable to convince EMTs she didn't need to go to the hospital.

For being shoved down a flight of stairs and hitting virtually every concrete step on the way down, Lydia knew she'd been lucky. She'd examined deaths from falls of lesser heights. Somehow, she'd managed to avoid a serious head or neck injury. Lydia had a hard time not assigning divine intervention. Fortunately for Lydia, she was a nonbeliever. She could move all her limbs and extremities. Hurt like hell. But she could do it. Nothing broken. A forensic specialist and biology expert, Lydia accepted the EMTs were correct to overrule her. Now to rule out internal bleeding and, more likely than not, a concussion.

At the hospital, Lydia played musical beds, transported across boards, slabs, stuck in tubes, rolled back and forth between mattresses and pads while doctors ran tests. Given her position within L.A. law enforcement, Lydia was able to jump the line and get treated right away.

The X-rays and various exams did not show a concussion, which seemed to surprise all parties involved. The doctors stuck her in a room, requesting she relax a few hours so they could monitor her. At least they gave her a room with a view. On a floor high up, the whole of L.A.'s skyline shone panoramic. Office buildings, skyscrapers, hotels, a thousand flickering lights huddled together, encased by surrounding mountains, mesas, cliffs, buttes, valleys, life contained via giant glowing goldfish bowl.

Though Lydia had avoided major injury, the same couldn't be said for her iPhone, which had shattered against the wall, exploding in a million tiny, little pieces. Without the mind-numb of the internet to distract her, Lydia had a lot of time to think about the attack. The *why* was easy: she'd touched a nerve. The *who*, not so much. Cam Rawls. Donnie Simmons. Shane Ellet. Such a violent reaction from any of the three felt forced. There also existed the possibility of an unnamed player, a person who knew her but whom she did not know. That was the scenario that frightened her most: the unknown.

This was Lydia's job, solving puzzles, taking jumbled fragments, presented however haphazardly, rearranging them in cogent fashion until they formed a complete narrative. She had dozens of mismatched pieces, out of time, place, all floating around her brain, leaving her waking and sleeping hours (what few there were) consumed by the process of trying to reassemble these scenes back together to tell a linear story. Memory doesn't work that way. An event twenty-five years ago can leave a deeper imprint than what happened this afternoon. As such, time itself isn't a straight line. Once a moment passes, it gets relegated to the past, where our minds assign importance, slotting each occurrence into a more autobiographical, imperative order. What occurred ten years ago affects both what took place five years later, and the ten years before that. In this regard, time rewrites itself, continuously, no moment stationary, progression fluid, flowing back and forth. Everything is a chain reaction. Remove, reorder, rearrange one spot on the timeline, and a new one emerges, with myriad different outcomes and possibilities. That was the part about investigation that fascinated Lydia. How the past not only changed the future but how the future could also change the past.

Whatever painkiller they'd given Lydia had her floating on a pillow of winds.

That's when the last two people she'd expected to see together walked in.

Hello, Mom and Dad.

Lydia couldn't recall the last time she'd seen Alan and Gloria Barrett in the same room. And alone? No Richard. No Heather. Just her mother and father, the sight so odd, so jarring Lydia would've laughed if it didn't hurt so much.

"Richard's parking the car," Gloria said, refusing to acknowledge her ex-husband. "The hospital garage is closed for some reason." Then, because she couldn't resist, she cast a side-eye sneer at Alan. "I didn't know *he* would be here."

"Nice to see you too, Gloria? How's the house?"

"Not as big as yours. How's your high school girlfriend? Does she have her driver's license yet?"

"Jesus," he scoffed. "Heather turns fifty this year."

"Maybe it's time to trade in for a newer model."

"Can you two please please please knock it off? You're giving me a headache. And my head already hurts enough."

Lydia's plea evoked a competition to see who loved their daughter more, each parent taking a side to assist with pillows that didn't need adjusting, asking questions about whether Lydia was thirsty, as she lay there with the cup of water and straw in hand.

Lydia wriggled and fidgeted until they stopped invading personal space.

It was startling enough seeing her mother out of the house. In the light of day, the cracks and crevices were more obvious, Gloria doing her best to avoid staying stationary long, turning her head faster than a jittery house cat bolting for another room. For his part, Alan had the upper hand in any interaction with his ex-wife. He didn't call attention to it. He didn't have to. Alan Barrett had been a big deal in movies when they were married. He became a much bigger deal after they divorced. He was wealthier, better dressed, stood straighter, and because he was a man, he aged more gracefully, full head of silver hair, mannerisms distinguished, dignified. Women didn't enjoy that luxury. Maybe Lydia had jostled her brain loose during the fall. She didn't often think about being thirty-eight or outdated societal constructs like old maids or biological clocks. Some parents brought out the best in their children. Alan and Gloria were not those kinds of parents.

There was one blessing, albeit with a touch of gray. Alan and Gloria showing up at the same time saved Lydia the hassle of having to explain the story a second time. In a way it was touching they'd both come running so fast. Never the warmest family, the three remaining Barrett members being in the same room moved her. Even if she wasn't sure *where* it moved her to.

Lydia didn't remember putting either down as emergency contacts—that honor would've fallen to Maureen, or Gil, if she'd forgotten to update a list. She didn't know who told the hospital to call them—maybe in her painkiller delirium she had? However they'd gotten there, Lydia had to admit a part of her took comfort, feeling like a little kid after she'd skinned a knee or been sent home with a bellyache. In the beginning, it wasn't all bad. There was a time, long ago, when Alan and Gloria weren't forever at each other's throats. Snippets of faded memories returned: red bicycles and blue trampolines; she and Jess in atrocious matching denim outfits; old plastic Halloween masks that could give you nightmares. A pleasant Thanksgiving. An Easter that wasn't a total disaster. Christmases that didn't totally suck.

Standing by their daughter's hospital bed, Alan and Gloria almost seemed to remember that. Cease fire issued, a moratorium placed on the war so enemy troops could enjoy some turkey, cranberry, and stuffing cordially before they returned to trying to kill one another tomorrow.

Her parents listened to Lydia talk about what had happened. She left out parts that might scare or overwhelm them, steering clear of any reference to her dead sister. They didn't need to be reminded of that loss right now. Not that they ever forgot. Such pain was everlasting. Because the mind can't experience endless anguish without going mad, trauma has a way of receding, settling, and if we leave it undisturbed, it'll adapt to its new surroundings, until it becomes another damaged part of us, damned and disfigured but incorporated. Like how a sapling will grow around an abandoned bicycle or through a signpost.

A moment later, Richard came huffing in the room. "Hey, kiddo. How you holding up?"

Even though her parents had been getting on fine, Richard's presence changed the dynamic. As if someone opened the door on a cold, rainy night letting the icy winds rush in, the room turned frigid. Gloria retreated, glowering at her ex. You could feel the venom stewing, forked tongue waiting to spew, hoping it scarred like acid. Lydia answered Richard's question. Or tried to, joking it only hurt when she laughed, which was Richard's type of humor.

"Oh, shut up, Dickie. Can't you see she's not up for talking?"

"I'm fine, Mom."

"I'm not." Then turning to Richard: "Dickie, take me home." Before directing her disgust at Alan, adding, "I feel sick."

Her father excused himself before things got more awkward, kissing his daughter on her forehead and telling her to rest. He shook Richard's hand goodbye. You could see he wanted to do to the same with Gloria, maybe not a handshake or hug, but an acknowledgment he was leaving. Knowing any such expression would be met with scorn, Alan didn't bother, exiting without another word.

"Mom," Lydia said. "Do you think it's safe to go back to the house?"

"What kind of question is that?"

"I talked to Gil earlier."

"I still don't understand that relationship."

Staring at slumped over, poor Richard, the on-call, faithful lackey forever by Gloria's side, Lydia wanted to point out pots and kettles.

"You were dating. Almost engaged. Then you break up? But still live together?"

"He said that the wildfire is getting bad."

"Nowhere near us," Gloria said, swishing a hand with haughty dismal, as if the mere concept of fire were a hoax.

"The air can't be good to breathe—"

"Don't worry about me," Gloria said. "You stay out of trouble." She pecked the space near her daughter's cheek. "Come on, Dickie."

They hadn't been gone long before the two plainclothes officers entered. Lydia had been at this long enough to know this wasn't the reception one receives for a run-of-the-mill assault and battery.

Homicide detectives don't show up at your hospital room at two thirty in the morning unless they believe they are needed.

CHAPTER THIRTY-ONE

Cam was drenched in sweat, favoring his side and breathing heavy.

"Where were you?" Dell asked.

"I went for a run."

"At midnight?"

"I couldn't sleep."

Dell gestured around the bedroom. "I was picking up your laundry. This place is a pigsty." He held out the broken half locket for Cam to see, watching his boy's eyes for giveaways, telltale signs of guilt, as if he was sweating out a regular suspect and not his own flesh and blood.

"Whose is this?"

A stupid question. Dell never saw Cam wear a necklace, let alone one with a locket; and the jewelry wasn't the kind a boy would wear anyway, the style and feel distinctly feminine.

"Jess." Cam's face fell flat. "I bought it for her."

"It looks like there's blood on it."

Cam snatched the broken locket, staring at it, squinting, dismissive. "Yeah, I guess there is."

Dell eyed his son. "If it's Jess', why do you have it?"

"Because she gave it back to me." It took Cam a moment to catch on. "I was bleeding, remember?"

"Yes, I do."

Cam looked down on his father. "I fell, scrambling from your deputies. Ricky what's his face and that other guy."

"Why do you have Jess' locket?"

"I told you! She gave it back to me. I went to the tower because I was worried about her." Cam winced. "I thought we already went over this? I tried talking to her. I told her I knew about her and Mr. Pearce. She stormed off. Next time I saw her, she was hammered, barely able to stand. I wanted to make sure she was all right. I tried to see if she needed a ride or whatever. We were getting on fine. At least I thought so. Then she got pissed all over again, swearing and calling me... I said I wanted the necklace back. You guys showed up. She tore off the necklace and threw it at me."

"Where's the other half?"

"I don't know." Cam grew aggravated. "I might've ... torn ... it, y'know? The necklace. It ... broke. We both fell. When I got up, I had this half a heart in my hand." Cam grimaced, clutching his side.

Dell furrowed his brow, nodding at his son's wounded ribs. "Still hurts?"

"Worse than before."

"Let me see." Dell approached Cam, inspecting his ribcage, fingertips grazing flank, causing Cam to shudder. Dell looked up. "I think you might have a fracture."

"It was killing me to run."

"You ran ... with a broken rib?"

Cam shrugged.

His father continued to inspect the damage, shaking his head with parental disapproval, despite being secretly proud. *My boy is one tough mother…*

"We need to get this checked out at the hospital."

"You don't think I did something to Jess, do you?"

"No, son, of course not."

"The last I saw Jess, she was running along the ridge, into the canyon. Everyone else was going the other way. I ran with them. I swear."

"I believe you, son."

"Last I saw her she was all right. Drunk but alive."

Dell said nothing.

"Dad, I swear on Mom's life."

Dell reassured his boy, hugging him, gingerly, telling him he loved him more than anything in this world and to put on a shirt. Be careful. Take his time. They were going to the emergency room.

While Cam got ready, Dell carried the laundry to the garage to start a load, pausing on the top of the stairs, struck by one of the most disturbing thoughts he'd ever had. The last thing Cam said in his room, swearing on his mother's life.

What's the value of wagering words on someone who's already dead?

CHAPTER THIRTY-TWO

NOW, Saturday, July 23, 2016, 2:20 a.m.

Despite having worked as a coroner's investigator for over ten years, Lydia had never met this pair of detectives before. That wasn't too strange. Los Angeles County was huge. It comprised eighty-eight cities and over a hundred unincorporated communities. Regions had boroughs composed of neighborhoods, each with its own police force, which broke down into assorted departments, many of these with their own specialty units or task forces, divisions within divisions. You were never going to meet all the players in regional law enforcement.

After introductions, Detectives Rod Yu and Terrance Williams, who worked the big cases downtown, took her statement. Though the assault had occurred in San Perdida, the municipality was still considered part of greater L.A. County. There could be any number of reasons why downtown detectives had been assigned the case. Lydia could hazard a guess. She wanted to believe it was because she had friends in high places. Instead, she feared her assault was being treated in conjunction with the Rhona Clarion homicide, Lydia now a vital witness, despite never having met the woman.

When it came to providing a physical description of her attacker, Lydia didn't have much to offer. The assault happened fast. The assailant was big like Detective Williams, husky, broad shouldered. Other than that? Lydia might've avoided a concussion, but the lack of sleep and head trauma wasn't helping with recall. A figure, shrouded in black, blindsided her, out of the shadows. A blur. Useless. Lydia didn't get a look at a face, couldn't even offer a definitive race, height, weight, or any of the characteristic markers that would help the two detectives do their job. The man was big. That was it.

Fortunately, a neighbor had gotten a partial on the license plate of the car seen speeding away after the attack.

"Is there anything else?" Detective Yu asked. "Besides what we already know regarding the Clarion case—anything that might lead us to catch who tried to hurt you?"

There it was. At least there were no more secrets. Everyone was on the same page. Maureen was right to report the call from Rhona Clarion to supervisors. Lydia had let personal interests interfere with a murder investigation. Let the chips fall where they may.

Lydia shared everything she knew. She talked about Shane Ellet and Donnie Simmons, doing her best to convey the lack of threat she felt conversing with each, speculating about possible motives while trying to exonerate both in the process. A fine line. She didn't think either fit the physical description of the man who attacked her. But, no, she couldn't be certain. Shane was an oddball fascinated by the morbid, Donnie a drug-dealing, degenerate creep. She still didn't believe either shoved her down a flight of stairs. That left Cam Rawls.

She shared these concerns, echoing Shane's claims from his show. The longer Lydia spoke, the more she realized the evidence against Cam was circumstantial. Secondhand innuendo.

"Unless you can say with absolute certainty that it was Cam Rawls who attacked you," Detective Williams said, "I'm not sure there's any-thing we can do on that front."

Lydia couldn't say that, not with any certainty, which seemed to relieve the detectives. Cam might have to answer formal questions down the road. Cop on cop. No one wanted that. In the end, Cam Rawls was an officer of the law, one with an impeccable record and, thus, above reproach. Even if Cam *did* match the size of her assailant, unless Lydia had hard evidence, police weren't going after one of their own. Not yet. And Lydia didn't have hard evidence.

"I think we need to talk to Ellet and Simmons," Yu said.

Detective Williams nodded in agreement.

The door pulled open. Lydia anticipated another nurse returning to check vitals or stick more needles in her arm. Instead, she found Maureen Gearon, hand over mouth, face ghostly white.

"This is my fault." Maureen didn't care that the detectives were there or that her statement could be held against her in a court of law. She came to Lydia's bedside. "I shouldn't have let it go this far." The guilt on her face broke Lydia's heart. The one person who never had to apologize for anything was Maureen. She'd been more than a mentor, teacher, parental figure—she'd been the best friend Lydia ever had. At least since Jess.

If the two detectives made assumptions, they didn't let it show. They were all part of the same—for lack of a better word—brotherhood. Yu, Williams, Mo, Lydia. Officers of the law, they constituted a tight-knit crew, banded by blue.

"It's not your fault." Lydia reached for her old professor's hand, feeling the tiny bird bones she hadn't realized were so delicate, brittle, frail. There was a reason Maureen ached for Lydia to take over the job. She'd seen enough horror to last a lifetime. How long could one be expected to stare into the face of death and remain unaffected?

All along the hospital corridor you could hear the beeps and blips from the latest devices designed to prolong the inevitable, muffling the screams from patients as doctors patched them with stents, screwing new metal rods into old, rusted sockets, sewing ripped flesh with a needle and thread, stabling sutures shut, repairing the damage man and his creations had wrought.

After Maureen gave Lydia's hand a loving pat, she turned to the two detectives.

"How are you, Rod? How's Xiao?"

"Getting big."

Then Maureen reached in for a big hug from the bigger man. "Terry," she said. "Do you still wish you were playing?"

"Sometimes. But, y'know, the NFL, the average career is what? Two, three years? At most? I put in another ten here, I walk away with most of my brain function intact."

"What's left of it," Yu joked.

All three laughed. The fact they knew each other shouldn't have been a surprise to Lydia. Maureen was chief medical examiner for a huge chunk of the city. For as much time as Lydia and Maureen Gearon spent together, her role model had an entire life Lydia knew nothing about. The familiarity between the detectives and Mo allowed Lydia to relax. Earlier, she'd been worried about being jammed up; now she saw a new pair of allies. Maureen and Lydia could use all the friends they could get.

"I hear you got a partial," Maureen said, referring to the license plate of the assailant who'd knocked Lydia down the well, leaving her to die.

"Closer to complete," the detective now known as Terry said. Maybe it was the crack about playing ball and alluding to the NFL. It was hard not to think about Cam, another athlete who had a shot at going pro but chose the PD over CTE. Although back then, we didn't know what we do now regarding brain trauma. You heard about it on the news, the tragic downfall of certain ex-players, living to the ripe old age of suicide.

There was a reason not to play these days. Back then, Cam had to trust his gut, walk away from the game he loved and a possible big payday to protect himself in the long run. Had Terry reached the same conclusion? That he had better odds of survival as a cop on the mean streets of Los Angeles?

"Waiting on DMV," Detective Yu said. "Should be getting a name any minute."

"How confident are you?"

"Six out of the seven letters and numbers? Almost a full plate. Make, model." Yu spread his arms. "A matter of time."

"Thank you for doing this," Maureen said.

Lydia's initial intuition had been right. L.A. detectives don't drop everything for an assault and battery in San Perdida. They do when the vic is a friend of Maureen Gearon.

A call came in on Terry's cell. He held up a finger, stepping into the hall, uttering a series of affirmative grunts before returning, broad smile carved on his big face.

The other three looked on as Terry tucked away his phone.

"And?" Yu asked.

"We got him," Detective Terry Williams said, still grinning. "We got the sonofabitch."

CHAPTER THIRTY-THREE

It's not easy being different, is it? Oh, we all think we're different. And we are. We are all unique sunflowers! One of a kind. Just like everybody else. I suppose that should offer comfort, right? That we're not alone? That we share in our suffering. I'm not trying to oversell personal pain.

Something changed in me when I turned sixteen. Hard to describe it. But I'm going to open up here because maybe some of you felt it too. That is the meaning of life. Shared experience. Community. We are stronger together than we are alone.

When I turned sixteen, I felt my world grow darker. I don't know if you know who Rod Steiger is. He's this old, old actor. He was in On the Waterfront *with one of my favorite actors ever, the great Marlon Brando. What are you rebelling against? What you got? That's not from* Waterfront. *The line from that one, the one everyone knows and quotes but I don't think fully understands: "I coulda been a contenda." Which makes me think of the best Christmas song of all time. "Fairytale of New York" by the Pogues. "I could've been someone." "Yeah, well so could anyone." Steiger was also in* In the Heat of the Night, *the movie not the TV show. But I saw this interview with him, Steiger that is, not Brando, though I could talk about that "contenda" line all night. But we're talking about the change. In me. Maybe in you. Steiger suffered from depression, see, and he called it the Black Dog, and this Black Dog was mean because it had been neglected, left in the basement to starve, so when it got out—and eventually it always gets out—it was vicious, vengeful, furious for having been denied so long. It went on a rampage. I think that's what happened to me. I have a Black Dog. I don't know if it's depression or rage. Then again, what's that they say about depression? Anger turned inward. Yeah, I got an anger burning in me. And I want it gone. I don't want it coursing through my veins, because I can see where it will deliver me. See, that's the thing with this Black Dog of mine. It's mean, ornery. And now that it's loose, I can't contain it. And the fucker is ravenous... And I have it good! I'm an upper-middle class kid like you. The world is made for people like us and I want no part of it. Go to college, pick a career, find a family, work your fingers to the bone, for what? Not weekdays. Those are shot. Factor in waking up, brushing teeth, brewing coffee, voiding bowels, shoving food down your throat as you rush out the door to sit two hours in traffic. Why? To make money for someone else. Until, spent and exhausted, you turn around for another two-hour commute home. For what? Maybe dinner with the wife and kids? Too tired to participate in real conversation. All the shit you take from your boss, your coworkers, clientele, customers. You don't have a week. You have a two-day weekend, the first of which is spent recovering, the second dreading what's to come.*

For the first time, I can truly see. I am not the Black Dog, but the Black Dog is me. I've been let out of the basement. The fury I feel isn't right. My desire to hurt those who have hurt me, not good. But it fuels me, gets me out of bed in the morning, this desire to survive out of spite. To keep fighting even though I know I can't win...

There's going to come a day I fear, where someone will say the wrong thing at the wrong time, and that'll be it. I'll snap. Beat a mutherfucker till he can't see straight. Figuratively of course. I don't need the police tacking on more bullshit charges. I'm not inciting. I'm not encouraging riots, and I don't want to see anyone get hurt. It's the monster in me I feel. Do you understand? Do you feel it too? Are you with me? What we've been conditioned to believe isn't real. Brad Pearce talks about it all the time. Hey, teacher, leave those kids alone! They saddle you with debt you can't escape, running up credit card APRs, student loan interest rates, tacking on late fees for late fees, and heaven forbid you get ill in America. Richest country on Earth. You'll go broke fighting leukemia. Welcome to the American Dream. Just don't wake up.

Where's your passion? Will you get a chance to discover it? I know, I know. "Shut up, Rider," they say. "What are you complaining about?" But that's the rub, isn't it? You complain about inequality when you're poor, they call you jealous. Complain about it when you're rich, it's, "Hey, man, why do you care?" I care because I'm part of a generation—maybe the first in American history—that won't be able to do better than our parents. We are part of a collective awakening. Where's that leave us? How outraged are you gonna get? Christ, we just got done with Reagan who managed to convince millions of working-class gullible fools that if he gave tax breaks to the super wealthy, so many crumbs would fall to the floor, we could drop on our hands and knees and lap up the remains till our bellies were full. Get a taste of the good life. And y'all ate that shit up! Down and out, destitute fuckers believing they're gonna own a horse or a yacht someday. Don't touch my tax dollars for socialized medicine. Bro, you ain't gonna have no horse. No boat. But, hey, look over there! That immigrant is stealing your tomato! Democracy. Vote. Change is possible. Yeah, right. Let me ask you something. Why would the Powers That Be, the ones in control, implement a system by which they could be removed from their positions of authority? I'm not telling you not to vote. I'm not telling you not to pray. Vote. Pray.

Do jumping jacks. All the same, man. I'm saying if voting changed any-thing, they wouldn't let us do it. I'm not saying grass roots can't work. Just that it requires too much work to make it work, forty hours a week, and we the people ain't got the energy left to fight a parking ticket. They have been dividing us since the start. Instead of fighting the Powers That Be, we fight each other or strangers overseas. We need to fight the real enemy. What I am trying to tell you—what I've been trying to tell you—what I can now say—what I can guaran-fucking-tee you, gentle listeners, is that one day you're gonna have to find that hill you're willing to die on, drive a stake in the cold, hard ground, and prepare to defend it with your life. Will it be for the company store? God, country, and apple pie? Or are you gonna risk dying to fight for the life you want and deserve, one free from the wage system, capitalism, and the folly of their manipulated market? Will you do what must be done to feed your soul?

They keep telling us this war is ending. We know better. Even if it does end, how soon till the next one begins? Kids like us don't go. We get defer-ments. We can make up shit like bone spurs or flat feet or some other horseshit. Let them sign the wretched and hopeless. Hit up South Central, sell them that pipe dream. Hey, don't get blown up, you might get to go to college!

Or maybe we were lucky this time.

I've rambled too long. Maybe I've been smoking too much. Hope I didn't bring you down. Y'know, this past year, I almost feel like I've had a purpose. I've almost felt like being alive is worth it, like we could make a difference. There have even been moments when my Black Dog obeys my commands, curls at my feet, takes a nap. In these moments I feel like maybe it's not too late—like we can do something great.

So, thank you, all who listen. I hear you in the halls. I hear you in the square. I hear you over lunch. I hear you talking about this show on your way to class or after school in the parking lot. Man, it's nice. It's nice to mat-ter. At least for a little while longer.

All good things must come to an end, friends. Until then…
Rider out!

A MOTH TO FLAME

All good things must come to an end, friends. Until then…
Rider out!

CHAPTER THIRTY-FOUR

NOW, Saturday, July 23, 2016, 3:21 a.m.

"Does the name Mark Burns mean anything to you?"

Lydia tried to think. Maybe? It was a common enough sounding name. A lot of years. Same likelihood as meeting a Rhona Clarion. But if Lydia had met someone by that name, she couldn't tell detectives Terry and Yu when or where, or why he'd want to run her over and throw her down a flight of stairs. And she could only think so hard before her head started to hurt.

"Mark Burns is a lowlife, an addict, a bum," Detective Terry said. "Spotty work history. Criminal record. Petty crap. Breaking car windows, boosting. Right now, he's living in an SRO hotel downtown."

Single room occupancy. Lydia was familiar with those dismal holes in the wall. These squalid, skid row closets were rented by the poorest of the poor, state-supported derelicts trying to stay alive between the first and fifteenth until the welfare kicked in. Lydia had been called to these rat traps more than once. Didn't matter the name, which were often deceptively cheery. The Sunshine Motel. The Radiant Inn. The Royal Palace. They were all the Million Dollar Hotel, places where you went to die; hospices for those saddled with the condition of being unwanted, unusable. Downtown Los Angeles was overrun with SROs. Like refugee camps. They were filthy, grimy, violent, a roof over your head with a communal bathroom down the hall, and not much else. Beat the alternative of the Mission Street Shelter or, worse, Tent City. Welcome to the modern wild lawless west. You didn't live in an SRO unless you were a dope fiend or a prostitute, and if you were one, chances were you were both.

"Still nothing?" Detective Terry asked.

Lydia could only shake her head, mentally revisiting the wretchedness from times she had been summoned to retrieve a body from an SRO. She still recalled one morning five or six years ago. Some young, ratty, backwoods hillbilly. A single gunshot between his eyes. The way the Southern California sunlight streamed in, illumining the dust mites and dead skin flakes, floating like snow, the overpowering scent of urine from in-room sinks where residents relieved themselves to avoid an uncertain trip down that long, dark hall.

Detective Terry turned to Yu, before both turned to Maureen, communication conveyed via secret hand signs, touch your nose and blink twice, cough to continue.

Whatever the code, Terry had been given permission to carry on. "Lydia," he said, with tact and sympathy, taking his time, as if this next part would require her coming to terms with harsh, unpleasant truths. "Burns did some work for your family."

Lydia couldn't hide her surprise. "*My* family?"

Terry nodded, grim. "Would've been years ago. Apparently, he had better days. When they got the hit on Burns' car, our boys downtown pulled his records, criminal, tax, W-2s. He didn't work for your family long. Would've been a few months." He stopped, waited, gathered to present the most harrowing particulars. "Early nineties."

Around the time Jess died.

Lydia remembered the mangy day laborers hanging around the house back then, Richard's charity projects, trying to push aside prejudice, reminding herself that everyone deserves a second chance; that a history of drug addiction didn't preclude a person's return to polite society. Often survivors had a tale to tell, one worth sharing because it might offer hope to another, save them from suffering. She knew Richard was in Alcoholics Anonymous. He was proud of his decades of sobriety. Which made his relationship with Gloria, she of the evening bottle of wine, all the stranger. Lydia felt rotten thinking about it like that, who was and wasn't redeemable.

Feeling obligated to offer more to the conversation, Lydia supplied a quick rundown of what she could recall, how Richard frequently helped those in need. Back then Richard spent half his time shuttling workers to and from AA meetings. Richard Fontaine was forever picking up scraps off the heap, trying to help, give back, pay it forward. Lydia detailed the physical attributes and character traits of a dozen men who could be Mark Burns, each looking like they'd just hopped off the back of Tom Joad's pick-up rattling its way to the promised land. Broken men with sad eyes and abysmal posture, less meat on their bones than a drowned, skinned rat.

She watched the detectives' reactions, which gave away nothing. Burns—if she had the right man—was slight, undernourished and frail. The opposite of her attacker. Or had she ascribed heft and size where there was none? Could a man that small knock her over so easily? Probably. Lydia was average size—she didn't inherit Jess' flagpole height—or maybe she'd assumed her assailant had been bigger because it made more sense. Truth was, she hadn't gotten a good look at whoever knocked her down. Figure cloaked in black, running in the dark. Happened fast. 1991 was twenty-five years ago. People change. Maybe Mark Burns had bulked up in prison. Maybe it wasn't Mark Burns at all. What reason would Burns have for hurting her or her sister? What reason or rationale guided any of this?

"What do you think it means?"

"A connection like this isn't random," Detective Yu said, voicing what everyone in that room had to be thinking.

It was Maureen who dragged the ghost into the light. "Those dates coincide with when your sister—"

"Went missing," Lydia finished.

Like she could forget? Lydia peeled back the sheets, wincing from the contusions and banged-up body parts, minimal movement agonizing.

She didn't get far before Maureen placed a hand on her shoulder. "You've got to be kidding."

"I'm fine. I've been here for hours. The doctor said I don't have a concussion. They're not admitting me. If this Mark Burns knows something about Jess, I can't lie here."

Detective Terry gestured to stay put. "Mo's right. You rest." He winked. "That's what we're here for. An APB has been put out for Burns' car. We have units heading to his hotel." He reached for Lydia's hand, clasping it. "We've got this."

After the two detectives left, Maureen pulled up a bedside chair.

"I'm sure you need to go back to sleep," Lydia said. "Promise. I'm not going anywhere."

"Neither am I." Maureen's decisive voice matched the determination on her face. "You know you're like a daughter to me."

Lydia was painfully aware of the fact. Gloria may have carried the pregnancy to term, which Lydia wasn't discounting. Not that she could if she wanted to, Gloria forever revisiting the destruction wreaked on her body. After giving birth, however, her mom didn't seem thrilled with the job. She wasn't adept at caretaking, nurturing, forming a bond. When they were small girls, just asking for food seemed to irritate their mother. Nowadays, come Mother's Day, Lydia phoned Maureen before she did Gloria. Maureen was the mom she never had. There was nothing in it for Mo, not that Lydia could see, investing so much time in developing, harnessing, and mentoring a stranger, and from the start—while Lydia was still in boarding school, in fact. Lydia didn't know what she wanted to do with her life. She had the grades, mind, and money to do anything, seas wide open. But she was directionless, rudderless. Maureen Gearon had been a guiding light, assuming the helm senior year, steering her ship toward postmortem medicine.

Her final year of high school, Lydia helped her squad win the National Science Bowl. That's when she first met Maureen Gearon, who sat on the regional board of the CA Office of Science, a recent offshoot of the Office of Energy Research, a program borne from the Energy and Water Development Appropriations Act. Every year this board offered a scholarship. Lydia didn't need the money, but the prestige of winning that scholarship led to her chosen profession. Taking her sister's place at UCLA, Lydia graduated from the rechristened David Geffen School of Medicine. It was doubtful Jess would've chosen that path, medicine. But who knew? Other than picking a college, her sister never got the chance to decide on a future for herself.

"What do you think any of this means, Mo?"

Maureen, still holding Lydia's hand, squeezed tighter.

"You're the one who told me: in the world of investigation, there's no such thing as coincidence."

"There's not."

"So, this all connects … somehow? My sister. Rhona Clarion. This … Mark Burns."

Maureen patted her hand, opening her mouth to offer comforting words but stopping short of filling air with the superfluous.

At that moment, neither of them had any idea how this was going to play out.

"Get some rest," Maureen said. "This will all be here in the morning."

Lydia knew her friend was right.

With or without sleep, the nightmare wasn't ending anytime soon.

CHAPTER THIRTY-FIVE

When a third day passed and Jess still couldn't be located, Brad Pearce was convinced to return to Southern California, his lawyer present, to face an informal inquiry. They could make it messy up north. Or Brad could come to them, willingly. Pearce caught the last flight to Los Angeles that Sunday.

The moment Pearce stepped into the station, with his aloof, cool-kid style, George Michael five o'clock shadow, sunglasses at night, Dell knew he had his man.

Had they met up? Was it prearranged? Consensual? Was he hiding her? Had something unforeseen and wicked happened? These were the questions besieging the police chief, fueling urgency. Come midnight, the girl was eighteen years old, and without Jess' corroboration, "statutory" would become much harder to prove.

Brad Pearce projected arrogance. As if just by walking in a room he'd done you a favor. Whoever decided to unleash this guy on high school girls defined oblivious. Burgeoning hormones, love story fantasies, and then this handsome stranger waltzes in? A wolf in the henhouse, or however that saying of his daddy's went.

Right off the bat, a revelation dropped: Brad Pearce was twenty-eight, not twenty-five, as Dell had been led to believe. *That was a lie he told students so they'd think he was one of them.* The former Pasa Ardo English teacher stuck to his story, admitting nothing inappropriate, all relationships with his students strictly platonic and professional. With Jess Barrett missing, there was no one to refute those claims. Outside of Cam, the sheriff's son. A tough sell.

"But, please," Pearce said, feigning decency. "If I can be of any assistance, let me know. Jess is a terrific student and wonderful young lady. I want to help." Then he flashed a megawatt smile that could have him starring in a thousand toothpaste commercials.

Brad Pearce acted like he should be working over the range in Hollywood. But not as movie star leading man. More soap opera heartthrob. The looks were there. The chops weren't up to snuff. In the sterile gray interrogation room, Brad's game was strictly B-rate, which was why he didn't prey on women his own age—they'd see through the smoldering façade, this manufactured revolutionary manifesto about taking the fight to the streets, because for a man like this, the streets were paved with gold. The effortless fashion choices, part Sonny Crockett breezy, part L.A. trendy, linen pants rolled at the cuffs, Brad Pearce invented a persona, sold the story he was one of you, down to the uncombed hair designed to look like he didn't put any effort into his appearance when you knew full well it required endless hours of manipulating styling gel. The harder one tries to come across like they don't give a damn is a mathematical equation that proves the exact opposite.

"My client is more than happy to cooperate," Susan Carlson said. "However, I ask that you keep the questions as they relate to Ms.

Barrett and any knowledge my client may have as to her current whereabouts." Before adding, with a smirk, "Of which, as we've stated multiple times, my client has none."

Susan Carlson didn't come cheap. She wasn't an attorney a high school English teacher could normally afford, which told Dell something else: her services had been secured by a man with money. Mommy and Daddy bailing out their little boy were always the toughest cases to prosecute. Unless Pearce was independently wealthy? Endless motions and injunctions, bullshit addendums and requests. Stall tactics. Anything to gum up the works and draw out proceedings. Like an enemy with a limitless supply of rations when you're down to a handful of nuts and the storm's a coming—they don't need to beat you; they only have to wait you out.

From that point on, Dell knew he'd lost. Any leading question shot down, Dell wanted to tell them he didn't care if Brad Pearce copped a feel or received head. Of course Dell cared—forget his job, a twenty-eight-year-old man abusing his authority for sexual gratification was as low as low gets. Right now, Dell was willing to sacrifice the battle to win the war.

There was still time to find Jess alive. That was the goal: rescue, not recovery.

The pieces added up—Pearce *had* to know *something*. Hotshot lawyer or not, the guy was in trouble, and a lot of it. These latest allegations, Dell hoped, would open the vault of past transgressions at the other schools. Even if those charges had been swept under rugs, prosecutors often stipulated the right to revisit in the event of recidivism. Prison time? Doubtful. But it wasn't out of the realm of possibility he'd have to register as a sex offender. Dell put it on the table, assuring Pearce the district attorney might be willing to negotiate in exchange for Jess' whereabouts.

"Ms. Barrett's current location," Susan Carlson said, emotionless, "is not something my client can help with. And," she added, "there's been no admission from my client nor accusation from Ms. Barrett that she and my client had a relationship that was anything but professional."

"This would be easier to confirm," Dell said, "if we could speak with Ms. Barrett."

Reaching in her big, black bag, Susan Carlson proceeded to produce assorted receipts, notarized eyewitness testimony, videotape from bougie San Francisco hotels and restaurants, timestamped toll booth footage. Following his dismissal, Brad Pearce had run back to his Marina home on the San Francisco Bay, back to his cushy life, abandoning his followers to worship their false god *in absentia*. Brad Pearce hadn't been in SoCal for weeks.

Dell felt like a small-town yokel, having failed to do his research first. He was getting a firsthand schooling now. Carlson could've told Dell this over the phone. She'd waited to deliver the knockout blow in person.

So, Dell tried another tack, a last-minute Hail Mary in the hopes of appealing to Brad Pearce's humanity. Let a mother and father know their child was all right.

"Can you tell me anything?" Dell said, addressing Pearce, not as cop to suspect, but man to man, human being to human being, though he knew Susan Carlson would, as she'd done all meeting, object before he got too far. "Friends? Boyfriends? Even rumors. At this point, Mr. Pearce, I'll take all the help I can get."

Before Susan could interject, Pearce held up his hand. This was the moment he'd been waiting for, and Dell, the fool, had walked right into the setup.

"It's okay, Susan." Brad Pearce looked Dell Rawls square in the eye, unable to hide the gleeful gloating. "She is close with your son. Cameron. I think they were dating? Cam *suspected,* erroneously of course, that my relationship with Jess was more than teacher and student."

Susan Carlson touched Brad's arm. He glanced over, nodded, cooler head prevailing.

Brad returned to smug, self-assured. "Ask anyone. I don't think it was a secret. Your son and Jess were dating. Or seeing each other. Whatever kids do these days."

Kids? Dell thought. *This asshole was a kid himself.*

"They'd broken up. I know Cam was very, *very* upset." Brad Pearce forced a laugh. "Of course, you'd know all about that. You're the chief of police. You're also his dad. I'm sure you've talked to Cam about his relationship with Jess. He could tell you more than I."

And with that, the interrogation was over.

CHAPTER THIRTY-SIX

NOW, Saturday, July 23, 2016, 7:12 a.m.

"Dude!" Donnie said, opening his apartment door shirtless and bleary eyed, reeking of cheap liquor and stale cigarettes, a lowlife's bargain cologne. "I was sleeping."

A blood red sun, obscured by smoky cloud, fought through angry skies, announcing the reckoning on the horizon.

"We need to talk." Shane brushed past him.

"Sure," Donnie said. "Come on in. Welcome to my shit hole."

The apartment, a dismal, squalid, one-bedroom dump, was littered with old takeout boxes and wrappers for food you heated up in a microwave to eat alone on disposable plates. Cigarette butts were stubbed out on assorted filthy, scarred black surfaces. When Shane picked up weed from Donnie, they tended to meet at a neutral location closer to Shane's place. Yes, Shane had been in Donnie's apartment before to buy pot and pills. Shane remembered the place wasn't the Wilshire Hotel. He didn't recall this.

"What the fuck are you doing here?" Donnie fired up a cigarette. "It's seven in the morning. Don't tell me you smoked everything I sold you. 'Cause I got nothin'. I'm not reupping till tomorrow—and why the hell do you keep bugging me? Your doctor will literally write a cannabis script for a headache."

"I'm not here for that." Shane scrubbed the back of his neck, raking dry skin with ragged fingernails. Face-to-face confrontation had never been his comfort zone. "The thing is…"

"What thing?"

"I've been up all night working on something—researching. Old case. Multilayered." Shane stopped. "Your brother."

"My brother? Ricky. My dead brother. You came to my apartment at seven in the morning to ask me questions about my dead brother Ricky?" Donnie stared, without expression.

"I'm not trying to bum you out."

"No," Donnie said, words dripping sarcasm. "Just what I want to be woken up for, hung over and coming down after a long night of losing a buttload of money." He made a grand show of clearing clutter off his foul-looking couch. Patting the cushions, Donnie sent unpopped kernels and other miniscule foodstuffs into the air like hyperactive fleas at a discount circus. "Please, won't you have a seat," Donnie said, affecting airs. "Shall I put on tea?"

"There's this girl. Woman, I mean. Lydia—"

He wasn't able to get that last vowel out of his mouth before Donnie was up in his face. "I knew it! I fucking knew it! You sent that bitch—"

"She's not a bitch—"

"Dude, she's a fucking cop."

"No, she's not. She's a medical examiner." Shane waited. "I think. Or she investigates murders for the medical examiner."

"That's called being a 'cop,' asshole." Donnie plucked a tee shirt from the back of a chair, sniffed it, tossed it aside, tried another, slid it on. "Jesus, Shane. Ask what you came here to ask, man. I need to go back to sleep. My head is pounding." Donnie made for the kitchen, having reminded himself to hydrate fast if he hoped to thwart a miserable hangover.

There was a pass-through window that separated the kitchen and living room. While Donnie pounded tap, Shane approached it to finish conducting the interview. The small, clear square reminded Shane of a prison visit. Not that he'd ever visited anyone in prison. The layout was the kind you'd see in a movie about visiting someone in prison.

Donnie refilled a tall glass, twiddling his fingers to encourage Shane to hurry up.

"Remember when we talked about your brother for my show—"

"You don't have a 'show.' You videotape yourself talking to yourself about stupid shit and then upload it to the internet."

"I have over ten thousand subscribers."

"I give a shit."

"Listen, man, you helped me out with that webisode. The one about Jess Barrett."

"Like I said: I give a shit. How long ago was that anyway? Why are we talking about it?"

"I wouldn't jeopardize your anonymity as a source—"

"The hell you wouldn't. You sent that dead girl's sister to a bar to find me!"

Shane didn't have a defense for that. He'd violated a sacred tenet of journalism: never reveal your sources. Of course, like Donnie kept reminding him: Shane wasn't a real journalist. That left wiggle room, one of the benefits of operating outside the system.

Donnie filled another glass, chugging it, before making a show of looking up at the clock on the wall.

"I need to see it," Shane said.

"See what?"

"The proof. The evidence Dell Rawls hid and your brother stole."

"Are you fucking serious? That's what you woke me up for?"

"Yes."

"It's a fucking piece of paper."

"From the morgue, right?"

"Yeah. I already told you. The death certificate or some shit. You're not gonna know what it means any more than me."

"I'd like to look at it. Then, promise, I'll go."

Donnie slammed down the glass, violently enough to shatter in shards but somehow it remained intact, and then he bolted from the kitchen, leaving Shane to stare at water stains on the ceiling. A cockroach the size of a small mouse sauntered across the tile, pausing long enough to have its picture taken. Shane turned to the living room window, eyes following orange and red tracer lights behind the thin, threadbare sheet being used as a curtain, making him wonder just how stoned he was.

Donnie didn't come back right away. Shane waited. He didn't want to piss off the guy more by hollering after him or traipsing through his dirty, depressing apartment. Shane started seeing double. He hadn't slept. Researching lead after lead had left him dizzy. He had so many threads running through his head, connecting this to that, that to this. Trying to keep it all together, this giant ball of twine. It was enough to drive anyone mad.

Ten, twelve minutes later, a pissed-off Donnie returned with a large white envelope, passing it to Shane.

On the front, a name: Jessica Julia Barrett.

"Ain't been through my dead brother's shit in years. So, yeah, thanks for that."

Shane peeled back the flap, which wasn't glued but was still sticky because time, stubborn pulp remnants remaining, sticking and ripping.

What he retrieved wasn't a death certificate but an autopsy report. He looked at Donnie. "What's this?"

"I told you. A death certificate."

"No. It's an autopsy report."

"What's the difference?"

"One is a document stating someone is dead. The other is an explanation *how* they died."

"What do I care?"

"Why did your brother hold onto an autopsy report?"

Donnie shrugged.

Shane studied the document. "This isn't the final report. There's no county seal."

"Beats me. All I know is Ricky was with the old man when they found the body. Said Dell acted weird as hell. After the doctor determined that girl fell and broke her neck, my brother got the axe."

"Why?"

"Dell said he was stealing from petty cash."

"Was he?"

"My brother was a lot of things, thief included. But he wasn't a liar. He said Dell used it to can his ass." Cigarette stump burned to the nub, Donnie pointed at the envelope. "Claimed that was evidence of a cover-up. Ricky took that with him. Swiped it from some old doctor who worked for the town. Louie something. Said it was insurance."

"Insurance? For what?"

"Fuck if I know." Donnie lit another cigarette, aiming the cherry-red tip at the document Shane held. "Blackmail Dell Rawls, use it to get out of trouble? You remember Ricky. He always had some big plan to get rich. I loved the guy, but he was a fuck-up, my brother. Night he died in that motorcycle accident, he'd been doing, like, a buck twenty on back streets, no streetlights, no helmet, gacked out of his skull." Donnie took a drag, thinking. "But I tell you this. If Ricky held onto that, it's worth something."

Shane stared at the white envelope. "What am I supposed to do with it?"

"How the hell should I know?"

"This is the 'proof' you said you had? Did you even read it?"

Donnie went to snatch it back. "If you don't want it, leave it here."

Shane held up a hand, motioning to calm down. He returned the report to the envelope, folding it, and sticking it in his pocket.

Shane didn't know his next move. All he had was a promise he'd made to himself many years ago. To be a real investigator. A legitimate reporter. No more getting stoned, filming bullshit, fishing for "likes" from strangers. He'd solve this damn case.

For years, Shane had skirted by on the cult of personality, pretending to be someone he wasn't. Maybe Shane wasn't to blame for what happened to Jess Barrett that night. He also wasn't innocent.

It was time to start paying back the hurt he owed.

"Almost forgot," Donnie added, reaching in his dirty jeans. "Found this in Ricky's things."

Shane outstretched his palm, and Donnie passed along the torn necklace missing half a heart, big ol' crimson-stained fingerprint in the center. And on the inside, a dedication.

"I told your lady cop friend Ricky didn't have it," Donnie said. "I'm not taking heat for some bullshit my dead brother did twenty-five years ago."

Shane read the inscription to himself.

From Cam to Jess.

CHAPTER THIRTY-SEVEN

**THEN, Six Nights After the Disappearance,
Wednesday, March 20, 1991, 2:19 a.m.**

Dell Rawls followed the direction Cam told him Jess Barrett had fled.
She'd been missing almost a week. Dell arranged a search party. Less
a search party, and more secret mission, just he and one of his men,
Ricky Simmons. They went late at night. Or early morning, depending
on how you looked at these things. Ricky didn't ask why they hadn't
conducted the search during daylight hours. Ricky Simmons wasn't
the kind of worker to ask such questions. On his best days the guy was
shiftless, lazy. Dell wouldn't have been able to answer anyway.

It had been a rough few days for Dell after he and his son visited the
ER, where they learned Cam had, in fact, been walking around with a
fractured rib. They stabilized the rib best they could, prescribing rest. If
Cam needed to cough, doctors said, he should hug a pillow.

Dell and Cam had had plenty of time to talk. About the water
tower, Jess, Rose, beloved wife and mother, the hurt they both carried,
Dell leaving the door open for Cam to share anything—*anything*—
with him. Dell never, for a second, believed Cam could've harmed Jess,
the mere idea preposterous. Cam was a monster on the football field, a

ferocious warrior on the wrestling mat, and the rest of the time one of the kindest, most gentle souls you'd ever met. Even during their recent arguments, where Cam was throwing out words like "fascists" and cursing, he sounded like a boy trying to convince himself. Still, Dell had put off making this trek, waiting a couple extra days, scared of what he might find.

This was all Brad Pearce and his corruptive agenda. Alibis aside, Dell wasn't ruling out Pearce having done something horrible to the Barrett girl. He shuddered to consider. Dell's hands were also tied, position compromised. By bringing in Pearce, interview on record, Dell had placed his son in a precarious position. The last thing a Pac Ten school would want—and Dell was still holding out hope Cam would change his mind about playing collegiate ball—was a new player coming in with that much baggage. And bags didn't get any heavier than "questioned regarding possible homicide."

Both Shane Ellet and Brad Pearce pointed crooked fingers at his son. Cam stuck to his story. Following the raid, he'd watched Jess run in the opposite direction, away from town and toward Cripple Creek Preserve. He never saw her after that.

Dell would prove his boy right.

By the time Dell roused Ricky from the station and told him to meet at the leaning water tower in Soledad Gorge, the night was darker than dark. The skies appeared free of cloud, clear, and yet Dell couldn't see a single star up there. Light pollution, they called it. Dell wasn't a science guy. All he knew: you couldn't see two inches in front of your face.

Dell told Ricky to take the north side, while he scouted the ravine. Dell and his men had already covered considerable ground. This time, Dell instructed Ricky to keep walking, all the way to Cripple Creek, which was miles away. There was no reason for Jess Barrett to have wandered that far, which was in the opposite direction of her friends and town. Dell was leaving nothing to chance.

Ricky slogged off, only to return ten seconds later to say his flashlight went out. Dell snatched the flashlight from the kid's hand, smacked the head, and the beam returned. Ricky wasn't just lazy; he was on the stupid side. Dell knew he'd have to let him go. He'd already caught the kid pocketing petty cash. Called in sick half the time. Dell also had a soft spot for guys like Ricky, who was forced to be a surrogate dad to his little brother, Donnie, after their parents died in a car crash. Dell tried to give Ricky a break, help him out. Dell could hear his beloved Rose's voice: *You can't save the world, honey.* Ricky wasn't a cop, hadn't been issued a handgun, had no official training, held no official title. Dell had hired him as a jack-of-all-trades to babysit the station on the overnight shift, follow up on public disturbance calls, easy money, but the guy was a class-A screw-up.

As Ricky ascended the mountainous shelves, Dell wielded his own flashlight, its wide beam spreading over rocky terrain and scrub brush, between big leaf maples and black cottonwood, the ground overrun with invasive species of fuzzy mosses and creeping thyme. Navigating the uncertain drop-off from earthen berms, Dell used the roots of coastal sage to keep upright, rappelling, zigzagging toward the basin. Mid-March, precipitation had been spotty, sporing a ripe tang of moist fungus and mold in the perpetually lightless shadows. A pungent mulch overpowered the more pleasant scents of cowboy cologne.

As Dell walked, he talked to himself. He walked much farther than he could conceive Jess Barrett having walked. Miles, it felt. The pre-dawn valley chilled, air crisp. Hitting a soggy patch of bog, Dell muttered a curse, extracting his big boot from the sluggish stillwater.

No more fragrant foliage or fauna. All he could smell was the industrial sewage from Cripple Creek's facility over the range.

He tried not to dwell on Jess Barrett's life. Dell didn't know the girl well, better acquainted with her family's history, her parents' divorce small-town infamous and ugly. Dysfunctional families yielded problem children who made bad decisions. A sad, sobering thought hit Dell: maybe they were fortunate Rose passed away young, while they were still in love, before familiarity had a chance to breed contempt and they became one of these couples who stayed together for the kids, putting on happy public faces that couldn't mask the silent disdain each held for the other. Dell saw it all the time. Drive down Main Street on any given Sunday morning, and you'd see these couples, late forties, early fifties, their best years gone, sitting wordless over meals, each reading a different section of the paper, catching up on the latest subjects they couldn't care less about to avoid conversing with one another.

In a way, Brad and Jess running off together was the best-case scenario. And not because the thought didn't disgust Dell. It would explain where Jess was, would tell him she was alive. She'd made a stupid, foolish decision, perhaps under duress, which gave them time to find her and bring her home.

Since the investigation began, Dell had learned a great deal about Brad Pearce, though often getting that information was like pulling teeth, another of his daddy's favorite sayings. So much sealed and hidden. Records showed a previous marriage, there were multiple accusations from other parents, at other schools, a long, sordid history of inappropriate relationships with underage, susceptible girls. With each scandal, he—or his family—bought his way out of it, had the charges dropped, suppressed, redacted, expunged, leaving Brad Pearce free to prey, stalk, select his next victim. That cycle was about to stop. Dell Rawls would make damn sure of that.

Jess was still young enough that she could have her life back. Barely eighteen, she had her whole life ahead of her.

If Dell could find Jess. If she was still alive…

Now in the lowlands, boots mucking through marshes and sloughs, Dell sought out the driest parts, feet wet, soaked through two layers of thick socks. Former riverbeds rose above banks, silt a few inches higher than that, cutting into rocky terrain, leaving little room to navigate or maneuver.

Clouds settled in the gulch. The darkness, already prohibitive, became an impenetrable wall, impervious to flashlight, atmosphere drenched as more fog rolled in.

Given dropping temperatures and the distance covered, Dell had hit the point of no return. He had traveled farther than he'd intended, and if he didn't turn around now, he feared he lacked the strength, energy, and willpower to make it home.

He was about to head back when he saw the sign for Cripple Creek Nature Preserve, its seldom-used pathway overrun with unruly foliage—yarrow, chaparral, mugwort—clogging the entryway. His eyes pushed through the sealed-off opening, past the expansive, trumpet-like flowers dangling from sagebrush, down the dark trail.

And there was the body.

At first, he wasn't sure it was a body. His mind tried to convince him it was anything but. An unfortunate tangle of knotted branches, felled limbs. Or if it was a body, it was that of an animal. They had mountain lions out here. Bobcats tended to leave people alone, but they'd drag a deer into the bushes, pick a carcass clean.

Easing down the stony embankment, using thick weeds and roots as footholds, Dell descended the ravine. The closer he got, the harder it became to lie to himself.

It was a human body. Female. Young. Eighteen seemed right.

She was dressed, jeans still on, not that sexual assault could be ruled out. Her tee shirt, a band Dell had never heard of, was torn, fabric ripped from where animals had started feeding. Decomposition had set in, the stench overpowering. Dell realized that wasn't the Cripple Creek sewage facility he smelled. The rotting corpse had chunks of meat missing, wildlife invited to nibble, chew, feast. The flesh around the fingertips had been gnawed off. Insects crawled through the vacuous eye sockets, soft tissue the first snack for hungry critters.

Dell had seen plenty of dead bodies. He didn't remember any this shade of deep purple, so purple it was almost black. The odor intolerable, Dell stretched his tee shirt over his nose and mouth to use as a makeshift mask, inching closer.

A glimmer caught his eye. Between bony appendages, something metallic shown. Dell looked up. The moon and stars had come out of hiding, the heavens parting to shine a glorious spotlight. Dell bent down to inspect further the object in the girl's hand. It was … a chain. With a heart locket. Or rather a chain with half the heart left. The necklace wrapped around stiff fingers. The inscription came into focus.

From Cam to Jess.

Dell looked toward the top of the rocky ridge, picturing a boy trying to hold onto a girl, a girl who maybe had too much to drink, losing her footing, the pair clutching opposite ends of a heart pledging eternal love.

Even if true, the alleged altercation had taken place miles behind him. *What was she doing out here?*

No, Dell thought, that constituted an accident. Even if someone sustained a head wound and wandered for hours before succumbing to internal bleeding and collapsing. That wasn't premediated. *Witnesses saw them fighting.* Dell couldn't be sure this was Jess Barrett's body. *Of course it is, honey.*

Who's to say Dell was ever here?

He'd send his men out when it got light. No one could help the poor girl now. A few hours, a day or two, would allow Dell to formulate his thoughts, cement a course of action.

He heard the crunching of branches behind him. Spinning around, flashlight aimed like a gun, Dell watched Ricky Simmons emerge above the rocks.

Before Dell could think about retrieving the necklace, Ricky approached, hand on radio, calling in to report they'd found the remains of Jessica Barrett.

CHAPTER THIRTY-EIGHT

NOW, Saturday, July 23, 2016, 10:54 a.m.

By the time they'd picked out a new iPhone, it was over.

Maureen had finished guiding a banged-up Lydia into her apartment when Detective Terry called. Mark Burns' rusted Honda was spotted outside the *El Capitan Hotel* on the edge of Skid Row. When no one answered the door, the desk jockey let police into the room. And there he was, slumped in a corner, needle dangling from arm, cold flesh a ghastly shade of blue. Looked like he'd been dead several hours.

Lydia asked if it was an accidental overdose or a suicide. Detective Terry said he wasn't sure how the M.E. would classify it, but it appeared intentional. Mark Burns had injected a sizable amount of heroin—"enough to kill a horse"—mixing it with ammonia, leaving nothing to chance.

When the call ended, Lydia sat in the living room La-Z-Boy, while Maureen made up the couch—Mo already told Lydia that the only way she was leaving the hospital was if she stayed with her. They both needed sleep.

"I don't get it, Mo," Lydia said. "Why would this man…"

Maureen Gearon sighed.

Lydia recognized that sigh. It told her Maureen had been holding back unpleasant news. Used to happen all the time in medical school. Like when academic politics denied Lydia an award she deserved or funding for a project fell through. Maureen, forever protecting Lydia, shielding her from the harsh realities of a cruel world.

"I was waiting to share this," Maureen said. "Until they'd caught him, when I knew we were alone and safe from interruptions—"

"Stop it, Mo. You're scaring me."

"I don't know where to start."

"The beginning is a good place." Lydia tried to smile. Right now, even that hurt.

"I was able to get my hands on Rhona Clarion's records, like you asked. Her professional notes from the clients she'd been working with. Including Mark Burns." There was that sigh again.

"Where are the records?" Lydia asked. "I want to see them."

"I had to turn them over." Maureen patted Lydia's hand. "We sat on this too long, you know that."

Lydia did, which made her feel worse. She'd taken advantage of Maureen's friendship and kindness, asking her to violate principles, risk her career. Lydia couldn't find the words to show appreciation or apologize before Maureen continued the wretched, tragic demise of Mark Burns.

"Don't worry," Mo said. "I read everything in those records. Rhona Clarion worked hard with Burns. Did her best to get him back on his feet. The notes were extensive. They talked. Often. In depth. I must say, Rhona was quite good at her job. Compassionate, kind. She got Mark Burns to open up and confide in her. These weren't official therapy sessions, you understand?" Maureen waited. "They weren't far from it."

Lydia didn't need clarification. *Not official* translated to no client/patient privilege to circumvent. No bureaucratic hassle. No hoops. *Not far from it* was the caveat: using them in legal proceedings would prove difficult if not outright impossible.

"Why do I get the impression you're not telling me everything?"

"You know Mark worked for your family?"

"So I've heard, yes. Richard hired people like that. Recovering addicts, alcoholics. Like I said, I don't remember anyone by that name."

Maureen caressed Lydia's hand. "For the best. Mark Burns was a bad man. Long criminal history. Violence. Restraining orders. Estranged from his own wife and children. When he was fired from working for your family, I think he saw an opportunity."

"Opportunity?"

"Money. Extortion." Maureen delayed. "Kidnapping."

"Wait. Are you telling me this Mark Burns confessed to ... abducting ... my sister?"

"I think that's what Rhona Clarion's notes imply. Burns was besieged by guilt. Rhona pressed him. He talked about this well-off family in Santa Clarita's valley and a seventeen-year-old girl matching your sister's description, a job he had back in nineteen-ninety, and how when he was let go, at rock bottom, broke and needing money, he hatched a plan. Not a good one. Mark Burns wasn't a smart man. It sounded like he had a partner, someone with a better grasp on reality, perhaps. Anyway, his plan went sideways."

"Sideways?" Lydia didn't ask it like a question.

"Again, Rhona's notes are nonspecific. If I had to infer... This isn't official. My take—"

"I trust your take."

"This girl he took—this unnamed girl matches… He took Jess, kept her in an old shack on the Cripple Creek Preserve for a couple days."

"Did he…?" Lydia wasn't sure she could handle hearing the word *rape*.

"Oh, no," Maureen said. "Extortion, a play for money. Nothing more. Rhona asked the same question in her notes. Then I guess before he could figure out a way to get your family a ransom demand, Jess broke free and made a run for it. Burns chased after, caught her. There was a struggle on the top of the ridge. He swore it was an accident, that she fell."

Lydia felt numb. All these years, waiting for an answer. Night after sleepless night, her subconscious stirring, searching for a solution. The night terrors. The nyctophobia. The fear. Jess being drunk and careless? That never felt right. Did this? Was this the moment of clarity Lydia had sought for twenty-five years? It felt so anticlimactic, unsatisfying. Lydia soon realized why. She hadn't just wanted someone to pay—an ammonia overdose was a painful way to go, like the knot that snapped Brad Pearce's neck—she'd wanted to be the one to do it, to administer the retribution, not through the courts or natural selection but with her own two hands around their throat. Vengeance. For someone to hurt like she had, to suffer.

"Are you okay?" Maureen asked.

Lydia couldn't answer that right now. She wasn't sure if she'd ever be able to. "I should call my mother. My dad. They deserve to know."

"I'd say hold off? I know that's hard. There still must be an official investigation, an autopsy on Burns—i's dotted, t's crossed. Your parents are going to have questions—questions you don't have the answers to. And, Lydia, I didn't break the law to get this information. I didn't play by the rules either. Understand?"

The last thing Lydia wanted was getting Maureen in more hot water.

"That's why Rhona Clarion called me?"

"I'd say that's a sound hypothesis. Maybe Burns let a name slip at some point?"

"Was Jess' name in her files?"

"We don't know yet. Could be. This has all happened fast."

"I thought you read everything?"

"I did. I can't say I read it as thoroughly as I would've liked. There wasn't much time."

"So, Burns knows Rhona called me, and he…" Lydia was reconstructing the pieces aloud in real time, needing to complete this arc from the loose, scattered fragments remaining.

"We don't have all the answers yet," Maureen said, trying to sound as comforting as possible. "We might never. I think your theory is accurate, though. The guy had been in and out of prison. He was looking at the possibility of going back for good. Maybe he knew Rhona called you. Maybe he feared at some point she would. But, yes, I think it's safe to say Mark Burns killed Rhona Clarion."

"He was trying to kill me too?"

Maureen released her hand. "It's going to be weeks, maybe months before we know what happened, if ever. This should be enough to let you rest, no? Get some sleep?" Maureen clasped both hands on Lydia's shoulders. "Lydia, you *need* to sleep. I can see it in your eyes, you're not taking care of yourself. Be honest: when was the last time you slept?"

Lydia didn't answer. She didn't know.

Right then Lydia wasn't sure she'd ever sleep again.

When Lydia woke, she thought it was morning, the blinds being lifted on another day. She expected to feel refreshed, see the sunlight creeping over the desert and mountains, a rare night's rest conquered. What she thought was dawn she soon discovered was dusk, evening gloam settling prematurely with the invading smoke. Her fear of the dark returned. No reprieve, no mercy. The answers Maureen offered hadn't changed a damned thing.

Lydia turned on the lights in every room.

At some point, Mo had gone home. Like a good mom, she'd started a pot of coffee and left an encouraging note. Her time off over, Lydia was scheduled to return to work at eleven. She didn't have a chance to make it to the cupboard before her new cell chimed. She hadn't imported contacts or personalized the ring tone yet, the unfamiliar numbers and noise contributing to her confusion. She recognized the Pasa Ardo area code and swiped to answer, caught off guard by Cam Rawls' voice.

Her first thought was her mom and the wildfire.

"The fires?" she said.

"They're getting closer. Smoke is making air quality hell. We're safe. No evacuation orders. Won't come to that. Never does."

"That's good to hear," Lydia said. "I was talking to my mother yesterday." She didn't see any reason to explain why she'd gone there, but sleeplessness and pain pills had her oversharing. "I tried to get her to leave the house—"

"Are you free?" Cam interrupted.

The question caught Lydia off guard. Disoriented, she'd forgotten she was talking to a man she'd suspected of murder just yesterday.

"To do what?" she asked.

"I have something I think you need to see."

Three cups of strong coffee, a couple painkillers, and an hour and a half later, Lydia had descended Santa Clarita Valley, floor consumed by the stubborn haze of auburn smoke, a noxious cloud spreading. If the fires were still that far away, she hated contemplating the hellscape should they get closer.

Entering Old Town, Lydia pulled into the parking lot of the decrepit Pasa Ardo Community Center, which had been converted from the defunct grammar school built eons ago. For a town with as much funding as Pasa Ardo, the broken-down, brown brick building stood out as an eyesore. They'd been talking about demolishing it and constructing a new one since Lydia was a kid. Voters could never agree on its fate. Library. Senior Living Center. Tennis courts. So there it remained, a massive reminder of people's failure to agree on anything.

When they were kids, Lydia and Jess used to bike out here. The Community Center had a small weight room, with ancient dumbbells and stationary machines from the 1970s, where the older high school boys would come to work out. There was a rec room, too, with ping-pong tables and a coin-operated arcade game. Or there used to be anyway. Lydia hadn't been to the Community Center in ages.

On the drive over, Lydia reassured herself she had nothing to worry about. This was Cam Rawls. Town cop, old acquaintance, all around good guy. He'd never have hurt her sister. He posed no threat to her. Her suspicions of him, pure paranoia.

Shane's claims of hidden evidence came via Donnie Simmons, a stone-cold drunkard, gambler, and pothead—evidence she never actually saw. More important, they'd identified the man who had murdered her sister—the same man who'd killed Rhona Clarion and who may have intended to make Lydia his next victim: Mark Burns. And Mark Burns was dead.

Yet, Lydia couldn't shake the urgency fueling Cam's voice. What could be so important that he'd need to see her now? Panning around the remote location, isolated from downtown, Lydia opened her glove compartment, tucking her firearm in the belt behind her back, sliding on her windbreaker.

Cam stood behind the glass door, waiting to unlock it since it was after hours. He held open the door and flicked on a light, revealing dirty tile, dust bunnies rolling like tumbleweeds.

With a head pull, he silently directed her down the dim hall. Half the overhead fluorescents flickered, the other half blown out. Shadows invaded. Darkness enveloped. Far off, water dripped, plopping in puddles, echo reverberating down the corridor. Lydia felt her steps slowing. She reminded herself not to let her imagination get the best of her. *There's a phone record of Cam calling you.* That reassured Lydia until they hit the top step of the black well. *Yeah, and they have a phone record of Rhona Clarion calling you too.*

"Sorry," Cam said, taking out his phone to power on its flashlight. "Fixture is busted." He held out a hand, shining the path to follow. "Been trying to get maintenance to fix it forever."

"They still use this place?"

"Barely. Weight room's still here. High schoolers and cheap old people. These days it's mostly storage for parks and rec." He held out a hand. "Watch your step."

A short stairwell delivered the pair to a sunken, cold concrete room, overstuffed with odds and ends. A rake, a shovel, an old push mower. Some traffic cones. A deflated basketball. In the middle of the room sat several desks, the kind Lydia remembered taking tests on, tan surfaces carved with bad kids' initials. In one corner stood the old arcade game, *Asteroids*, gathering dust. In an opposite corner, a pair of rusted green filing cabinets. The bottom drawer of one had been left open.

Cam pointed at the cabinets. "Records," he deadpanned.

On top of an old school desk rested a large white folder. Official hospital stamp, labeled with her sister's full name and social.

"After we talked, I reached out to Shane Ellet, told him to delete that episode about Jess."

"You watched it?"

"You told me to." Cam stopped. "You also knew Shane was calling me a murderer."

"Not in so many words."

"He accused my father of hiding evidence."

"Yeah," Lydia said, feeling the guilt sink in. "That was lousy of him."

"Lousy," Cam echoed. "But he might not have been wrong."

Lydia leaned back, letting her hand hang lower, drifting toward her waistband.

"A call came in," he said.

Lydia wasn't sure if this was a confession, a setup, or something unforeseen and therefore worse. The devil you don't know.

"Earlier today. Over the tip line, voice disguised."

"Shane Ellet up to his old tricks?"

"That'd be my guess. Sounded like the same garbled modulator from his Rider days."

"What did the caller say?"

"This is the official autopsy report," Cam replied, ignoring her question, placing a finger on the white folder. "I assume you've seen this?"

Lydia relaxed enough to retrieve the large envelope from his possession, slipping out the M.E.'s findings. No one had ever passed along an official report of how Jess died. No reason to. Everyone knew the cause of death: fractured neck.

"This afternoon has been hell," Cam said. "I've wrestled with what to do, y'know?"

No, I don't know.

From the sunken dwelling, Lydia could see the darkened sky glowing between the slats of blinds, fiery red framing a mushroom cloud blooming. Her pulse quickened as the room fell darker and the distant wildfires blazed more ferocious. They were still far away. Right?

A world going up in flames was still preferable to the other option rattling around her skull: having to draw on a fellow cop.

Then Cam reached behind his back.

Lydia went for hers.

Cam eased off, slowly showing his hands, in which he produced another envelope. Same size, color. Cam placed it on the desk beside the formal findings. "Read that one."

Lydia slid out a second report. Same M.E.—Dr. Louis Lowry— same letterhead and approximate length, same number of indented paragraphs, identical signature.

"Notice anything different?"

Lydia was supposed to see they weren't the same. That was the point. Like one of those games in a magazine, spot the difference, omission or addition, depending on point of view, subtle. She perused the two, focusing on the official report first. Seeing the cause of death in medical jargon was jarring. Which might've been why it took a few seconds to see it. Shane hadn't been lying. *How did he know?* It was right there. You had to understand the intricacies in interpreting a report, be intimate with the specificity of the field.

Jess' neck *had* been broken.

But that wasn't what killed her.

What had Cam's father done?

CHAPTER THIRTY-NINE

**THEN, After the Body Was Found,
March 20 – First Couple Weeks of April 1991**

When Ricky Simmons emerged from the woods to find Dell with the
necklace, it was too late for Dell to hide the evidence. That was what
had been on Dell's mind. If he could think back and accurately recall.
The ordeal had been overwhelming. That night, he'd been wandering
in the dark so long, so many swirling, conflicting ideas floating in and
out of his head, remembering Rose, worried about Cam, the air crisp,
nippy, fragrant aromas of desert fauna, seepage of industrial sewage, the
stench of a rotting corpse, rendering the experience part dream, part
nightmare.

The Pasa Ardo PD arrived on scene, everyone getting their hands
dirty. From that point, Dell had to play it by the book.

Dell had a plan. A simple plan. That was the problem with those
simple plans. They always seemed fastest to fly off the rails.

The necklace was logged into evidence, where it would remain,
safe and secure, because Jessica's Barrett's death would soon be ruled
an accident. She'd broken her neck. Time of death was placed several hours after witnesses had seen her with Cam. *Estimated* time

of death—because "estimated" was the best they were getting. After almost a week, it had been too long to pin down an exact time.

Dell never once, not for a second, believed Cam could've hurt Jess. Dell also knew how people thought and reacted. Might've been his greatest strength, really. His ability to read the room. Pasa Ardo was simmering after Jessica Barrett's death. They wanted *someone* to pay. And with Brad Pearce ruled out and safely ensconced in San Francisco, Shane Ellet's involvement wiped clean—both parties safeguarded by the powerhouse law firm of Carlson & Associates—Dell couldn't shake the fear someone would come for his boy. Though much of the region prided itself on progressive politics, racism still existed; it didn't matter whether the town sheriff was black or blue.

For the first time in his career, Dell decided to break the law. First, he had to fire Ricky. Finding just cause was easy. Close your eyes and point. Stealing. Clocking out early. General incompetence.

Not long afterwards, Dell went to retrieve the necklace and locket. Only to find it … missing. The obvious culprit: Ricky Simmons. Getting down to the Pasa Ardo evidence room was about as difficult as sneaking into the Community Center after hours. This wasn't a town where people locked doors or got murdered. Dell was kicking himself for not taking the necklace sooner. He didn't want to draw attention by acting out of recklessness. There were other officers at the station. No reason for anyone to be digging around the evidence locker. Give it time. Let a couple weeks pass. Except Ricky got there first. Dell already suspected Ricky of using drugs, meaning he'd snatch anything to hock. Guy wouldn't get much for a busted locket, but the white gold was worth something.

From there, the situation only grew worse.

County doctor Louis Lowry had been handling Pasa Ardo's life and death matters since before Dell was born. He birthed babies. He wrapped up the dead. Lowry was well into his eighties, long past retirement age. But the man loved the work.

Dell could navigate a missing necklace. Ricky would pawn it sooner or later for quick cash. There was only one pawn shop in town. And every item they procured made it into a weekly report that landed on Dell's desk. If Ricky Simmons got motivated enough to try his luck in another town, that just put more miles between them.

Then came the day Louis Lowry phoned Dell, and the police chief was forced to question whether he'd been wrong about everything.

"Hello, Chief," Lowry said. "I've finished the Barrett autopsy."

Unlike the big city, there was no rush to wrap up such examinations in Pasa Ardo. Once the cause of death was determined, Louis would take his time before filing the official certificate. The old man worked at two speeds, slow and sleep.

The chief wasn't worried. Louis had sent over preliminary findings, which the autopsy confirmed. Accidental fall. Broken neck.

Except now Lowry added a small wrinkle.

"What are you saying, Lou?"

"Well now, Chief, I'm not totally sure. To be clear: I am not calling this foul play. This bone I'm talking about, well, breaking it *is* rare. But not unheard of. Even if a person *is* murdered. I only bring it up because, well, I started thinking about it. We have that pervert teacher, and I know how much you want to nail his, pardon my French, balls to the wall."

"Have you written this up?"

"No, sir. Not yet. I have the notes I've been keeping." Louis stopped, as if struggling to remember the exact order of events. "Put some findings to paper. Takes a while to finish a final report." Louis laughed, which turned into a raspy cough. "I revise a lot. A bit of a perfectionist." The doctor paused. "The wife used to say I was like a squirrel hiding acorns…"

By this point, Dell had stopped listening. He had a choice. It wasn't a difficult one to make. Louis was a long-time employee, a trusted doctor, and a friend. It was a simple request.

"When you file the official report," Dell said. "I'd like you to omit what you just told me." He paused. "As a favor."

Dell was prepared to launch into a speech about allowing the town, community, and Barrett family to grieve, heal, accept, and move on, how introducing this new, small, inconsequential detail would only needlessly open another can of worms, muddying already murky waters, maybe toss in another fishing analogy. He didn't have to.

"Whatever you say, Chief."

And that was that. Dr. Louis Lowry wrote a new final report.

Over the course of the next several weeks, Dell kept an eye on Ricky Simmons, checking in with local pawn shops. No necklace nor locket was ever unloaded. No one questioned the new autopsy report. The death certificate was filed. In a crooked system, sometimes we must bend rules to ensure justice.

In the end, Dell's concerns were all for naught.

Several months later, Ricky Simmons, screw-up that he was, got high on methamphetamine and rode his motorcycle headfirst into a tree.

The cancer came for Dell not long after. The end was quick.

The ex-police chief died without guilt, harboring no shame over what he'd done, believing his secrets—and son—would be safe.

CHAPTER FORTY

Lydia pointed at the line of text that stood out. A few extra words. But choice words that made a world of difference.

"It's not in the official report," she said.

"Not the one that was filed, no."

Lydia studied both documents. All but identical. Jess' death still ruled an accident. Same toxicology report, what could be gleaned from a body gnawed by vultures and rodents, the hair fibers that retained the benzos' long-acting half-life. Along with multiple eyewitness reports of Jess' alcohol intake, an accidental slip added up. The spot where her body was discovered, over two miles from the water tower, on the edge of Cripple Creek Preserve and adjacent wastewater facility, did not. This fact wasn't addressed in either report. Common sense implied her sister, high and drunk, had wandered, gotten careless. That's how she fell, slipped, fractured her neck and spine, C4, C5, that precious, narrow margin, which if damaged translated to death or lifelong paralysis.

Same situation. Same write-up.

Save that one small difference…

The hyoid bone in her sister's neck had been broken.

"I had to research what the hyoid even was," Cam admitted.

Lydia did not have to research a damn thing, biology fresh on the brain. She could almost recite her medical texts on the subject, verbatim.

The hyoid bone is a small, solitary horseshoe-shaped bone that floats free in the middle of our throats. Considered an unconventional bone, it sits between our larynx, pharynx, and tongue. It assists with opening and closing our mouths, biting, masticating, and swallowing. The tiny U-shaped bone also helps us breathe, speak, and throw up. Versatile. Resilient. Hyoid bone fractures are uncommon. Perhaps its most useful function is found in forensics, postmortem. Specifically in homicide cases, where one wants a murder to appear as a suicide or an accidental broken neck…

When the victim had, in fact, been strangled.

And Lydia had encountered this same M.O. twice in as many days, albeit in cases twenty-five years apart.

"Nobody lied," Cam said. "But no one announced it either." You could see Cam was desperate to believe. Would it have made a difference? True, his father suppressed this report, removing any mention of the hyoid fracture. His son was dating the victim. Technically unethical. But understandable.

Lydia had considered the possibility Cam was involved with Jess' disappearance and death. She'd grown suspicious because Shane Ellet said Dell Rawls covered up evidence. This was part of that evidence. If Cam *was* guilty, why was he showing it to her?

"Where did you find this other report?" Lydia asked.

Cam pointed to the corroded filing cabinets, the bottom drawer pulled and left open.

"Why would your father keep this here? Why not destroy it?" Lydia read the name of the examiner. Dr. Louis Lowry. Lydia didn't know the fate of every resident in Pasa Ardo. She knew Lowry's. He'd been a well-known, respected doctor in town. He died a while ago. After twenty-five years, so many players were gone, six feet under. Did she really want to tarnish legacies? "Do you think Dell was trying to protect Lowry's reputation?" The question didn't address every concern, but Lydia was giving Cam an out.

He didn't take it.

"I don't think so," Cam said. "It was hidden."

"Hidden?"

Cam nodded. "Back of that drawer, tucked in a corner. Never would've thought to look."

"Your mystery caller?"

"Told me where to find it."

Lydia pointed at the white envelope, not as aged, sullied, or yellowed as one would expect a twenty-five-year-old parcel to be after spending two-plus decades in a musty old cellar.

"Who has access to this room?" she asked.

"Look around. This is a glorified storage shed." Cam pointed at the cabinet. "Nothing in here worth stealing. Those files? Duplicate copies of schedules for summer programs in nineteen ninety-six. Receipts for ice cream cones the Little League team bought. Nothing important enough to keep under lock and seal. During the day, those doors remain open." He pointed to the other side of the hall. "The weight room is over there. Parks and rec pick up or drop off sporting goods for town events. People come in and out all the time."

On the surface, there was nothing deceitful about the original autopsy report. Neck and head trauma had still occurred. Only a trained eye would draw a correlation between strangulation and fracture of the hyoid bone. Lydia possessed that trained eye. Now. Then? She was a thirteen-year-old grieving sister.

"Dad must've known." Cam looked pained. "This was a homicide."

Lydia removed her glasses, pinching the bridge of her nose, searching for the right words to ease Cam's burden. But she wasn't going to lie.

"Why wouldn't my dad pursue this?"

"You were a good kid," Lydia said, neglecting her own doubts. "The first person they'd look at would be you."

"A couple days ago, you thought I had something to do with Jess' death."

"A lot has changed in a couple days, Cam."

"I can't keep this a secret. My father broke the law."

"They caught the guy."

"Who? Pearce?"

"No. Not Brad Pearce. You're right. My sister was murdered. By a man named Mark Burns." Lydia went on to explain Burns' backstory, his crimes and comeuppance.

When she stopped talking, it looked like a light switched on in Cam's eyes. "You never got a ransom note?"

Lydia shook her head no.

"Your sister was missing how many days?"

"Mark Burns wasn't the sharpest tool in the shed."

"He holds her, never requests a ransom, and then, what, decides to kill her?"

"From his social worker's notes, it sounds like he was keeping Jess in a shack out by Cripple Creek. She ran. He chased her down."

"And strangled her."

"From this report, I'd say that sounds accurate."

Cam didn't look satisfied. Lydia couldn't understand why. Shouldn't he be relieved? Cam had to know, by outing Dell, he was putting himself in harm's way. He was right. After the riots in '92, it's not like race relations got better around here. Or anywhere. Just look at the current state of America. This should've offered solace. Cam's expression conveyed the opposite, as if the revelation created more problems.

Cam waved her along, beckoning to follow upstairs. He unlocked the main office, making for an old, dust-covered PC, where he pulled up the online obituary for Mark Burns. Lydia sidled up beside him, reading over his shoulder. There wasn't much in the database. A brief description of the sad life and times of Mark Burns.

"What do you know about this Mark Burns?" Cam asked.

Lydia repeated the few concrete details she had. Hired as part of Richard Fontaine's not-ready-for-primetime crew. While Burns was at their house, she said, parroting Maureen's theory, he must've sensed a payday.

"I don't remember him," Lydia said. "My mother has kept that house in a continuous state of renovation since the divorce. Dad is on the hook for repairs. Part of the settlement. He doesn't fight it. He's got the money. Gloria's kept Richard employed for a quarter century. It's a source of pride for my mother."

"Twenty-five years?"

"Hell hath no fury."

"That's not what I mean. This guy was a junkie, living hand-to-mouth, skid row hotels, homeless. You're telling me your mom—Gloria—refined lady of sophistication"—Cam and Jess spent a lot of time together; he knew the type of woman Gloria was—"she's hiring a man like Burns?"

"No, that would be Richard. Like I said, he's Gloria's general contractor. More like on-call handyman. Sometimes friend with benefits. I think. He chooses his own crew."

Cam knew about Richard Fontaine, who had been hanging around Lydia's mother and the house since before Cam and Jess got together.

"Mark Burns," Cam said, "doesn't sound like he could tie his own shoe. Richard on the other hand…"

It took Lydia a moment to catch on.

"Not a chance," she said.

"Hear me out. I was at your house often. Your mother was always complaining about not getting enough money in the divorce. And there's Richard doting on her, trying to win her affections—"

"Richard Fontaine is the nicest guy I've ever met." Lydia held up a hand. "No offense to present company."

"None taken. And yes, I agree. He's super nice and supportive, and no offense to *you*, anyone who can put up with your mother for three decades *is* a saint."

He wasn't wrong. Lydia thought about it often, how grateful she was to have Richard around because without him taking care of Gloria, the thankless task would've fallen on her shoulders.

Cam scratched his chin. "You're saying Mark Burns is now the number one suspect in the murder of your sister?"

"It's more complicated than that." Lydia leaned over and typed in Rhona Clarion's info, waiting as Cam read. "This was the social worker assigned to Burns. Rhona called me before she died, wanting to talk. About Jess. Then she turns up dead."

"How long ago did she die?"

"Rhona? A few days ago. Before you and I talked."

That hung in the air, the fact that Lydia hadn't mentioned any of this to Cam, fueling speculation just how much she suspected him.

"Cam, nobody has to know Dell hid anything."

"This isn't about my dad. Cards on table? I can't sit on this report. It was left for me to find. Which means someone else knows about it. And when it comes to light, there's going to be inquiries, questions about me. In this town, during times like these? These are questions I'd rather avoid. They say Mark Burns is good for two murders? Great. I'm just asking what anyone is going to ask. How would a part-time gopher junkie screw-up like Burns know Jess' schedule? Know where to stash her while waiting for the ransom? Get a letter to your dad? When you see stuff like this, Lydia, ninety-nine percent of the time, it's an inside job."

Before Lydia could object, Cam held up a hand.

"I'm not accusing Richard or your mom of malice. I'm asking for your help talking to them. It goes easier for me—and them—if we keep this informal."

Lydia begrudgingly nodded. It was the least she could do after suspecting the guy of murder. Although this detour was putting a serious dent in her evening plans, like showing up for work on time.

Lydia phoned Ward to tell him she'd be late, then she rang Maureen, who'd made her promise to keep her abreast of all movement, worried sick after last night's attack. No answer. Lydia left a short, succinct, nonurgent message, doing her best to hide the fear in her voice.

She sensed they were nearing the truth.

Only this time, Lydia wasn't sure she wanted to learn it.

CHAPTER FORTY-ONE

NOW, The End, Pt. I, Saturday, July 23, 2016, 9:12 p.m.

"Oh, my," Gloria said, palming a glassful of white wine, pulling the door wide. "This is getting to be a regular occurrence." She feigned surprise. "And is that Pasa Ardo's finest, Cameron Rawls? Dickie! Come say hello to our sheriff and my daughter." Then to Lydia: "You are looking spry for being thrown down a flight of stairs."

Cam turned to Lydia, who realized she'd skipped over that part. She didn't have time to delve into it now.

Richard Fontaine emerged from the back room, shirtless. A shocking sight. Towel in hand. White hair and wrinkled skin, he sported a formidable barrel chest and broad shoulders, muscle mass still intact, carved from decades of manual labor.

Before Lydia could speculate if Gloria had broken down and allowed Richard in her bed, her mom corrected any misassumptions. "Dickie's been painting all day. He needed to scrub up before we got dinner." Turning to Richard: "Did you order yet?"

Richard stared, dead-eyed, focused on the town cop. "No. Not yet."

"Will you be joining us?" Gloria asked. "We're having…" Her face pinched quizzical. "What did we decide on again?"

"Japanese," Richard said. "Sushi."

"I don't think anyone is delivering food." Lydia gestured out the large glass wall. Plumes of dark gray smoke plugged the sky, glowing red ash replacing stars, drifting like hell's snowflakes. "Not in the middle of a wildfire—"

"Sushi?" Gloria made a stink face at Richard. "Doesn't travel well."

"Mom. We—I—wanted to talk to you about something." Lydia waited long enough for her mother to process the request. When you redirected Gloria's attention, you needed to give her time to come around, to exit her perpetual resting state of blunted and numbed, let her eyes fix on you, command them to return to the present. "About Jess."

The way Gloria glowered after that made Lydia's heart seize up. She'd violated the sacred rule: never speak that name. This couldn't have been the only time. It must've come up at *some* point, every now and then. A holiday dinner, evoking a pleasant memory? A sister and daughter who'd been part of their everyday life all those years doesn't vanish from existence.

Her mother huffed, groaned, evidencing the ache, turning in pain. "I can't believe you…" She let those words fade away, leaving her remaining daughter to wallow in shame and regret. "You," she repeated, turning, before gulping more wine. Paired with too many pills, Gloria lost any remaining inhibition. "You, Lydia, should've told me your sister left that night. If you had, she'd still be here."

Cam Rawls stepped forward. In his tight police uniform, the big ex-football star still cut a commanding presence. "Mrs. Barrett—"

"Don't call me that," Gloria said. Whether it was the *Mrs.* or Alan's last name or both she objected to, Lydia could not say. Her mother had kept the last name. She'd had opportunity to change it back to "Dunn," her maiden one. Divorced women did it all the time, especially when they hated their ex-husband. Then again, the Barrett name came with perks, admission to sold-out shows, preferred seating at the best restaurants, rushed delivery, which Gloria was happy to exploit.

A singed mesquite wafted. Lydia inhaled a lungful of smoke, clearing her throat.

"You smell that?" Lydia said. *That can't just be the vents, can it?* "Is there a window open?" Then turning to Cam: "Has there been an evacuation notice?" Lydia went to the window, peering over the mountaintops. A brilliant strip of dark orange glowed above the crest. No flames were visible yet, but red ash continued to flurry the grim sky.

Cam shook his head no, before stepping to Richard, speeding up inquiry. Time was no longer a luxury they enjoyed. "Do you remember an employee named Mark Burns?"

"Yes," he replied, without hesitation. If Richard had an escape plan, feigning ignorance was not part of it. "Conflicted young man."

Young man? Mark Burns had not been a young man. Then again, perhaps when you reached Richard's age, everyone was a "young man."

"He's dead," Lydia said, the words spat like a challenge. No, Lydia didn't believe Cam's theory that Richard had enlisted Mark Burns' help kidnapping Jess, which was unfounded, unprovoked, speculative nonsense. She didn't *not* believe it. At this moment, Lydia wasn't sure *what* she believed. "Turns out my sister's death wasn't an accident. She didn't slip and fall. It's true she broke her neck. But that was *after* she'd already been strangled."

Richard's dead eyes gave away nothing.

Gloria, never short of histrionics, fell into a chair. "Why? Why would you do this, Lydia? How dare you come here, with this, this … cop." The way her mother wielded the word *cop*, it might as well have been a racial epithet or slur.

"Stay calm, Mrs. Barrett," Cam started to say.

Until Gloria cut him off, screaming, "I told you once! Now I'm tell-ing you twice! Do not call me that! Do not! Not ever! It's not nice!" The unintended cadence and rhyme echoed old Dr. Suess books that house-keepers used to read Lydia at naptime.

With everyone watching, Gloria regained her regal composure, smoothing her fuzzy collar, cinching her sash. "Does your father know?" she asked, before sipping her wine.

"No," Lydia said.

"Thank heaven for small miracles."

In Gloria's twisted world, being first to learn a daughter's death resulted from a homicide and not an accident constituted victory.

"How did he die?" Richard asked, circling back to Mark Burns, face catching up with the reverent mourning he wished to express.

"Overdose," Lydia said. "Intentional."

Richard shut his eyes tight, pinching away the hurt. His mouth fell open. No sound came out. Lydia tried to deduce why the news, while sad and unfortunate, hit Richard so hard. How could Richard, who employed dozens of derelicts over the years, recall Mark Burns? This was decades ago. He hadn't worked for him long. A few months buried among eons of experience. Lydia couldn't recall the names of several people she met last week.

The scorched redolence of dry sage brush and creosote grew stronger, making breathing difficult. Hacked coughs echoed from all corners.

Lydia turned to Cam. "I don't care about evacuation orders. We need to get everyone out of here. This can't be healthy for them to breathe."

"*Them?*" Gloria snapped. "Richard and me? Why? Because we're so old?" She couldn't keep her eyes open, swaying unsteadily, nodding standing up. Richard caught her by the arm before she could fall and break a hip.

Lydia never called Gloria on her alcohol intake, nor steady diet of benzodiazepine, muscle relaxants, and anything else she could coerce her pill-factory doctor into prescribing. For those of means, the world is an oyster shell filled with opiates.

Enough was enough.

"Mom, you're drunk." Then to Richard: "Pack whatever she needs—"

"How dare you," Gloria seethed. "Who do you think you are? Talking to me like that—"

Cam addressed Richard, palms open, cards on table. "I'm going to ask you something, man to man. I got a message today. A tip that said you and Mark Burns were attempting to extort Alan Barrett for money." He paused. "By holding Jess."

"Of all the outrageous, slanderous…" Gloria stopped mid-sentence, unable to harness the requisite vocabulary to illustrate how offended she was.

Lydia turned to Cam. "Shane told you that?"

"No," Cam answered, eyes still fixed on Richard. "An email. Later. Anonymous. Just before you showed up."

"You never told me that," Lydia said.

Without missing a beat: "Not sure you want to throw stones, Lydia."

The doorbell rang.

"Richard," Cam said, "I need to hear it from you. You tell me it isn't true, good enough for me."

No one moved. Not Gloria, huffing and panting, in between reaching for wine; not Richard, who held her up, locked in a death stare with Cam; nor Lydia who remained standing still, observing, searching for clues before all evidence was destroyed.

After the bell rang a second time, Lydia peeled off from the conversation.

When she opened the door, seeing Maureen Gearon standing there wasn't the biggest surprise. Lydia had left a message, explaining where she'd be. Of course Maureen would drive into the valley, risking a wildfire to make sure she was okay.

The real shock was the man who materialized behind her, emerging across a charred battlefield triumphant, unable to hide the look of smug satisfaction on his face.

The mouthpiece that started it all.

The Rider on the Plain.

The Moth.

Shane Ellet.

CHAPTER FORTY-TWO

NOW, The End, Pt. II

Shane came up beside Maureen, standing there on the porch, both framed by the encroaching fires burning in spread-out patches, consuming brushland, painting the hillside in swirling European oils, all Halloween orange and chimney red. The flames had made it over the crest.

"Are you two together?" Lydia asked.

"I don't know this man." Maureen peered over her shoulder. "He was pulling in as I was parking."

Shane didn't say anything, but the look in his eyes told a different story. "Yes," he said, correcting Maureen's version of events. "I mean, I followed her here."

Lydia interpreted Shane's statement to mean he'd used Maureen's taillights as a guide. The large house sat below the road, its view obscured by woolly yarrow and blue fescue. There was scant streetlight. With the hills burning, you couldn't see twenty feet into the lowlands through the thickening smoke. Lydia didn't have time to reexamine her assumption, before Shane breezed past Maureen, beyond Lydia, entering the house without being invited, joining the rest of the party. He looked frazzled, fried, mismatched clothes untucked and wrinkled, as if he'd pulled an all-nighter before the big exam. There was something else in his eyes, a glimmer not present during their night over pie and coffee at Bob's Big Boy Broiler. Lydia couldn't read what that was. Shane couldn't stop himself from grinning. *How high was he?*

The heat in the room swelled, temps now sweltering. Lydia removed her windbreaker, wrapping the gun from her waistband in it, setting the scrunched bunch on the counter. She fanned the air around her face. It felt like the thermometer had risen ten degrees in ten seconds.

Cam's phone buzzed and he glanced down, catching Lydia's eyes first. "County's issued an evacuation order for Pasa Ardo. Effective immediately."

Gloria, white wine in hand, eyelids fluttering open and shut like a faulty camera shutter, said, "I'm not going anywhere."

"Don't be stubborn," Richard said.

"Oh, shut up, Dickie."

"Why did you leave the apartment?" Maureen asked Lydia, who had started coughing. "You need to rest."

Lydia backed away. "I have too much on my mind right now, Mo."

"Yes, you are dealing with a serious head injury." Maureen motioned toward Cam. "You heard him. Evacuation order. Smell that smoke? That's why you're coughing. I listened to the radio on the way over here. The fire breached containment. Where's your car?" She gazed out the large paned windows, now opaque and fogged with smoke, an impenetrable wall sealing off borders north, east, and west. You could feel its heat on the other side of the glass, like putting your hand against an oven on broil. "Never mind," Maureen said. "I'll drive you home."

"What are you doing here?" Cam asked Shane.

"You were right," Shane said. "When you stopped me the other night."

Lydia, bent over, hands on knees, glanced up. "When you said you 'reached out,' I didn't realize you pulled him over."

"I wanted to talk to him. After we met for lunch. When you told me about his internet show and what he was saying about me."

"I deleted the episodes," Shane said.

"I'm grateful." Cam didn't appear grateful.

Lydia stood, wiping sweat and surveying the dysfunction. You had Cam and Shane and their antagonistic dance in an ongoing feud, clipped conversation an iceberg theory on display, seven-eighths contextual backstory hidden below the surface. Whatever their beef, Shane appeared ready to make amends—had sought out Cam to do so, in fact, as natural disaster lay waste to the land. You can apologize over the phone via simple text or email. If Shane got his hands on the altered autopsy report, he'd met with Donnie. So where was the necklace Ricky stole from the evidence room? That piece of evidence was far more damning. Against Cam. *Unless Shane had changed his mind, had come to believe that someone else was involved in her sister's death…* Either way, Cam wasn't accepting olive branches. Maureen had also made the trek—a much longer one—slogging L.A. gridlock, over the mountains and through the valley, driving straight into the storm. No surprise. Maureen Gearon would move heaven and hell to make sure Lydia was all right. All the while, Richard Fontaine pleaded with Queen Gloria, who posed center stage, demanding all eyes on her, every huff, moan, and hand gesticulation delivered with an Oscar-worthy performance. Given the bizarre dynamic, Lydia half expected her father and Heather to pop in any minute.

Cam clapped his hands, drawing attention, corralling troops. Speaking to Richard: "You have bags packed? All your things?"

"Dickie doesn't *have* any things. He doesn't live here. He works here."

"Jesus, Mom—"

"Oh, *I'm* the problem? We live where it never rains, some idiot flicks a lit cigarette into dry grass, and this is my fault?"

"No one said it's your fault. There is a fire. We have to leave—"

"I was wrong to accuse Cam," Shane said, broadcasting to the room, catching up to a conversation two minutes ago.

"All good." Cam slashed a hand through the air. "Apology accepted—"

"I was wrong to accuse you," Shane repeated, sliding past Gloria, stepping to Cam, halting further objections before the town cop could raise them. "But I wasn't wrong about Jess being murdered—"

"We know," Lydia said, interrupted before she could supply the name Mark Burns.

"Who are you?" Gloria asked Shane. "How *dare* you mention my daughter's name—"

Maureen waved her arms above her head, trying to seize control. "The man responsible has been caught," she said, piggybacking on what Lydia had started to say, only to be cut off as well.

"My name is Shane Ellet. I used to have a radio show—"

"You never had a radio show," Cam said. "You illegally hijacked airwaves, violated a dozen FCC laws, and if your folks didn't hire an expensive legal team to bail your ass out, you'd still be in prison. But people like you don't go to prison, do they, Shane? Rider. Moth. Whatever stupid nickname you've made up for yourself this time. Dude, you're the same age as me. Forty-two is too old to be acting like a punk."

"I'm forty-one."

"No one cares. Stop smoking weed."

"I'm going to get the bags," Richard said.

Watching Richard walk away, Lydia felt that tickle at the base of her skull, intuition on high alert, zeroing in on minutia like pace of steps and tone of voice. She tried to remain open-minded to Cam's theory, however rogue or far-fetched. Maybe Mark Burns didn't work alone. Maybe snatching Jess wasn't his idea. Lydia wasn't ruling out a partner. But watching old Richard Fontaine plod down the long hallway, she couldn't accept his being involved, in any capacity. It had nothing to do with logistics or denial, and everything to do with his character. She could sniff out an actor playing a part, separate real tears from the manufactured variety. Sights, sounds, sixth senses. Then again, right now, how could Lydia trust any of her senses? Eyes tearing, skin flushed, she could taste the burn.

The fire continued its methodical march, propelled by a dry, desert heat, like a bucket of water had been poured on desiccated wood in a sauna, steam sucked up before it could rise, suffocating feeble attempts to inhale.

"Yeah," Shane said, "you're right," this time conversing with carcinogenic air. "I didn't have any 'show.' Not radio. Not TV. My whole life I've lived off my parents' money, getting stoned in their guest house, pretending I was a journalist. I wasted my life."

"Thanks for sharing," Cam said. "Tell it to your group counselor." He offered an affirming thumbs-up. "I'm sure this will be a real turning point in your life."

"Why do you hate me so much?"

"Besides accusing me of killing my ex-girlfriend?"

Gloria tilted her head. "You never *dated* my daughter."

"Mrs. Barrett, don't you remember how often I was over at your house?"

"Don't call me that! Do not! Do not! Do not! I am *not* 'Mrs. Barrett'! I haven't been married to that sonofabitch for twenty-eight years!" Then to the smoky heavens: "The *happiest* twenty-eight years of my life! The *best* decision I ever made!" Gloria made for the white wine, which was empty. Ignoring the chatter and commotion behind her, she staggered to the pantry to open a new toasty bottle.

Lydia' face beat red, mortified. Gloria's memory wasn't slipping. Her dismissal of Cam as an ex-boyfriend had nothing to do with diminished faculties or illusions Jess died a pristine virgin. Gloria was exclusive, an elitist, classist. A racist.

From down the hallway returned Richard, laboring with two heavy suitcases, overstuffed with rainbows of fabrics pinched in the zipper.

Flashing a cursory glance, Gloria dropped ice cubes in her chardonnay. "I told you, Dickie. I am not leaving my house—"

With that, the power went out, all light extinguished.

Lydia's heart beat faster. She wasn't alone, which kept the worst of the anxiety at bay, but the panic remained along the peripheral, taunting, threatening, and Lydia had to focus on her breathing, already no easy task, or risk being swallowed by the void.

Beyond the big glass wall, forked flames devoured blue beaked yuccas and buckeye, timbering sweet bay, swallowing deciduous valley oak whole. Lydia sought out the fire, willing her eyes to adjust to its light. She needed the hellish inferno as a beacon to lock onto. She couldn't let her phobia get the best of her now.

"Mrs. Barrett—" Cam caught himself. "Gloria. You are getting in Richard's truck. Or the back of a squad car. Your call. Either way, you are leaving. Now. We can finish this conversation at the evacuation site or behind bars."

Lydia's balance started to waver. Maureen tried to grab her hand, but Lydia shook her off. She needed to concentrate on her breathing, keep count in her head, her only defense to stave off darkness' tightening grip.

"Evacuation site?" Gloria said. "If you think I am crowding into some gymnasium, shoulder to shoulder with illegals, you're as delusional as him." Gloria didn't specify which *him* she was referring to.

"Then drive to Beverly Hills," Cam said. "Pick a five-star hotel. The Ritz, Wilshire. I don't care. But get in a vehicle and drive away from the fires, understood?"

Richard came beside Gloria, trying to take her arm, an effort she initially rejected, before relenting.

"We're right behind you," Maureen said.

During these assaults by the dark, Lydia's mind could lose focus. Getting her mother out the door safely was a welcomed distraction. "Do you need me to get anything?" Lydia said. "Keepsakes? In case—"

"Get anything? Yes, Lydia." Her mother's voice imbued with disgust. "Everything! I want it all! This is *my* house!"

"The photo albums are in the guest room," Richard said. "First floor. End of the hall, on the left. The blue room." He looked at the thin wall separating them from the encroaching blaze. "Insurance will cover any other loss—"

"Insurance, Dickie? You can be so obtuse sometimes." Gloria snagged the bottle of white to take with her. Richard let it go, like he always did. It was the only way to survive life with Gloria.

"Get those books," Cam said at the door. "You don't have long before every road out of here will be blocked. Meet us at the precinct. That's seven miles south, atop the hill. It'll buy us time. We'll know more about the fire's path and expected arrival."

Gloria muttered she wasn't going to a police station. Lydia confirmed she'd be there. Cam pulled open the door, and there it was, tall columns of flame, climbing, marching over the ridge, seizing high ground.

Lydia watched as Cam herded Gloria and Richard outside.

"I'll help you get those photobooks," Maureen said to Lydia, who stared at the closing door, wondering what Cam was going to do. Was he really going to let Richard drive away if he suspected him? Or was the evacuation a ruse to get Richard to the station? Cam didn't believe her mother had anything to do with this, did he? *She didn't, did she?*

Shane remained in the middle of the room, silent, ignored, rendered all but invisible. No one had told him to leave or stay, as if his fate was the least of anyone's concern.

Maureen wrapped her arm around Lydia's waist, guiding both toward the guest room and the photo albums, Lydia peering over her shoulder at Shane, who stood stone-like.

"I followed her here," he said.

Lydia stopped moving. *Shane wasn't talking about using Mo's brakes as guiding lights.*

He pointed at Maureen. "I've been following her for the past twenty-four hours."

Maureen's mouth dropped, gobsmacked. "Why on Earth would you be following—"

In the dark, Shane counted on his fingers. "Maybe twelve? I suck at math. I saw you talking to that black detective. Not Cam. The other one, in the suit, outside that hotel downtown."

"I don't have any idea—"

"I could've been a journalist," Shane said. "If I applied myself. I can write. I see what others don't." He breathed heavily out his mouth, halting a coughing fit. "I've always been lazy. Took the easy way. Shortcuts. Any advantage or exception I could exploit. The right way was too hard. I liked admiration, lacked ambition. Didn't care about respect. That's not a good formula."

Lydia flashed between him and Maureen, before returning to Shane, wondering if she was witnessing a breakdown. Hair unkempt, big bags and dark circles under his eyes, pallid face refracting flickering yellow, orange, and red, he embodied a madman, one of the myriad ragged individuals you found throughout Los Angeles County. Bedraggled, broken, a shell of a former human being pushing a shopping cart, muttering nonsensical obscenities, grinning like a fool during dire negotiations with the invisible.

"Shane," Lydia said, voice calm and compassionate. "I can see you're going through something. I am happy to listen. Once we are safe—"

"*El Capitan!*" Shane said. "That was the hotel." He pointed at Maureen. "Where I saw her and the detective."

The SRO where they found Mark Burns' body? Black detective? Not Cam. *Detective Terry Williams from the hospital.*

"That thing your mom said—" Shane continued, striding closer, standing taller.

"I think this can wait for another time," Maureen interrupted, so stern and maternal, Lydia prepped for the ultimate school marm dismissal, "young man."

"—about hating her married name." Shane was undeterred. "It was ironic. Or should I say well-timed?"

Lydia realized she'd been mistaken. She wasn't witnessing a breakdown; this was a comeback.

Maureen yanked her arm, trying to tug her to the guest room. "That man is crazy."

Lydia remained rooted. "What are you talking about, Shane?"

"That's how this started. How I figured it out." He pointed at Maureen, chuckling to himself. "It wasn't hard. Sure, it was buried—a good lawyer can fix a lot of shit. Trust me, I know. Brad Pearce and I shared the same one. Well, not the same *lawyer* but the same firm. I just had to send an email. Took some persuading. A long phone call. Believe it or not..." He laughed. "I can be charming when I have to be.

Once I established that connection, the rest was *so* obvious." Staring at Maureen, Shane showed his hand. "I don't have any proof, so I'm not accusing you of anything. Not yet. But it would be one weird coincidence—"

Lydia stepped to him. "Whatever you're trying to say, say it." She stabbed a finger out the smoky glass wall, into the firestorm engulfing the night. "I'd rather not get burned alive."

"Her last name," Shane responded. "She changed it back to Gearon after the divorce."

Lydia waited on Maureen, who said nothing.

"Maureen Gearon is Brad Pearce's ex-wife."

CHAPTER FORTY-THREE

THEN, Two Weeks Ago, Saturday, July 9, 2016, 8:12 a.m.

"When does Dan get back?" Maureen rolled out of bed, slipping the robe up over her naked shoulders, glancing back. The ascending morning light in the cottage shown perfectly off the smooth linen sheets, the gentle folds, the gradation of easy slopes.

"Week and a half or so," Rhona said, barely covered and unashamed. "Conference. New Orleans. The girls are at a friend's house." She laughed. "Not that they worry about where Dan or I go these days. Might as well be living on their own. They're seldom home over the summer."

"How is Dan?"

"Busy. Working on a new patent."

There was no animosity toward Dan Clarion, neither from Maureen nor his wife Rhona. The married couple was at an age where they'd made the transition from lovers to friends to coworkers, wrapping up the contractual obligation of raising children, sleeping in separate beds, a business agreement. Dan seemed to have lost interest in her sexually years ago. Not that Dan would've condoned infidelity any more than Rhona would. Neither asked the question nor sought the answer. Maureen understood. Rhona longed for intimacy, the transformative power of the human touch but without the strain of dependency or impediments on freedoms. They were the same that way, Rhona and Maureen.

They'd met several years ago. Both worked for Los Angeles County, if in unrelated capacities. Their paths didn't cross. Until one night they did. A random fundraiser at the MacArthur. That's how the Universe works. A chance meeting at a social function. Stars lining up. Time. Confluence. Objective chance. A disorderly pattern that adhered to a strict set of rules we are not meant to understand. They didn't keep their relationship secret out of shame or because of any taboo—this wasn't the 1940s. Rhona was married, and Maureen? She relished her privacy, seeing no reason to broadcast whom she was sleeping with any more than she'd snap a picture of what she was having for dinner to share with strangers on the internet. That was the nice part of growing up, not needing to seek the approval of others.

There was a myth about the way men aged being more dignified, their wrinkles adding an air of regality, sophistication. Anderson Cooper was a silver fox. Kathleen Turner stopped receiving movie offers. Women were supposed to fade away sexually, cast adrift on the cold seas like aged Eskimos on an ice floe, frigid and forgotten. To Maureen, Rhona grew more beautiful every day.

"You are amazing," Rhona said.

Maureen didn't shy from the compliment, peering over her shoulder, with eyes that said she felt the same about her lover.

Hollywood sold the glamour of sex, glossing over its messy realities. In movies it was flawless physical specimens or, more accurately their body doubles, a comingling of the best flesh choreographed with appropriate sultry soundtrack. There were none of the embarrassing parts, the sounds and odors, the escaping air, soiled sheets or damp spots.

Maureen Gearon had lived a full life, robust with lovers, men, women. Gender had little to do with it. That's what made what she and Rhona had so special. Having someone you could trust with your whole heart and life. At this stage? A rare, precious gem.

The cottage where the two had been meeting belonged to Maureen, a rental property, one of several she owned, which she never rented out. They met when they could. There was no pressure for more. A mutually beneficial arrangement. They cherished their time together. And savored their solitude apart. The relationship worked because of how in sync those needs were.

"Macchiato?" Maureen asked, walking to the kitchen, opening the fridge, already retrieving the organic whole milk and raw cane sugar, sweet, coarse molasses crystals that would melt like fire-torched crème brulee in the hot foam. You could only find the special beans at the farmer's market on Sunday. Maureen could admit it: she was a coffee snob.

The rental property sat in Laurel Canyon, modest but not lacking style, tucked off the road, secluded in the forest, which added to its fairy-tale aesthetic. A home away from home for Maureen, who found peace here, with or without Rhona, solace unavailable at her main residence in Hidden Hills in the city. Like a less neurotic Winnie the Pooh, she considered the cottage her thinking place. She kept several personal items here—computer, books, writings. Sometimes Maureen wondered why she didn't sell her big house and move here. She didn't need the money, for one. And if she were being honest, she liked the big house on the hill, the status symbol and prestige it invited, which owed more to birthright than profession.

"What's work looking like?" Rhona asked from the bedroom.

"Death?" Maureen responded, deadpan, a form of gallows' humor that earned a polite chuckle, as she ground the beans, the full-bodied aroma of kopi luwak, robust enough to rouse the dead.

Maureen frothed the milk, expressed the beans to crema, filled two tiny cups, and returned with them on small saucers.

Maureen passed along the macchiato. "Lydia's coming in to assist me, this week or next."

"Any closer to filling those big shoes?" Rhona smiled.

"She will," Maureen replied with confidence. "Someday."

"Soon?"

"I hope." Maureen slipped back into bed, unable to hide the pride she felt toward her protégé, steam rising from the rich, creamy milk, sugar caramelizing on top.

"You act like she's your daughter." Rhona shut her eyes, an oversell of how good that first cup in the morning was. Or maybe her expression perfectly captured the moment.

A lazy Saturday of Ranwick Bells, SoCal sunlight slicing slats and coffee in bed. Did it get any better?

Maureen slid closer, allowing Rhona to rest her head on her shoulder, stroking her hair. "In a lot of ways, she is."

Rhona sipped her hot cup, silent but glancing up, a foreign, uncertain expression puzzling her face. "There's still so much I don't know about you."

Maureen didn't have a response. There was much she didn't know about Rhona. That was part of the appeal she supposed, the air of secrecy, or rather mystery. Once the mystery is gone, there's nothing left to solve. That unknown quantity was to be celebrated. Keeps the spark alive. Familiarity breeding contempt. This morning, however, Maureen felt lured to be more open, forthright. Perhaps this was how not to stagnate a relationship. Don't hold back *too* much. There was a fine line between independence and making your partner feel unessential.

Maybe it was the good coffee on an empty stomach, the perfect mix of dopamine and serotonin that comes with caffeine and postcoital bliss. Maureen felt like talking.

A wave of silver sun highlighted the curve of Rhona's body beneath the white sheet. Maureen sat up on the bed, cradling Rhona's head in her lap.

"What would you like to know?" Maureen said.

"I've told you about my daughters," Rhona said. "Tell me about Lydia."

"She's a remarkable young woman. Like you said, the daughter I never had."

"Do you regret that? Never having had a child? A biological one, I mean. Of your own." Rhona halted, fearing she'd overstepped bounds.

Sensing this, Maureen assured her all was fine.

"What was his name again?" Rhona asked. "When you were married?"

"That was so long ago, I was a different person."

Maureen didn't hate him. Not anymore. He was long gone. True, for a while she harbored resentment. Not over the money. Or even the time and house he stole. It was the dignity he took. He was like a cancer that never went into remission. Even after he threw her away, he'd reappear, catching her when she was weak, worming his way back into her life. He was a master at manipulation. He'd come calling after his latest disgrace, bailed out yet again by family money and clout, swearing he'd changed, begging for another chance. She couldn't say no to him. She never stopped loving him. If he was the disease, her unwavering devotion and willingness to forgive was its worst symptom.

But a heart can only break so much.

That last time pushed her over the edge. She was already entrenched in her career, a respected woman of power in the Los Angeles medical community. Through all his head games, she never lost sight of that, rising above the hurt and the pain, remaining focused, eyes on prize, until she came out on top. Chief medical examiner. She was a survivor. And then he did it again. One last summer of tainted love and promises broken before he took that teaching job, doing what he did best: conning impressionable kids with heroic tales of antinomianism, seducing young girls with cult leader precision. He got his, though, she made sure of it. There was poetry in the broken neck. All these years later, she could admit she may have lost her mind there for a while. Now that she'd found it again.

Rhona waited for Maureen to say more, to answer her specific question. This was an opportunity to grow closer.

"I don't regret a thing in my life," Maureen said. "Lydia, for all intents and purposes, is my child. Her parents…" Maureen punctuated the statement with a hard, remorseful stop.

"Not in the picture?"

"No, they are. Unfortunately. Which takes its toll on Lydia." Maureen cradled her palms around the coffee, inhaling its earthy fragrance.

"How did you two meet?" Rhona asked.

Maureen didn't think about that part often, the complicated origin of their lifelong bond, suppressing it, burying it. Funny, how from small mistakes big things grow. Collateral damage that allowed splendor and beauty to bloom, blossom, flourish. One little sin… Since coming into Lydia's life, Maureen had more than made amends for what she'd taken.

Rhona gazed up at Maureen. "What is it?"

"What do you mean?"

"Your face … it grew sad, baby." Rhona slipped out of Maureen's lap, sitting up, taking her hand. "Talk to me."

Maureen had never told anyone, had never spoken about that night, the jealousy consuming her. The weeks, months of stalking him. Her. Like a comic book villain in a ballcap and sunglasses, on the boardwalk, at the high school, the water tower, after he said he couldn't love her, could never love her, watching him with those girls. And that's what they were: girls. Not women. Girls. *That* girl. That one girl. He always came back after the others. This one was different. This one he said he loved. She couldn't let him do that. She'd wanted to make it right, see the sick bastard pay. Only a sicker part of Maureen still loved him, or rather was under his spell. Control. A form of emotional abuse. Years of keeping it in, trusting no one…

Gazing into Rhona's loving eyes, secured by her tender touch, Maureen longed for someone with whom she could share the tremendous onus. She'd carried it for years, decades, all alone. Was it time? *Unburden yourself.* A confessional. Maureen didn't have religion. There was no priest. She didn't believe in magic men with white beards sitting on clouds surrounded by winged creatures playing the harp. She enjoyed fairy tales. She didn't live by them.

"Baby," Rhona said, looking deathly serious. "You know you can trust me? You can tell me anything."

Wouldn't that be nice…

CHAPTER FORTY-FOUR

The End, Pt. III

You could hear the fire crackling, consuming the hillside's parched kindling in the dry, acrid winds, the lack of movement suffocating in its stillness. Cam had set a speculative timer, a guesstimation of how long they had until the conflagration swallowed them, but time seemed to hold, issue a stay of execution, sizzling meat removed from a burner, gas stove left on. Time never stops. There are no reprieves. There is only stalling the inevitable.

That was the logical, reasonable part of Lydia Barrett's brain talking, the prefrontal cortex, interior frontal gyrus, the temporal lobe, that prudent parts of the human mind responsible for making sound decisions based on science and not swayed by impulse.

The left side of her brain didn't stand a chance.

Smoke continued to infiltrate, dry ice on the concert floor, choking the air. The dark shows no mercy.

Lydia didn't think about Brad Pearce often. She knew, of course, what everyone later learned, rumors of Pearce's inappropriate sexual relationship with Jess, innuendo most certainly true if never proven in the court of law. They'd found Jess' writings. She never wrote "Brad" anywhere. She wrote of Cam and Rider. Brad was always "he" or "the one," a nameless entity that would never be confirmed because Jess Barrett went missing before her eighteenth birthday, was found dead after it. Jess had been their best chance of putting a pedophile and sexual predator behind bars. Then Brad Pearce removed any hope of justice when he slid that loop around his neck and kicked out the chair.

This was what Lydia was thinking, the rippling butterfly effect of carnage one man left behind, trying to hold steady, remain calm and not let her anxiety get the best of her.

With all these swirling thoughts, Lydia, as she so often had, turned to Maureen for guidance, advice on how to proceed. Mo was her glue, her rock. She would make this all right. But Maureen had left her side, turned her back on Lydia. She appeared to glide across the floor, weightless, ghost-like, until she reached the counter by Lydia's scrunched-up windbreaker. Hallucinations were a side effect of the nyctophobia. Lydia knew she couldn't trust her own eyes. But that's what Mo looked like to her in the moment: an apparition.

Lydia waited, silently begged for reassurance from Maureen that what Shane had said was a lie, one big misunderstanding. Brad Pearce's ex-wife? Not possible. For starters, Lydia knew Maureen was gay. Or had she inferred that? What did Lydia know about Maureen's life, sex, personal, or otherwise? For as close as the two were, Lydia always sensed a part of Maureen remained cloistered, sealed, closed off.

"Mo?"

Maureen lifted her head, craned her neck, slowly meeting Lydia's gaze. One look in Maureen's eyes confirmed everything Shane said had been the truth. This was why he'd offered up the autopsy report but not the necklace and locket. *Only one person was guilty.*

"They'd already gotten divorced by the time he was teaching here." Shane pulled out a tiny notebook from his back pocket, a reporter's timeline. "It's a little unclear. Because I think they were still living together. Off and on, even after the split. They had a house in San Francisco—"

"*I* had a house in San Francisco," Maureen said, breaking her silence. "Marina District. Two million. Worth five times that now. Stolen. I was too naïve to have a prenuptial agreement. Brad came from money. Lots of money. Inherited a fortune when his parents died young. Played the poor little orphan card. And he made even more money by stealing it. A born grifter." Maureen spun around to face Lydia, earnest, yearning for understanding. "He had done this before."

"This?" Lydia weighted the word with expectation bound to disappoint. *This? Seduced women, stole their money, took young hearts, destroyed lives? Raped? Murdered?*

The bright orange and hellish reds from the blaze refracted off the windows, glass, and other shiny objects, a kaleidoscope of the warmest colors on the palette wheel alighting the room. Smacking off ivory lamps and copper sculptures, the gaudy gilded golden frames of American splendor, nature's viciousness and impartiality boasting its inability to be tamed.

Now you could see the brushfire eating the garden, the tool shed, barn, cabana, where flame met the concrete walkway of the pool, before splintering off in furious directions to devour more flowers, trees, weeds, and other wild things.

"We should go," Maureen said.

Lydia didn't respond, couldn't move.

The two women stared at one another, the eyes of each aching to convey more than eyes or words ever could.

"All I wanted to do was make it right," Maureen said.

Lydia stared at her former mentor and role model. In the smoke, she looked aethereal, her silver hair and visage displayed the dignity of aging gracefully, no toxic fillers like Gloria, each imperfection only adding to her natural beauty. Then something strange happened. As Maureen came closer, she adopted a more concrete, earthly form but her perfect posture and poise began to break down, shoulders curling forward, spine contorting crooked, a body collapsing in on itself, head unable to be held high, a witch shriveled by a bucket of truth.

"It wasn't the money Brad took." Maureen's composure continued to erode, which was shocking to witness because if there was one thing Maureen Gearon always possessed it was composure, class, grace under fire. "He stole so much more." In front of Lydia's eyes, the tall, elegant woman she admired, revered, and thought she knew, appeared to tie herself in knots, compacted bones gnarled. Lydia knew it was a trick of the brain, perception and reality impacted by the gravity of the situation and her condition. But she saw what she saw.

Lydia turned to Shane, a pleading look to say he'd been mistaken. Despite Maureen's admissions, a part of Lydia was insistent he must be wrong. If Shane could retract his claims, then those allegations wouldn't be out there, none of it true. Life, as Lydia knew it, would continue.

Shane couldn't do that.

Which forced Lydia to confront this new world order as remnants of the old one burned down around her.

"He wasn't as young as he told people," Maureen said. "He lied about everything. Brad lied about lying. He was incapable of being honest. I wasn't that much older." She stopped, momentarily transfixed by the fire beyond the glass wall before her voice escalated in urgency. "He was a student of mine. Did you know that? One semester. Long ago. While I was teaching in grad school." Maureen laughed, an unhinged, shrill skreich. "Your sister wasn't the first. He did this to others. Brad was a predator. He glommed onto anyone willing to try and love him, until he sucked them dry, peeled off remains, tossed them aside like garbage.

He was assured but unassuming, gregarious and charming, so beautiful. When you were under his spell, you never saw a creature so beautiful…" Her voice tailed off as Maureen's soft gaze shifted to the now blinding light. "Such a fantastic lover."

"Mo, I don't understand—"

"I wanted to make it right. It was a confluence of timing, events, a…"

"Coincidence?"

Maureen smiled. It was a sad smile all the same. "No," she said, admitting the truth that had been there all along to see, how Lydia had been duped, bought, manipulated.

"I sought you out," Maureen said. "I was on the board. You did well in science. I could help, financially—"

"We had money."

"I know. But a scholarship—you earned that."

"Did I?"

"Of course! You were brilliant. It felt like destiny."

"Which part, Mo? Where you strangled my sister, killed Rhona Clarion? Mark Burns?"

Shane reached for Lydia's hand, taking hold, urging her toward the door, until Maureen brought up the gun, the one she'd pulled from beneath Lydia's windbreaker, and everyone froze.

"Oh, honey," Maureen said. "You have the story all wrong. No, that's not how it happened. Rhona Clarion did work with Mark Burns. And a lot of other derelicts. I knew Rhona. Well. We had … dinner … often."

Lydia was putting it together but didn't get the chance to finish before Maureen grew impatient.

"We were … close! She kept notes. I had access to her computer files. I picked Mark Burns at random. He was a nobody. When I saw he worked for your family, I had an out. Dates didn't exactly add up. No one was going to scrutinize. A means to an end."

"But why—?"

"Yours won't be the only number they find in Rhona's cell phone records. I needed to wrap this up quickly."

Behind them, beyond the home's north wall, a structure collapsed, the roof from the shed or maybe the detached barn Richard used to store lawn equipment. It was a loud, startling sound, the crash a sonic boom, whooshing a rushing wave of heat.

"If Rhona hadn't called you…" Maureen sighed. "That was difficult. I should've known better. I opened my heart."

"To confess?"

"I didn't tell her anything." Maureen's eyes began to tear up, the gun shaky in her old, clawed hands, arms sagging under the weight. "I didn't have to. Rhona spent a lot of time at my place. She was jealous of my relationship with you. She snooped. Found something I'd written a long time ago. Her decision to call you was … unfortunate. When I found out…" A single tear ran down Maureen's face. Remorse? Or was it sweat from the heat? "It was an accident."

"What was—"

"Rhona fell. We'd been arguing."

"You strangled her. Like you did my sister."

"No, she fell."

"Who? Jess? Rhona?"

"Rhona hit her head on the edge of the bed…"

"And Jess?"

"Both were … accidents."

After that, Maureen's entire disposition changed, no longer emotional, switching to clinical M.E. mode, matter of fact, detached, arm and hand suddenly straight, steady, stiff. "The rest was easy. I have friends on the force. Men like the ones you met, Terry Williams. This is L.A. We take care of our own. Sometimes you need to cut corners to ensure justice. You were never meant to get hurt. Just scared off. Losers like Mark Burns die every day. He was barely alive as it was. We did him a favor putting him out of his misery. I knew you'd recover Rhona's body. It was your jurisdiction. I could manage that part."

"Everything Cam said about Richard hiring Burns. All that business about holding a girl in a shed for days—"

"A story." Maureen sighed, waved it off, a senseless tragedy effortlessly explained. "An anonymous email to a small-town rube," she said, before turning to Shane, the silent observer, watching this unfold, the repercussions his revelation had unraveled. "You," she said, shaking the gun like a strict teacher's ruler. "You?" That was her only question to Shane. *You? Of all the people to be outsmarted by, of all the minor inconveniences, inconsequential, irrelevant, pains in the ass...*

"Lydia, dear, we need to go," Maureen said. "We'll talk about this later."

"Later?" Lydia's eyes grew wide.

Maureen took a step toward her.

Lydia retreated. "I'm not going anywhere with you."

Maureen maintained her sad smile as she lowered the gun to her side, the expression on her face a mix of heartache and silent resignation. Even now, Lydia wanted to reach out, fix this, rewind time and bring back better days. But time doesn't work like that. It moves forward.

Shane, whose hand still clutched Lydia's, tugged, impelling them toward the door, a gesture that made Maureen blurt out laughing for some reason.

"I was supposed to meet Brad at the water tower that night," she said, unable to walk, body bent, twisted, crooked. "He had remained up

in San Francisco, staying with his friends in *my* house in the Marina."
Maureen lifted her gaze and that sad smile morphed into petty smirk.
"I never got it back, that house. But he got his."

"He didn't really hang himself, did he?"

Maureen didn't answer right away. She didn't have to. The hyoid
bone broke in a hanging or strangulation just the same. If an M.E.
wasn't looking for murder…

When Mo finally did speak, her face lit up with sick delight. "Lifeless
body swaying from the ceiling, final moments spent in agony. It's like
God Himself had intervened, cast His judgment, working through me.
A hellish, unspeakable way to go. If I ever allow myself to think of him,
that's the part I like best."

Lydia had so many questions, about Rhona Clarion, Mark Burns,
Jess. Maureen was trying to rewrite history, reorder events, disrupt the
narrative and picture that had taken so long to assemble. Lydia turned
to Shane, whose YouTube channel, *Night Shade*, a program about mystery and dying, started the closure Lydia didn't know was possible.
Speculation. Conjecture. Clues. They were all there. They had been there
all along, and they would still be there, left to be compiled and reassem-
bled later. Lydia could do that part. That was her job. What she needed
now was to hear how her sister died. And they were out of time.

Maureen didn't need the prompt. "We moved in the same … circles.
Brad and I. Financially. No matter how hard I tried to avoid him, I
could never leave him behind. Brad used me for years, coming in and
out of my life when convenient. Even after we were divorced and he
stole my house, humiliated me, he'd come back, usually after whatever
latest scandal he managed to buy his way out of, and I couldn't turn
him away. Can you imagine?" She cackled. "Look at me! I'm a successful woman." The shriveled, old thing withered further, a spine ravaged

by chronic scoliosis, arthritic hand tremoring, too weak to even hold the gun, which fell to the floor, landing on the hard wood with a thud. "That last time, the summer before he started teaching your sister, it was too much. It was like a game to him. To break me over and over. To get me to open my heart back up. I had money, prestige, respect. And here was this, this … I don't want to talk bad about your sister. But him? A charlatan, cad, whatever words kids these days use to describe men like that. Brad was a parasite. And *he* rejected *me*. For a high school girl. I saw *them*. More than once. It…" Eyes fixed on Lydia, desperate for understanding. "It broke me. It was beneath me. I lost my mind for a while there, I admit." Maureen held up her empty hands in the smoky air in mock surrender. "When Brad didn't show up at the water tower, I spied your sister leaving the party alone. I only wanted to talk to her."

"Why?"

"To help her! Like I've tried to help you! We women must stick together! Help one another! I planned to tell her what he was like. I tried. I tried talking to her. She laughed at me. Called me a sad, jealous old woman. Old? I was thirty-five. Ha! You're thirty-eight, Lydia. Tell me, do *you* feel old? But that girl, that little girl, that child, calling me old, after all I'd survived, after Brad had turned me away, again and again… The last thing I remember was…"

"What?" Lydia could barely speak through the wafting, curdling smoke.

"My hands around her throat."

Shane yanked Lydia's hand harder, pulling her to the door. The flames had collapsed the barn, chewing up the sky, climbing, consuming. You could hear ceiling beams starting to crack, dry wall splintering, foundation crumbling. "We have to leave!"

Together, they fled through the columns of flame to his Camry, fire blazing out of control all around them, licking skies. Trees, bushes, brushes, weeds, the boat on the side of the house, the garage, barn, shed, cabana, construction equipment all engulfed, save for the swimming pool shimmering, waves gently dancing in the backdraft.

Ducking inside the car, Lydia strapped in as Shane fired the engine, motor roaring. Shifting in reverse, he weaved backwards up the steep driveway, wheels taking air as he jammed the shaft forward.

Punching the car in overdrive, Shane pressed the pedal to the floor, tires squealing to gain traction, burning rubber on their way to freedom.

And just before they careened down the other side of the hill to safety, time and consequence seemed to grant a reprieve.

Lydia turned back toward her childhood home.

Maureen Gearon stood in the doorway, no longer bent and contorted but standing arrow straight, tall, proud, and elegant, shimmering silver hair lit aflame.

Lydia witnessed that grace, poise, and dignity as it was consumed by the fire.

ACKNOWLEDGEMENTS

Thank you to my lovely wife Justine and my two boys, Holden and Jackson Kerouac.

Thank you to my agent Jill Marsal, publicist Lisa Daily, and designer Christian Storm.

Thanks to my beta readers: Maureen Snow, Steven Davis, Suanne Schafer, Linda Bandy, and Charlotte Miller.

A shoutout to the rest: Melissa Greco, Kid Sofia, Celeste Bancroft and the Gang, and Lucky Dog, the greatest toy poodle a man has ever the privilege to know (I hope the old guy is still kicking by the time this makes it to press). Big hugs to everyone in the crime-writing community who helps prop me up when I feel like falling down.

And, lastly, a huge thank you to all my readers. A writer runs out of ways to say the same thing, but none of this is possible without you. As long as you keep reading 'em, I'll keep writing 'em...

We hope you enjoyed **A MOTH TO FLAME.**

Keep reading for an excerpt from the next
heart-pounding thriller from Joe Clifford,
I WON'T SAY A WORD

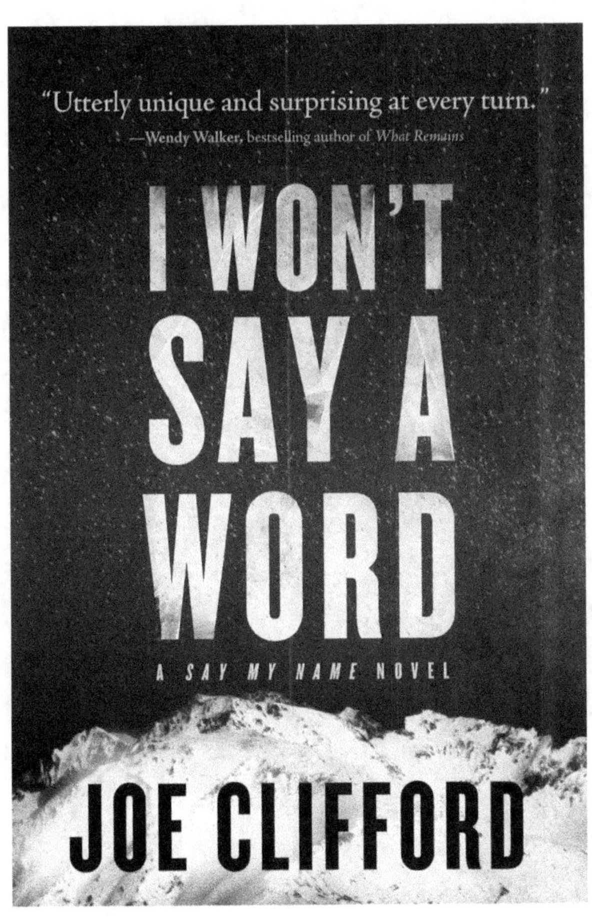

THE BEGINNING

ONE MORE CUP OF COFFEE BEFORE YOU GO

Today, Josh would put flowers on their mother's grave.

Jobs seldom delivered him this close to Bennington, Vermont, the small town where his mother Toni was born and now buried. Josh kept meaning to visit. At the end of each grueling day, he found new reasons not to. Sciatica flaring. Daylight fading. Depth charts to log, AA meetings to make. Bullshit excuses. Josh didn't visit Toni's tombstone because it would hurt too much. Especially sober. He didn't want to deal with the emotions it would dredge up—about his dead mother, his dead father, his big brother, who though technically alive was stuck in a hospital three thousand miles away with little hope of getting out.

The large diesel truck lumbered into the Shell Station on Farmington Ave., shuddering to idle in front of pump number eight. The early dawn sky glowed vibrant. Purples, reds, rose, orange. Sand layered in a mason jar. Like an art project when Emily was in elementary school. Now their baby girl was in college. White Mountain University. Her number one choice. Didn't even need a fallback. God, she was smart. A helluva imagination, too, a real gift for storytelling. Must've inherited the talent from her uncle, who had the way with the words. At least until the accident broke his brain. After work,

Josh needed to help Em finish that family tree project—providing the motel's wireless was working, which was no guarantee. A brainiac, Emily was already in New Hampshire, getting a head start on freshman year.

Slamming the door shut, Josh caught the company logo. For a second, he expected to see the familiar insignia for AC Victor.

You fucked that up.

These days Josh was back to being a regular employee on the clock. Paul was a good boss, JP Construction a good outfit. But JPC wasn't AC Victor, the drilling and splitting business Josh started and co-owned with his best friend, Freddie. Until drugs and alcohol grew into a beast too wild to tame.

Why was Josh doing this to himself? First thing on a Monday morning? Addiction, dead parents, brain-addled brother. Josh was staring at a long haul. Why add extra fuel to an already exorbitant guilt trip?

Josh slid the AmEx through the slot, flipping the gas cap, and jamming in the nozzle, prepared for the insatiable monster to gobble up a hundred-and-forty bucks' worth.

Stalking between islands, weaving beneath buzzing fluorescents, Josh shoved open the mini-mart door.

"What'll it be, pal?" the cashier, a man in his late fifties, asked. Must be new. For years, the same old lady, Betty, had greeted him behind the register. Why does everything have to change?

"Pack of Marlboro Lights." Then as if remembering he'd forgotten to take his heart medication, Josh added, "And a bottle of Advil," which was the strongest drug he was allowed to take for his perpetually barking back. "Oh, yeah, and a coffee."

An odd expression contorted the cashier's face. This early, they were the only two in the store. A strange tension filled the air. Probably sleep deprivation. Twelve-hour shifts were taking their toll.

The cashier pointed over the big guy's shoulder to the coffee station. "Made a fresh pot." He waited for a reaction. "Hear me? *Fresh* pot. For you!"

Josh flicked a thumbs up. *Okay, weirdo. Hazard of working the grave-yard. That much time in your head, you go insane. Just ask his brother.*

Outside, with his fresh coffee in hand, the early morning chilled, August dawn slow to warm. Josh toppled four Advil, popping them in his mouth, washing down the ibuprofen with scalding coffee. Replacing the nozzle—one hundred, thirty-nine dollars, and ninety-nine cents—Josh chuckled to himself. Back when his brother could read numbers, that figure would've triggered the hell out of his OCD.

The big guy climbed back into the big rumbler, pulling out of the lot, and making for the highway. GPS clocked the trip at three hours and change. Josh hated being away from his wife Amy, but it was nice knowing he wouldn't have to spend six hours behind the wheel. During the week, Josh stayed at motels up north, sparing himself the round trip back to Berlin, the heart of Central Connecticut—Berlin, like the one in Germany, but pronounced with the accent between syllables, like "pearl" and a preposition. And God forbid residents hear you pro-nounce it any other way.

Considering how badly he'd screwed up, Josh knew he should be grateful. To Paul, for giving him a second chance at JP Construction; to Debra, his father's second wife, and the closest thing to a mom Josh had left—his stepmother found the Bay Area Institute for People with Traumatic Brain Injury, paying for his big brother's care. Room, board, medical bills. A burden that lands on Josh's shoulder without Debra. He should be thanking her, not holding a grudge. That was the tough-est aspect of AA to stomach—besides the spiritual shit—gratitude. Josh didn't trust his stepmother, not after that funny business with the will. And once money is involved, family business only gets funnier.

Hitting the onramp for Route 9, Josh tamped down his pack of Marlboros. Thinking about family dynamics was giving him a headache. Even when his older brother *was* writing stories, he couldn't have dreamt up a crazier plot. Amy's maiden name was Fortman. It was a made-up family name, only a couple generations old; all Fortmans around here were related. Her father Andy started Fortman Brothers Construction, one of the biggest construction outfits in New England. Andy and his brother Ari—yes, *that* Ari Fortman. It was also the company his father Neil worked for when he contracted the myelofibrosis that killed him. Yeah, barbeques and family reunions were a blast.

Josh wished he could pin his dad's death on Ari—but by the time Neil was diagnosed, the slimeball attorney turned lobbyist was down in D.C., making in-roads, ascending Capitol Hill. And by the time Ari reached the promised land of Mar-a-Lago, Neil was dead. Truth was, there was no one *to* blame. Everyone got screwed on that deal, Andy included. The company charged with testing the soil failed to detect the radioactive materials. So, Dad and a lot of other workers had to die.

Shit happens. Then you die.

Gratitude? Fuck that. We survive.

If Emily hadn't sent those questions for her genealogy course, Josh wouldn't be thinking about any of it. Poking around the web, he'd expected to uncover a great great grandmother with Cherokee blood. Not this. Maybe it was inevitable, given the prominent stage his uncle-in-law Ari currently enjoyed. Is "uncle-in-law" even a thing? *Who knows? But "asshole" is.*

Connecting to Interstate 91, the big guy cracked the lid, steam rising. He fired up a smoke, first one of the day and the only high he was allowed to enjoy. Josh dialed in Howard Stern on Sirius XM, taking long, slow drags, waiting for the jolt that weirdo cashier promised.

The more coffee he drank, the more disoriented and sleepier he felt. Caffeine ain't got nothing on methamphetamine. Still, wasn't coffee supposed to *wake* you up?

Around Hartford city center, traffic slogged, lanes clogged. Riders and racing rats with the same idea to get an early start and beat the morning glut. Gridlock. Any delay would put a dent in the schedule. Paul would be pissed. This job had a hard deadline. Josh's new boss Paul was bankrolling a small empire in ski country. Vermont, New Hampshire, Southern Maine. Bretton Woods. Pats Peak. Sugarloaf. This current gig outside Magic Mountain? Third housing development this year. No rest for the rich. A lot of money to be made in those hills. Josh was hoping to see some of it. As soon as he finished crawling out of the red. What didn't go to Amy and family expenses got sucked up by bill collectors and whittling down credit card debt. Josh planned to start paying back Freddie the money he stole from AC Victor—as soon as he *had* extra money. When do we ever have "extra" money?

A wave of dizziness washed over Josh, and his lids fell heavy. Images, memories, invasive thoughts flooding…

Josh snapped to in time to slam on the brakes, only to have some nerd in a hybrid toot his tiny horn, shaking a furious fist. Looking down at the Connecticut River, Josh considered pulling over for a quick power nap. Power nap? At six in the morning?

Stop being a pussy…

Dad's voice never left his head. Just because people die doesn't mean they stop speaking to you.

Josh pushed aside the voices and memories. Only way to survive. You last long enough, you start to miss everyone. Not that forty-three was old.

Josh had his whole life ahead of him.

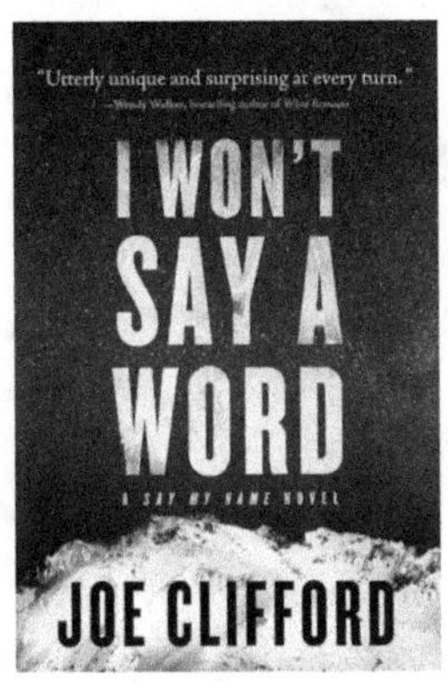

Keep an eye out for

I WON'T SAY A WORD

ABOUT THE AUTHOR

Joe Clifford is the author of several acclaimed novels, including *Junkie Love* and the Jay Porter thriller series. He lives in the San Francisco Bay Area with his wife and two sons. Joe's writing can be found at

www.joeclifford.com.